Empyrean

by

Nicole L. Bates

Dedication

This book is dedicated to my husband, Ben.
Thank you for showing me everyday what it takes to stop
chasing dreams and start catching them.

Copyright

Contents

PART 1

Chapter 1

Emergency alarms blared and red warning lights pulsed overhead as Jahira's boots pounded down the curving silver hallway of The Aquilo. Her sister's small dark fingers wove through her own and clung tight enough to make her hand tingle.

"This way, hurry up!" Jahira called over her shoulder. Her mother and father kept pace behind.

The white arch of the recessed elevator door finally appeared around the next curve. Jahira stopped, chest heaving, and pressed the white button on the wall. Before the door opened, she knelt down and wrapped her arms around Zarya.

"You go with Mom and Dad, make sure they get on board for me all right?" Jahira leaned back and looked at the small face creased with worry. She smiled what she hoped was a reassuring smile as she tried to smooth the wrinkles from her twelve-year-old sister's brow.

"Jahira, please come with us," Zarya pleaded.

"I've got to fly the Eagle out. I'll be right behind you. Everything's going to be okay."

Jahira pushed her sister gently into their mother's waiting arms, and then wrapped them both in a tight embrace.

"You be careful," her mother whispered in her ear.

"I will," Jahira whispered back.

Her father crushed her to him and released her quickly before she ushered them all into the waiting elevator. More families had gathered behind them. There was no time to prolong the goodbye.

"Get to bay four, Veronica's got a spot for you. I'll radio as soon as we're away."

Jahira's father nodded and pulled her mother and Zarya to the back of the elevator in order to allow more people inside. Tears formed in her sister's big green eyes, eyes that matched her own. Fighting back her own tears, she waved until the door closed.

"Please keep them safe," Jahira whispered. With the heels of her hands she wiped the wet tracks off her cheeks and then continued down the hallway, dodging the bodies of the other citizens of the man-made world.

The noise of the alarm increased in intensity. Jahira reached the forward emergency shaft, spun the wheel, and then pulled with all her strength. The hatch opened with a pop followed by a short hiss of air. Climbing feet first into the shaft, she was forced to look down to see where to place her feet. The ladder plunged downward into darkness. A wave of dizziness washed over her. Before she lost her grip, she looked up, took deep breaths through her nose and held on until the dizziness passed.

You'd think after six years as a pilot, heights wouldn't bother me so much, Jahira thought.

Once she felt confident that she could move without passing out, she lowered her left foot and right hand, then repeated the movement with the opposite hand and foot. Steadily, and with her eyes glued to the wall in front of her face, Jahira continued down to bay six. A long shuddering breath eased the tension in her chest when she finally placed both feet on the floor. She opened the bottom hatch, and walked out onto the loading dock.

The breeze created by the forced-air vents throughout the room cooled the beads of sweat which lined her jaw and forehead.

Magnar, her co-pilot, waved from beneath the Eagle.

"All suited up and ready to go," she observed as she reached his side.

"Yep, with ten minutes to spare. Get your gear on and let's move."

Jahira accepted the suit he held out for her. She stepped into the stiff boot covers, and then pulled the filmy material up her legs, worked her hands into the sleeves, and wiggled one arm at a time until she got the body of the suit up and over her shoulders. Skin the color of rich soil contrasted with the albescent sheen of the suit as she checked the seals before pulling on her gloves. Finally, she secured the hood, powered up, and ran a system scan.

"Ready to go," she said. Her voice echoed back inside her helmet.

"Help me with the last two crates." Magnar's voice coming through the speaker in her helmet seemed overloud inside the confines of her hood, but the comm-link checked.

Jahira grasped the opposite end of the crate which Magnar already held. Together they lifted and then loaded the cargo onto the platform. After the second crate had been loaded, she and Magnar balanced on the lift to either side of the crates.

"Take us up," Jahira said.

Magnar stepped on the green button on the corner of the platform and the rectangle on which they stood began to ascend upward toward the opening in the belly of the Eagle. Before the seal melded into the floor, Jahira stepped off and walked to the flight deck. She slid into the left seat. Magnar settled into the right seat. Their hands flew through the pre-flight checklist as the chatter from the big ships filled the air around them.

"Bay one, prepare to launch." Jahira heard General Thayer's voice over the comm-link in her helmet, followed by Gavin's response.

"Andromeda is away in five, four, three, two, one."

Jahira completed her checklist and gripped the yoke.

"Andromeda's clear."

"Bay two, prepare to launch."

"Fire's moving in fast General." Jahira recognized Kato's voice, the pilot of the Magellan. "Once we're clear you'd better send the rest fast. We're out in five, four, three, two, one."

Jahira's palms began to sweat.

"Magellan is clear."

"General, we have to go, now."

"That's Tryg," Jahira whispered.

"Bay three," Magnar replied.

His wife and Jahira's family were all aboard the Messier which still waited for launch in bay four.

"General, we've got fire!" Tryg's voice struggled to maintain its calm.

"Get out of there now!" General Thayer commanded.

Jahira's heart pounded.

"Seyfert, what's your status?" General Thayer asked.

Silence.

"Tryg, report!"

"Seyfert is clear. Some damage but it's contained. Get the rest out, now."

"Bay four, five, six, launch immediately," General Thayer ordered.

"Don't have to tell me twice," Jahira said. She keyed open the hangar door.

The moment the first sliver of black space became visible, she pressed the yoke forward. The Eagle shot across the deck and out the still expanding opening.

Jahira stayed on course until they were clear of the other ships, and then she banked right. A clear view of flames erupting and dying across the Aquilo filled the window. The fire worked its way up and through their man-made world, disappearing almost as fast as they appeared.

Flames died fast in space.

She pursued the bigger colony ships out to space, pressing forward until her radar confirmed she was clear of the hot zone.

The shock wave from a massive explosion rocked the Eagle forward. Jahira's eyes fixed on the enhanced viewing screen. The view from the rear camera showed the last of The Aquilo's walls rending apart before they shot out into the void.

In seconds it was over.

The sound of her own ragged breathing filled her hood as she watched the pieces of her world drift away.

Chapter 2

"Wow! You're huge!"

"That's not what you're supposed to say to a pregnant woman."

Jahira smiled, listening to the voices of Magnar and his wife drifting from the control room to the main cabin where she busied herself with an inventory check that didn't strictly need to be done.

They'd been on course for seven days, cramped inside the Eagle, rationing the packets of water-soluble protein powder they carried in one of the storage crates; but today they would finally be able to get out of this blasted tin can. She and Magnar were scheduled for two days of scouting the planet's surface before both of them could finally be reunited with their families. In the meantime, she wanted to give Magnar and Amara what little privacy she could.

"Sorry. I just can't believe you've gotten even bigger in only one week! It's beautiful though. You are beautiful." The last statement came out so softly Jahira could barely hear him.

"He's getting so big, too! I can see his little hand or foot sometimes pressing out against my belly. I can't wait to meet him."

"Me either." After a few seconds of silence, she heard Magnar's voice, reluctant now, "Ok, well, our time's up. Jahira's family is waiting. I love you."

"I love you, too. See you soon."

A few seconds of silence followed, and then Jahira heard boots cross the threshold between the two rooms.

"Your turn," Magnar said.

"Okay, thanks."

The portable data screen Jahira had been using to log the inventory passed between them as they jockeyed for position. A moment later Jahira lowered herself into the seat that still retained Magnar's body heat. She activated the comm-link to the Messier.

"Jahira!" Zarya's smile lit up the screen. The corners of Jahira's eyes crinkled as she smiled in return.

"What's up, Z?"

"Are you really going to see the planet today?"

"Yep. We'll be entering the atmosphere in less than an hour."

"Are you excited to see what it's like? I'm excited."

"Yeah, I guess I am." In truth, the chaos and sorrow of fleeing The Aquilo had been forefront in her mind over the last few days. She hadn't acknowledged her anticipation about exploring their new home until Zarya asked. Seeing the joy on Zarya's face made it feel less like a betrayal of her past to admit that she was excited about colonizing this new planet.

"They told us we only have a minute or two, so I can't talk long, but I love you and I miss you and I can't wait to see you soon. Mom and Dad want to say hi, too."

"Love you, too. See you soon."

"Hi, Jahira." Her sister's face faded from the screen and her mother's face appeared.

"Hey, Mom."

"Be safe, okay. I love you."

"Love you, too."

Her father's face pressed in cheek-to-cheek with her mother's.

"Find us a good spot, Jee."

"Will do, Dad."

"Okay, the light's blinking, our turn's up. Be safe."

"Bye."

Jahira barely got the word out before the screen went blank. She sighed, "Damn comm-lines."

"Tell me about it," Magnar returned from the main cabin and slid into his seat.

"Ready for approach checks?"

"Yep."

They ran their checklists, prepared the cabin, and double-checked everything they'd already done.

The giant orb of swirling colors loomed before them, beckoning.

"Countdown to atmo," Jahira said. "In ten, nine, eight...brace yourself."

Magnar tightened the strap across his chest before returning both hands to the console. Swirls of clouds rushed up to meet them. Jahira guided the Eagle through the atmosphere of KB-135Q, the nearest planet in the habitable zone of the binary solar system where The Aquilo had made her grave. Probes had been sent to the surface months ago. The decision had been not to colonize here due to the evidence of sentient life.

Not much evidence, Jahira thought, *but enough that it should have been a no land zone.*

That had all changed one week ago.

Jahira's body began to vibrate along with the ship as the Eagle descended.

"Think she'll hold?" Magnar asked.

"In one minute, I'll tell you," Jahira replied. She could sense Magnar's grin.

Clouds engulfed the tiny intruder, and spat her out on the other side.

"Decelerate and pull up," Jahira commanded.

Magnar's gloved fingers flipped a switch and then slid down a back-lit screen. The jet slowed. Jahira pulled the yoke slowly, leveling the Eagle out. A vast steel-blue sea blurred below them. The Eagle maintained a course toward the second of the three continents on this planet.

Waves crashed against a rocky shore. The rocks yielded to scrub brush, and brush eventually grew into a thick forest of dark trunks topped by wine-colored leaves. The ship skimmed over the land, recording everything. Jahira scanned the area for heat signatures and began to relax when nothing over forty kilos appeared in the database.

Magnar raised his hand and saluted. Jahira followed his gaze and saw the Falcon pulling up on their right wing.

"Anything interesting?" Tala asked over the comm-link.

"Looks pretty standard so far," Jahira replied.

"How far in are you going?" Leiko, Tala's co-pilot, asked.

Jahira pulled up her map on the dashboard, highlighted their route, and sent the link to the Falcon. In a matter of seconds she received a link back, which she opened and added to her screen in order to compare the routes.

"We should meet you at the rendezvous in about four hours," Jahira stated.

"Roger," Tala replied. "Holler if you need us."

Jahira waved before the Falcon banked and then pulled away.

"All right, start feeding our data to the KC. Let's find out where we're going to make our new home."

Magnar opened the link to the Kepler Colonizer and programmed the feed from their hard drive to copy into the file that would be retrieved by General Thayer on board the largest of the colony ships. The five big ships waited in orbit around the planet while the two smaller jets scoped out the prospects.

The forest finally began to open up about three and a half hours into the flight. Fingers of yellow vegetation crept up from the south and formed peninsulas of bright color across the dark landscape. Another half hour and the yellow softened to a mossy green. These grasses graduated to a deep gray-blue hue and finally overcame the thick forest to create a wide swath of open field big enough for all five ships plus the two jets.

"This is it," Jahira said. Her statement confirmed by a flashing green blip on the map.

Jahira brought the Eagle to land in the open field. The Falcon approached from the south. Tala landed as Jahira and Magnar unstrapped from their seats and prepared to deplane.

"We'll take the first tour," Jahira said after she'd opened the comm-link on her suit to the Falcon. "Stick tight and we'll survey the immediate area. We'll let you know when it's safe to come out and play."

"You bet," Tala replied. "Be safe."

"Always," Jahira stated.

Jahira stamped her feet and tried to shake the feeling back into her right leg before she joined Magnar on the platform.

"I can't wait to get off this thing," Magnar said.

"You read my mind," Jahira replied.

"Ready?"

"Let's do this."

Magnar pressed the release with the toe of his boot. Jahira bent her knees slightly for balance. Her stomach flipped once when the platform began to lower them toward the ground.

Magnar drew his gun from his belt. Jahira rested a hand on the hilt of her stun weapon but didn't release it from its holster. Nothing had shown up on the radar, but Jahira still felt a little twitchy. There were a lot of places to hide in that forest, not to mention the waist-high grass in this very field.

In unison, they stepped off the platform onto firm yet flexible ground. Jahira kept her back to Magnar's while they scanned the immediate area. The gray-blue fronds bowed in response to a breeze that Jahira could not feel.

Once it became clear that there was no immediate danger, her shoulders relaxed and she removed her hand from her weapon. Magnar lowered his but kept it in his hand. They headed northeast toward a river which sparkled in the sunlight as it flowed out from a stand of what looked a bit like trees.

"They're silver," Magnar whispered, echoing her own thoughts.

As they drew closer Jahira could see the spade shape of the individual yellow leaves. Nestled among the foliage were hundreds of bright red bulbs.

"Edible?" Magnar asked.

"Let's hope so," Jahira replied. "It'll take a while before we get any crops from our seeds."

Magnar shook his head.

"I can't believe the whole garden complex is gone."

"Me either," Jahira replied softly.

She'd always known she would get off The Aquilo someday. After all, that was the whole point. Certain individuals from each generation were presented with the choice of staying or colonizing each new world. Some people would have to stay aboard to keep The Aquilo going, but there were always people who feared the change and were more than happy to forgo the adventure. Jahira had signed up to colonize. She and her family had been scheduled to settle the next planet on the docket. Still, it overwhelmed her to think that The Aquilo didn't even exist anymore. She no longer had a choice.

"I wish we could try them right now." Magnar gazed with longing at the red fruits. "A week of protein powder does not exactly excite the palate."

"How long until we have our first harvest, do you think?"

"Amara said they're making pretty good progress with the seedlings. Maybe a couple of weeks for the radishes and leafy vegetables."

"How's Amara doing?" The best she could do was pretend she hadn't heard their entire conversation.

"She feels good, she's happy, and the baby is healthy. I couldn't ask for more than that."

Jahira smiled.

"I'll bet she misses you though."

"Meh, she's happy with her plants. Honestly, she's probably enjoying the break from me hovering around asking her how she feels every five minutes."

Jahira laughed.

"You'll be a good dad."

Magnar didn't respond, but she saw his shoulders straighten a bit and she smiled.

Jahira led the way east, along the edge of the silver trees toward the river. Flashes of light caught her eye. Sunlight glinted off tiny filaments which covered the leaves like peach fuzz. Darting in and out of the branches, strange looking bugs flitted and dove in erratic patterns. This place might not be so bad.

"Everything all right? What's your status?"

Jahira nearly jumped out of her suit when Tala's voice filled her hood.

"We're great, and it's beautiful," Magnar replied. "Amara will love it here."

Jahira grinned. She could imagine Zarya darting and swinging through these trees.

They made it all the way to the river before they turned and headed back to the Eagle.

"Nothing out of the ordinary so far," Jahira announced over the link to Tala. "Radio the General and let him know we'll scout for two days before we give him the green light."

"Roger that," Tala replied.

"So can we come out now?" Leiko asked. "I love this ship, but I think if I stay in here one more minute my butt is going to fuse to this seat."

Jahira chuckled.

"Now that's something I'd like to see," Magnar replied.

Before Leiko could respond Tala interjected with the response from General Thayer.

"The General says we've got forty eight hours."

"Sounds good," Jahira replied. "Why don't you come on out and stretch your legs."

"Amen to that," Leiko said.

"What about the suits?" Tala asked.

"Readings are all good," Jahira replied. "Take 'em or leave 'em."

"Here we come," Leiko announced.

Jahira watched the silver rectangle detach from the belly of the Falcon. Two sets of booted feet appeared, followed by two identical flight suits, and finally two beaming faces.

"What do you think?" Magnar asked, looking at her with one raised eyebrow through the clear faceplate of his hood.

"I think it's time to get some fresh air," Jahira replied.

Jahira released the seal on the hood and pulled it off over her head before powering off her suit. She slipped out of the filmy material and stepped out of the awkward boots. As she straightened back up she rolled her shoulders and reveled at the caress of the warm breeze on her face.

"I feel ten pounds lighter," Magnar said.

"I feel ten years younger," Jahira replied. She inhaled.

The scent of dirt and flowers filled her nostrils. Oxygen filled her lungs.

This might not be so bad at all.

Chapter 3

Without a glance at the other contestants poised on the edge of the ice-slick cliff, Krnar inhaled until his distended lungs strained against his ribcage. He held the breath and forced his pounding heart to a slow, steady cadence. Energy coiled in every fiber of his lithe frame. He waited for the signal to jump, ready to show his people what he could do.

There had been a time, not so long ago, when he'd hated himself. Hated the way people averted their eyes when he approached, then stared at his back. He had despised being different in a world of unbroken sameness. At least, until he'd discovered the advantages of being born without the devolved triangles of flesh on his back that his people called water wings.

An ululating trill broke the tense silence which permeated the still morning. Cries of encouragement resounded in the wake of the signal to begin the trials.

It's now or never, Krnar thought.

Krnar lifted his arms and bent his knees. Fur-covered feet pushed off the rocky ledge. His body arced and then sailed forward on the updrafts. When gravity began to pull, he aimed his fingertips toward the waves below. Like a sleek white arrow he raced toward the sea.

The cries from the spectators cut off abruptly as Krnar torpedoed into the icy water. The momentum of his dive carried him down, past the netting which held the ice floes at bay on this first day of the trials.

When his downward impetus abated, Krnar opened his eyes. He kept the tinted, protective second lens in place. Bubbles surrounded him, buoying his body as he began to kick. One arm at a time reached forward and then pulled back, propelling him through the salty depths.

It had taken long hours of practice to teach himself to swim without the water wings. Not able to imitate the movements of his peers or the adults in the community, he'd been forced to find his own rhythm by trial and error. Taunting from the other children had fueled his determination. The memory of those days drove him forward.

Shadows moved through the blue-white light shed by the snaking tendrils of glow-weed below. Some of the shadows began to merge and swirl in mesmerizing patterns before rising up out of the weeds. He could make out the occasional eyeball or flash of a tail from individual fish, but from a distance the approaching school appeared huge and menacing. A close-lipped smile split his face when the mass parted around him, and then came together again on his opposite side.

To either side he could make out spots of light moving through the heavy depths. The glowing forms of his competitors winked in and out of his peripheral vision. Krnar relaxed into the pace of his self-taught technique.

Satisfaction swelled in his chest each time he pulled ahead of one of those glowing dots in the distance.

Icy water coursed along his fur-covered skin. The taste of salt pressed past his closed lips and teased his tongue. Krnar reveled in the impenetrable, peaceful silence of the sea. The farther he swam, the more he felt cleansed of the dark, stale caves where he and his people had spent the long Season of Ice.

A new generation of The People had been born and half grown in the depths of the caves which sheltered them through the cold season. So many had lived their life without ever seeing the light of Mrkellan. He smiled remembering the looks of pure awe on the faces of the children who had survived the Season of Ice and climbed to the surface for their first Season of Light.

For an eternity, he raced forward, still submerged. Rays of sunlight filtered through the maze of cracks formed by the broken ice above him. A mild burn crept into his lungs, sending signals to his brain that it was time to surface. He ignored the discomfort and continued to push. The fiery sensation spread into his throat.

He kicked and pulled, one more body length, two more…dancing lights encroached on the periphery of his vision.

Pursing his lips against the urge to inhale, Krnar scanned the surface for a clear place to rise from the sea. Thighs and shoulders screamed in protest as he kicked and pulled with all he had left.

The sleek white fur of Krnar's head broke the surface. He opened his mouth and gasped his lungs full of air. Before he could turn to see how far he'd made it, a wave rebounded off the nearest ice floe and returned, catching him full in the face. Trying to breathe between spasms of coughing, he finally rid his body of the salt water. Fortunately, the ice floes surrounding him prevented any competitors from witnessing his ignoble finish.

They also prevented him from being able to see where he stood in the rankings.

Breathing steadily now, he placed both hands on the nearest chunk of ice and pulled himself to the top of the floe. The grey cliff where he'd started loomed in the distance. It hid the sight of the wall of ice beyond, but Krnar knew it waited for him, eager to test him.

He opened his mind and sought a link with the circle of elders. The whisper of another's thoughts entered his head, flavored with emotions that were not his own. He projected his location.

The tingling sensation left him as quickly as it had come. Krnar would get no clues from the elders.

A faint splash alerted him to the presence of a competitor, one who slipped into the water too quickly for him to identify. He scanned all around but saw no one else.

No point in delaying the inevitable, he thought.

Cold spread from his toes and up his legs like an uninvited touch as he slipped off the ice and back into the sea.

Fatigue, combined with a lack of the urgency he'd felt on the swim out, made the return trip considerably longer.

Distant trills and broken bits of conversation traveled on the wind, tickling the hairs which covered Krnar's ears once he'd reached the rocky shore at the base of the cliff. Fingers numb with cold sluiced water from the fur on his arms and chest.

Only one elder remained on the ledge at the bottom of the steps. Orvan nodded and extended his arms. A hide draped across long thin limbs, still ropy with muscle even at his age.

Krnar accepted the offering with a small bow.

The hide provided little warmth by itself, but it did block the wind. Added protection allowed his insulated hide to regain some measure of warmth.

Orvan turned without a word and led the way up the steep, hand-carved steps. A light dusting of snow coated the cold stone thanks to the ever-present wind on this Aruvel-forsaken continent.

Clusters of ice formed in the still-wet webbing between Krnar's toes. Daydreams of sitting by a fire with his hands wrapped around a bowl of steaming tea spurred him up the cliff.

Three steps from the top, Krnar's head crested the walls of rock to either side. Hundreds of fur covered legs blocked his view of the community cavern. His eyes strayed up and to the side, past the onlookers to the glistening blue wall of The Great Ice rising into the sky like a threat.

The crowd parted for the final pair.

Krnar followed Orvan into the cavern. They wove through the rock-lined hearths of his people until they reached the smooth open floor at the back of the cave.

Light and shadow played across the walls. The central fire flickered, beckoning him to rest in its welcome warmth. A large pile of vrmefur, crusty orange-tendriled and oil-filled inhabitants of the sea, burned slowly within the blaze.

Krnar seated himself in the single remaining vacancy, closing the inner circle of contestants which surrounded the fire.

He had arrived last. Did this mean he'd been last to surface or simply the slowest to return?

Impatience threatened to push him over the edge of acceptable behavior. He forced his body to remain still, eyes focused on the fire. He waited.

Six males and four females competed for the honor of being sent forth on the day of the junction, the day when the two suns of the solar system aligned on either side of Leron. The day of the junction also marked the midpoint of the warmest season on Leron's third continent, providing a narrow window of opportunity for the chosen to leave this barren world of rock and ice in search of the warm land.

Krnar longed to be chosen. He longed to prove himself worthy of this honor. Part of him also relished the thought of being alone and at peace for the first time in his life.

After an agonizing eternity, Ellall stood. Regal in her beaded robe, the Akaruvel's ice-blue eyes froze on each candidate in turn. Firelight glinted off the silver bands which encircled both of her biceps, both forearms, and a single finger of her right hand.

The five rings, representing the five sacred pools, were the only artifacts to have survived The People's exile.

Ellall lifted her hands. Silence filled the cavern. The sudden wail of a hungry babe was quickly hushed. Finally, Ellall lowered her arms and began the first ceremony.

"Today marks the end of the first day of the trials in this, our twenty-fifth Season of Sacrifice." Ellall paused.

Have we truly been trapped here so long?

Krnar began to calculate. *Twenty five Seasons of Sacrifice, which meant fifty Seasons of Light, separated by fifty Seasons of*

Ice. Each Season of Ice was four times as many moons as one Season of Light-

Ellall's voice interrupted his thoughts.

"Today we celebrate the first victory in the series of tests that will reveal which of our candidates is most prepared for the journey to the warm land, and which one has the best chance of survival...alone."

Krnar couldn't resist a glance around the circle.

Krag, youngest, boldest, and least experienced met his gaze briefly and then cast his eyes to the floor. No one else noticed him, their focus remained on Ellall.

"Krag, please rise," Ellall said.

The young man stood, squaring his shoulders against the good-natured jeers from the crowd. Called first to stand because he had been the first to surface during the swim, Krnar felt a pang of sympathy for his young competitor.

"Kllollan."

Only three moons his junior, Krnar had expected Kllollan to fare better, but she had been ill during this last Season of Ice. Perhaps she'd not fully regained her strength.

"Plldoll."

The youngest of the female contestants stood. She bowed low to Ellall, who bowed in return.

"Brdar *and* Grkar."

Even Ellall could not completely contain her grin as the two old men rose simultaneously. The best of friends and the fiercest rivals; Krnar could just imagine them waiting together below the surface, each trying to outlast the other.

Ellall paused between each of the next names.

"Trgor. Tllomell. Erget."

A thrill of surprise twisted through Krnar's stomach. He considered Erget his greatest competition, but only two names remained. The hairs along the back of Krnar's arms tingled when he heard Ellall's next statement.

"And in an unprecedented end to the first trial, we have another tie. Krnar and Allnall, please stand."

Krnar's knees threatened to give out as he rose on unsteady legs. Emotions warred within him. He kept his mind blocked in order to prevent anyone else from feeling his mix of shock, elation, and profound disappointment.

A tie, he mused, *and with Allnall of all people.*

Careful to keep his features under control, he stepped forward to receive his victory token with Allnall at his side.

The cool weight of the carved krska bone felt good in the palm of his hand. Sharing this moment with one of his greatest childhood tormenters did not.

As he returned to his place in the circle, Krnar scanned the crowd of onlookers until he found the familiar face of his hearth-brother. Arkan's slight nod was all the praise he would be able to receive, but it was enough. His brother by circumstance, though not by blood, had considered competing alongside him until he and his mate had taken in Ulletta's orphaned nephew.

Twenty five Seasons of Sacrifice; twenty five Lerroni who had departed from the third continent with a heart full of hope and determination. Not one of them had ever returned.

The ceremony dwindled to a close. Families retreated to their hearths and soon the cave became a miniature replica of the night sky, shadows dotted with myriad glowing forms trying in vain to keep the darkness at bay.

Chapter 4

Krnar woke with a start and lay for a moment, listening. The sound of even breathing filled the cavern all around him, punctuated by the distant groan of ice floe meeting ice floe in the sea far below.

A few deep breaths released some of the tension from his shocked-awake body, but his mind would not rest. Today the second trial would take place.

With a sigh, he pushed himself upright and sat with his legs crossed. Mingled light from The People's phosphorescent forms lit the cavern with a comfortable gloam. Most of those forms lay curled upon stone, ribs rising and falling ever so slightly in rhythm with peaceful dreams. One other sat erect, far across the cavern. Krnar could hear the faint scrape of bone against stone.

Erget glanced up and nodded, never pausing the steady movements of wrist and fingers as he sharpened his hunting knife.

Krnar checked his supplies. Everything was ready, just as it had been before he fell asleep last night. He made a half-hearted attempt at waiting patiently, but restless energy got the better of him.

With a light and expert touch, he pushed against Erget's mind, careful to do no more than make the man aware of his presence before retreating back inside his own skull.

Erget glanced up and tipped his head to one side.

Krnar gazed pointedly at the sleeping forms around him and then pushed again at Erget's thoughts.

Erget smiled.

After a bit of gentle mental probing, those nearest the two anxious contestants began to stir. Like a stone tossed in the sea, ripples of movement expanded until the entire world had risen to greet the new day.

Krnar gathered his supplies before moving to the mouth of the opening carved into the floor of the cavern. The long dark shaft led to the extensive cave system below ground, where The People hid...lived seemed too optimistic a description for the endless moons of dark and hunger... during the Season of Ice.

Before long, the other competitors had joined him. Fingers tested knife edges and steady hands looped gut-line through lizard-hide belts. Movement ceased when Ellall joined them. She spoke a blessing over each hunter in turn.

As Ellall's last words echoed off the cavern walls, Krnar led the way down the shaft. Allnall followed so close after that the fur on his fingers tingled each time her foot landed on the rung above.

Nervous sweat slicked his palms, causing Krnar's hands to slide on the bone-carved rungs of the ladder. Halfway down, he blinked back the secondary lenses which protected his light-sensitive eyes on the surface.

From the base of the first ladder, he continued down a short tunnel to the right until he reached the second shaft and ladder. Five levels of caves burrowed through the forward section of the cliff. The first level ran parallel to the surface. One end of the tunnel opened over the sea, the other eventually curved back toward the surface and opened into the base of the Great Ice. The second and third levels were short and narrow, mere passageways to the extensive system of caves and tunnels below.

At the end of each Season of Light, the entire community would make this trip back into the bowels of the earth. Krnar hated those days, hated even the memory of those days when darkness surrounded him, pressing against him with the threat of never returning to the daylight. If he succeeded in his mission, he would never have to make this trip again.

When he stepped off the ladder into the fourth level, deep shadows swallowed the blue-white light which formed a halo around his entire body. The shadows marked the empty hearths carved into the tunnel walls which were abandoned each time

Mrkellan returned to the third continent. Cold stone, worn smooth by the passage of a million footsteps, whispered as he walked. He proceeded with some trepidation to the gate which separated The People's territory from that of the krska.

The scratch of bone on stone echoed through the empty tunnels. Krnar cringed at the unwanted announcement of his arrival to any nearby cave lizards.

A brief glance over his shoulder let him know that Allnall did not intend to follow him. The sleek, glowing fur of her head disappeared into another vertical shaft. She'd apparently chosen to hunt on the fifth level. Whether out of personal preference or to give them both space to hunt, he appreciated the decision.

Krnar pulled the gate closed behind him and then wove the gut-line latch tightly around the bone frame of the gate.

On silent feet, Krnar crept forward. He unsheathed his knife and stone-tipped spear as he continued down the increasingly narrow corridor.

Lizards typically did not venture this close to The People's territory, but the Lerroni had been living on the surface for several moons now. Their lingering scent might not be enough to deter the creatures after so long away.

A shuffling sound ahead and to his right brought Krnar sharply back to the moment. He stopped to listen.

Silence stretched for several heartbeats and then another faint scuffle.

Moving forward, Krnar placed his feet against the stone soft as a whisper, careful to reduce any vibrations caused by his footfalls. After creeping along for about four body-lengths, he came to an intersection. One tunnel continued straight ahead, another directly to his right.

The intermittent scuffling emanated from the tunnel to the right.

Judging by the rapid narrowing of the opening along with the fact that the sounds neither approached nor receded, he guessed it must be a den.

Which means a female, Krnar thought.

He had no desire to engage any lizard in the confines of its den. If it proved to be a female with young, his sacrifice might not come in the form he desired.

Tingles traveled down his spine as the sensitive fur of his back brushed against the smooth stone of the tunnel wall. Krnar side-stepped, keeping his eyes on the entrance to the den. Hunters typically avoided female krska. They were more aggressive, less predictable, and ultimately necessary for the continuation of the species which their people depended on for survival.

The main tunnel curved to the left and began to shrink in on itself.

Forced to stoop and shuffle through the lizard-sized passage, a dull fire spread across Krnar's back.

Stale air hung thick with the smell of krska. The stench coated him. He crept forward, spear at the ready. Every nerve tuned to his surroundings. He noticed the change in the slope of the floor, the way the air ceased to move, a faint drip in the distance as water forced its way through rock. Mentally he gauged his ability to maneuver in the tight quarters.

A flash of movement caught his eye and then disappeared into the dark oval of another tunnel. Heart pounding, Krnar approached the opening.

The moment he set his foot in front of the entrance, a gelatinous mass barreled into his legs. Krnar staggered backwards until his shoulder slammed against solid rock.

Feathery growths, which sprouted from the lizard's body, twitched and quivered. Krska had no eyes; instead it picked up vibrations in the air. This particular male lacked the anemone-like appendages on one side of its head. Thick lines of scar tissue had replaced them.

Sharp teeth lined the inside of its triangular snout. Long curving claws extended from all four feet.

Those claws will make excellent ice-hooks, Krnar thought.

The prey-turned-predator twitched its tail, preparing for another run at the intruder.

The narrow passage limited his range of movement, so the spear was not an option. He'd have to wait for the lizard to come in close enough to be taken with a knife. Krnar wished for Arkan in that moment. The People typically hunted in pairs. One hunter created a distraction while the second moved in for the kill. The hunters today had no such advantage.

With a flick of his wrist, Krnar adjusted his grip on the smooth bone handle of his chosen weapon.

Make your move, he thought.

Shallow ripples travelled along the krska's skin. It feinted right and then, with surprising speed, came straight for Krnar.

The lizard's bluff worked. Krnar reacted involuntarily to the movement. When the charge came, he struck a second too late. The stone tip of his knife grazed the thick hide of the animal's neck.

His error gave the lizard enough time to lock Krnar's lower leg between its powerful jaws. White hot pulses of pain shot up his limb. Krnar growled before he drew back his arm and struck again. This time he did not miss.

The stone tip plunged into the soft spot between the krska's vestigial eyes, piercing the place where its spirit dwelled.

Bits of flesh tore loose from Krnar's calf as the lizard thrashed in its death throes. When it finally lay still, Krnar's leg remained trapped.

He considered prying the jaws apart with his knife, but the angle was bad. He would most likely slip and stab his own foot. No need to add humiliation to injury. Instead he rested on one knee and sawed at the lower jaw, careful to aim the blade away from his own hide. Once he'd created enough slack, he pried the mandible away with his fingers and then slowly extricated his limb from the creature's top teeth.

Adrenaline pumped through his system. It helped block the pain, but he knew he needed to work fast and get out before the smell of blood attracted more krska.

Using the length of gut-line looped through his belt, Krnar secured the lizard's body on his own back. He cursed when he realized that the shortest way out would lead him past the female's den.

After mentally rerouting, he decided to climb down one of the shafts near the lizard's lake and then continue out the fifth level gate. There was no guarantee this would be a safer course of action. He could only hope the other hunters would create the distraction that he needed.

Burdened and injured, it proved far more difficult to tread lightly. Krnar remained vigilant, spear and knife poised for action.

Fatigue burned the adrenaline from his bloodstream. Needles of pain drove into his leg with every step. The growing ache in his back tried to distract him as he walked, half-bent, with the weight of the dead beast pressing down on him.

Finally, he reached the Lerroni-carved shaft which led down to the fifth level of caves. The circumference of the passage would not accommodate man and lizard. Krnar worked the knots out of the gut-line and shrugged the heavy burden from his back.

A satisfied hiss escaped his lips as he stood erect and stretched his back. The relief proved short-lived. Krnar re-tied one end of the gut-line securely around his waist, the other end he lashed around the krska's front paws.

He lowered the lizard's body into the shaft, tail down, and then followed feet first until he felt the first rung of the ladder brush against his fur.

Once he'd found a foot-rest and a hand-hold, he bounced twice to test the structure with the additional weight.

Gut-line dug into Krnar's waist from the dead weight of the krska dangling from the other end. He tried to take shallow breaths as he descended.

The ambient light from his bioluminescent coat did not extend far enough for him to notice once he'd exited the vertical tunnel. A sudden relief in the pressure at his waist startled him. He glanced down to see the krska resting on the stone floor below. Able to descend more quickly now, Krnar alternated hands and feet down the last few rungs.

With the efficiency of long experience, Krnar lashed his kill to his back. Pain throbbed through his injured leg and his head spun from loss of blood. Hobbling and hissing he made his way toward the fifth level gate.

The soft sound of disturbed water alerted him to the fact that he passed near the lizard's lake. Something, or several some-things, had noticed his arrival.

He saw no signs of the other hunters until he reached the gate. Here a glowing form beckoned, illuminating the crisscross pattern of bones which held the lizards at bay.

Krnar's step quickened.

His fingers fumbled with the gut-line on the release. Krag, waiting on the other side, lifted his hands as if to help, and then quickly dropped them to his sides.

"Krnar, are you okay?" Krag asked.

Krnar stumbled past the gate. Forcing himself to pause and turn, he retied the line around the latch.

"Great," Krnar replied.

"You don't look great." Krag projected an image into Krnar's mind. He saw his own light masked in places by a thick coating of dark blood.

"I'll be fine. Most of the blood is from the lizard. You still waiting?"

"Yes. I didn't want it to get too crowded in there."

Krnar nodded. He longed to ask if Krag had seen anyone else pass through this gate, and whether or not they'd taken a sizable krska, but that would be going too far.

"Good luck," Krnar said, and then continued toward the oranlo.

The narrow tunnel soon opened into a vast cavern pockmarked with midnight circles on a black canvas. It was an eerie feeling, walking past the empty hearths of his people, as if he were the last person alive.

He followed the argent glow to the shore of the silver pool. Once again he released the lizard from its bindings and eased his burden to the ground.

Without preamble, he walked out into the middle of the warm, thick fluid. Heat surrounded his legs, concentrating on the wound in his calf. Krnar inhaled and exhaled through clenched teeth as the pain intensified. Eventually the feeling like a burning knife slicing his flesh waned to a mild throb.

He waited until sensation from the wound ceased entirely, then returned to the shore to assess the damage.

A large divot remained on his inner calf. The wound had sealed, but the liquid could not replace flesh, not in one visit anyway. It would be many moons before fur would regrow to cover the exposed skin. He would have to keep his leg wrapped well to prevent frostbite.

Before burdening himself once more with the heavy krska, Krnar decided to wash the remaining blood from his fur. Steady pain-free strides carried him to the clear pool at the far end of the cavern which provided drinking water during the Seasons of Ice.

The floor of the lake shifted as glow worms and cave crabs scurried before his footfalls. Before he tainted the water too profoundly, Krnar cupped his hands beneath the surface and then drew the brackish water to his mouth. Like a perfect icy kiss the liquid froze his lips and sent shivers down his spine.

Once he'd drunk his fill, he scrubbed and sluiced blood from his fur. A murky cloud spread across the surface in all directions, with him the nucleus.

Feeling revived, he retrieved his kill and steeled himself for the long climb back to the sunlight.

Chapter 5

"Kepler Colonizer, this is the Eagle, over."

"General Thayer here; what's the verdict."

"We are green for landing," Jahira said with a smile. "I repeat, the area has been deemed safe for settlement."

"Roger that, we're on our way."

Jahira left the comm-link open and waited in the flight deck of the Eagle. Anticipation bubbled inside of her as she listened to the radio chatter between the five ships still waiting beyond the stratosphere. She had long ago learned to filter through the acronyms and piece together the big picture of the messages buzzing through the comm-link. She listened to the commanders of the big ships preparing to enter the planet's atmosphere. The cryptic conversation soothed her.

Everything sounded routine until Veronica's voice came over the link a little louder than before, and full of tension.

"We've got debris, coming head on," Veronica reported.

Jahira straightened up in her seat.

"Messier, what do you see?" General Thayer asked.

"Looks like scrap metal. We were hit, but it glanced off. Wait –" Jahira leaned toward the console and held her breath. Veronica whispered, "Oh, God."

Jahira flinched as a loud crash echoed through the Eagle, followed by the blare of an alarm.

"What's going on?" Magnar asked. He entered the flight deck from the rear cabin.

Jahira reached out and grasped his hand, then pulled him down into the seat beside her.

"This is the Messier, we've got a breach. A big piece of debris cracked the front shield; we're entering atmo and losing pressure fast."

Magnar's grip on her hand tightened painfully.

Jahira squeezed back.

She listened to Veronica yell orders. The sickening scream of metal splitting apart drowned out the pilot's voice, and then…silence.

"Messier, come in!" General Thayer's voice cut into the tense silence and boomed through the Eagle. "Messier, I repeat, report!"

"Veronica!" Tryg's voice echoed through the flight deck. He called for his wife over the comm-link from the control room of his own ship. Tears began to roll down Jahira's cheeks.

"Please," she whispered. "Someone please answer."

Silence.

Jahira released Magnar's hand. Her fingers flew across the console. Finally, she pulled up the visual feed from the Kepler Colonizer.

She watched in horror as a streak of smoke rocketed through the clouds and exploded into a thousand pieces.

A sob tore from her throat as the pieces of what had been the Messier rained down over the western shore of the second continent. She didn't want to watch, but she couldn't tear her eyes away.

Her parents. Zarya.

Magnar pulled the seat-belt straps over his shoulders and buckled into the right seat. Without a word he fired up the engines.

"What are you doing?" Jahira asked.

"We're going," Magnar replied.

Jahira scrubbed the tears from her cheeks and nodded. She strapped in and within seconds the Eagle was airborne and headed for the sea.

EMPYREAN

Chapter 6

It was the longest flight of her life.

Jahira tried to keep it together, tried to believe there might be some chance that her family had survived, but deep down she knew. The video kept playing in her head; the smoke, the pieces. She'd been through those sims. She knew.

Glancing at Magnar for the hundredth time, she wondered what he was thinking. His face remained unreadable, as emotionless as if it had been carved from stone. The only evidence of his inner turmoil was his white-knuckled grip on the yoke.

"Magnar, I-"

"Don't," he cut her off sharply. "Just don't."

Jahira nodded and turned her attention forward. She didn't try to speak for the rest of the flight even though she wished desperately for a distraction from her thoughts.

"Eagle, this is the KC, what are you doing?" General Thayer's voice over the comm-link made Jahira jump.

"KC, this is the Eagle, we're headed to the...site...sir," Jahira replied.

"Eagle, your flight is not authorized. All ships are instructed to rendezvous at the landing coordinates."

Jahira glanced at Magnar before she responded.

"I don't think that's going to happen, sir."

"Eagle, I repeat, your flight is not authorized." Jahira heard the General sigh, and then his voice softened somewhat. "Look, I know, but we need to rendezvous and find out what happened. I can't afford any more losses."

"Sorry, General," Jahira replied. She closed the comm-link.

Magnar looked at her then, his expression didn't change, but he nodded slightly before his gaze shifted back to the horizon.

The forest below them blurred into streaks of dark plum.

Half an hour out from the center of the crash radius, Jahira started to see evidence of the disaster. Hunks of blackened metal and smoking remains of the ships interior littered the ground for miles. Her throat clenched as she decelerated and switched the view on the EVS to show her the images from the belly cameras. Scanning the wreckage for any signs of life, her last glimmer of hope fled.

She turned on the tracking device and immediately began to receive readings from the scattered ID chips which had been implanted in all of Aquilo's residents. A list of names began to scroll through on another screen as the ship's computer loaded the data. Jahira forced herself to read each name.

After forty five minutes they'd identified two hundred of the Messier's five hundred passengers, but still hadn't found the ones they needed to find. At some point Tala and Leiko had joined the search in the Falcon. Tala opened a link from the Falcon's hard drive to the Eagle's so that their list of names automatically uploaded to Jahira's feed. Jahira separated the names into two side-by-side lists, one from their search, and one from the northern quadrant.

"There," Magnar spoke suddenly and pointed to the screen.

Amara's name had popped up on the list coming in from the Falcon.

Jahira set a course for the associated coordinates.

As she prepared to land Magnar touched her arm.

Jahira glanced over, and then down to where he pointed.

Three new names had appeared on the list. Three names she'd been waiting for, and dreading.

Josephine A. Williams, Marcus D. Williams, Zarya F. Williams.

Tears welled in her green eyes and overflowed to create glistening tracks down her dark cheeks.

She managed to land, albeit with a little less finesse than usual. Magnar immediately unstrapped and stood.

"You coming?" he asked.

Jahira didn't have the energy to nod. With mechanical movements, she undid her harness and stood on shaky legs. Magnar already waited on the platform.

He offered her a hand-held tracker. She took it, though it seemed as if someone else moved her body. She couldn't feel the tracker in her hand; she couldn't feel the cloth against her skin. Maybe her mind knew that if it let her feel anything, her tenuous hold on sanity would be lost for good.

Magnar, on the other hand, looked determined.

He stepped on the release and they descended. Magnar headed east. Jahira watched him walk away, and then he began to run. She forced her feet off the platform and headed west.

The smoke and fumes made her eyes and the lining of her nose burn and begin to run. She didn't bother to wipe away the tears. After a few minutes she half-heartedly wiped snot from her upper lip with the sleeve of her flight suit before it ran into her mouth.

About half a mile from the Eagle, her tracking device began to beep. When the visual changed from one flashing green light to two solid green dots, she knelt down and began sifting through the ash and debris.

An involuntary gasp escaped from her lips, followed by a half-moan, half-sob as her fingers wrapped around a wide silver bracelet.

Zarya's arm cuff.

It had been a present from their father, made of the same material as The Aquilo, stronger than steel. Her sister had always worn it around her scrawny little bicep.

Jahira picked up the cuff and brushed dirt and ash from its surface. She released the clasp and then re-sealed it around her own wrist.

Tears and mucus continued to run down her face un-checked as she dug. She didn't stop until she'd found all three chips, each only a foot or two away from the others.

They died together.

Jahira held the chips in the palm of her hand and curled her fingers around them until the edges dug painfully into her skin. With her fist pressed against her heart, Jahira lay down among the ashes of her family member's remains. Sobs wracked her body.

She cried until she felt completely hollow inside, and then she cried some more.

Time ceased to exist. Sorrow and memories wrapped her in a cocoon of grief until her mind shut down and she fell into blessed unconsciousness.

When she was again coherent enough to become aware of her surroundings, she was surprised to see Tala sitting cross-legged only a few feet away.

"You found them," Tala said softly.

Jahira nodded and opened her hand to reveal the three implants. She stared at them, and then felt Tala's hand on her shoulder.

"I'm so sorry."

Jahira nodded once in acknowledgment.

"Do you want to come back, it's getting dark."

Jahira looked up, surprised to see no more than a fingernail of sunlight remaining on the horizon. The orange crescent shrank and disappeared into the sea.

Jahira stood and nodded.

She followed Tala back to where Leiko had started a small fire in a clearing between the two ships. Jahira sank to the ground. Flames danced around the compact brick of combustible material. The heat soaked into her fingertips and warmed her tear-stained cheeks.

"Where's Magnar?" she finally asked. Her voice sounded thick and raw.

"He's still out there," Tala replied, nodding her head to the east. "Closer than you were though; we'll be able to hear him if he calls."

"Should we go get him?" Leiko asked.

"No," Jahira replied. "Give him some time. He'll come back when he's ready."

A few moments passed before Tala spoke again.

"We checked in with General Thayer and let him know where we were. He's pissed but he'll get over it. There are a lot of people aboard the other ships clamoring to come out here."

Jahira nodded.

"Did he find out what happened?" Jahira asked.

"Pieces of the Seyfert," Tala replied. "Remember it was damaged during evac? Well, she made it through atmo all right, but some pieces broke off during entry. Those pieces…"

Tala's voice trailed off and Jahira nodded.

"I heard the rest."

EMPYREAN

Chapter 7

The towering expanse of blue-white ice loomed over Krnar, imposing, intimidating. With his toes a mere arm's length from the wall, its height seemed insurmountable. He knew better. He'd done this many times before, just never with the whole world watching.

A flick of his wrist brought one lizard claw into his right hand. He set the first hook and felt the pull of the gut line against his wrist. He repeated the motion with his left. Once his hands were secure, Krnar lifted one foot up to a slight ridge in the ice. The weight of his body pressed the lizard teeth, which he'd sewn into the bottom of his boot, into the ice. Muscles working in practiced harmony, he surged upward.

Krag and Kllollan made a great show of racing to the top. Krnar followed the lead of the veterans, picking his way carefully, steadily. It didn't matter who made it to the top first, it only mattered who could survive the longest.

Only seven of the original ten candidates remained. Young Plldoll and old Grkar had been seriously injured during the hunt and failed to return with a krska. They could never hope to survive the final trial without supplies. Trgor had never returned from the caves.

A collective gasp rose from the crowd at the base of the ice. Krnar glanced over and saw Krag dangling by one ice hook. While Krnar watched, the boy twisted, set his second hook, and continued upward at only a slightly slower pace. Krnar shook his head. Carelessness was not a desirable attribute of the one who would become the sacrifice.

The bulging pack on his back threatened to unbalance him on numerous occasions. Krnar hugged his body to the ice and he set each hook before lifting the opposite foot. He would need every last item he'd rendered from the flesh and bones of his kill if he hoped to outlast his competitors.

Finally, Krnar dug his hooks into the snowpack on the top of the Great Ice. Tendons strained as he stretched his arms to their limit before firmly setting both hooks.

Hissing and growling, he pulled with all his strength. Ice dug through his fur and into the skin of his chest and stomach as he hauled his body onto the surface. His heart thudded against his ribcage. Deep breaths drew icy air into his mouth and sent needles down his throat.

Moving one arm at a time, he pulled until his thighs crested the ridge. His arms remained in an isometric contraction while he bent his right knee and pulled his leg up onto the ice. The sharp teeth in the bottom of his boot bit into the crust. With one final heave, he drew his full length onto the surface.

Krag and Kllollan had already disappeared into the wind-swept horizon. Erget and Allnall stood three body lengths to either side of him. They tied strips of hide around their heads which had small eye-holes cut into front of the material. Brdar and Tllomell continued their climb to the top.

After retrieving and donning his own eye cover, Krnar drew his spear from its sheath which he'd sewn into the side of his pack. The tip of the spear broke through the crust at regular intervals as he began his journey across the ice.

Mrkellan pulsed in the clear sky above him. He probed the path ahead for fissures, squinting against the sunlight which reflected off the intermittently exposed ground around him. Swirling snow pushed by ceaseless wind made it impossible to hurry. When he glanced back toward the community cavern, neither rock nor sea were visible, only an endless river of frozen light in every direction.

What if I cannot find my way back? he wondered.

It happened every season. Some who set out to train, explore, or to survive during the final trial, never returned. His father had been one of these. Krnar's mother had died shortly after giving birth to him and though his father had never said it, Krnar knew he'd blamed his beloved wife's death on his deformed son. Why else would he have competed in the trials with a son barely old enough to hunt? Why else would he have given up out here rather than find the strength to return to an orphaned, ostracized child?

The tip of Krnar's spear bit violently into the frozen ground.

If it hadn't been for Arkan's parents taking him in, he wouldn't have survived that following Season of Ice. They'd been good to him and Arkan had treated him like a true brother, harassing him when they were alone but pummeling anyone who dared to tease him where Arkan could hear it.

The other kids had learned subtlety, Allnall had become a master. Granted, that had been many moons ago. They were grown now and over those childhood squabbles.

The first two sleeps passed quickly. Krnar found that solitude suited him. Alone with his thoughts, no one staring, no tingles of conversation buzzing against his mind, he could completely relax for the first time in his life.

After two handfuls of sleeps he began to feel a bit mad.

The landscape never changed. The wind never ceased. Sometimes when he woke he felt sure he still slept, dreaming a dream that kept repeating until he felt desperate to wake.

The daily decrease in the weight of his pack proved to be his one assurance of reality. A constant reminder that he still had to find his way home and, hopefully, have enough rations to make it there. Thinking about the lizard which had provided all of the meat and supplies he'd been allowed to take on this journey filled him with a surge of gratitude. He had an immediate advantage simply based on the size of the krska he'd taken down.

For another full sun, Krnar occupied himself by building an ice cave. He remained at this temporary hearth for ten more sleeps, passing the waking hours by carving small figurines from the length of krska bone he'd stashed in his pack.

Like a sea worm that had been prodded too many times, Mrkellan began to hide its light for longer stretches of time. Krnar lay with his head protruding from the entrance of his frozen shelter and stared at the night sky.

With his right index finger he connected the points of light that formed The Great Cave, The Spear, and The Oranlodi. The oranlodi, the five sacred pools. If he succeeded in becoming the sacrifice, he would be responsible for finding his way to the pools, and then finding a way to bring his people back.

Thoughts of his return, of being hailed the hero of the prophecy, became true dreams which morphed into strange images of twisted memories.

A tingling sensation along both arms forced Krnar awake. He jerked upwards, slamming his chin against the upper arch of his doorway. With hands and feet working together, he scrambled out of the shelter. Once free, he furiously brushed at his limbs only to discover tiny eroki which sought shelter in the warmth of his fur.

He paused, laughing at himself and his over-reaction, and then set about plucking the ice worms from his glossy coat.

"You gave me quite a scare, little creatures," he said aloud. He held the final worm aloft and peered at it with squinted eyes, trying to determine if it had a face, or any kind of discernable front and back. "Good luck my little friend. Burrow deep for the cold comes soon."

He placed the worm on the crust and watched it wiggle its way into the snowpack.

"You know you're lonely when you start talking to the worms."

After a breakfast of frozen meat washed down by snow, he decided it was time to head home.

With only a minor ache in his belly and a much lighter load, he began to walk. Snow squeaked beneath his feet as he took his first steps back toward civilization.

Chapter 8

Steady steps carried him for three suns before fierce winds forced him to stop and build another shelter. The combination of falling flakes from the sky and blowing flakes from the ground swirled together into a dangerous wall of white. It always amazed Krnar that if enough of them worked together, something as tiny as snow-flakes could pose a threat. If he continued in this white-out he ran the risk of traveling in the wrong direction or, worse yet, walking straight into a crevasse and falling to his death. Best to risk a few days of hunger at the end than to risk not making it back at all.

Once inside his ice cave, he removed his gloves and boots, leaving only his krska-hide leggings on for convenience more than warmth. It would be nice to have a fire. Unfortunately none of his supplies were expendable, or particularly flammable.

He waited out the storm for a sleep and another full sun.

Emerging in the silence of a bitter cold and windless night, his fur glowed a brilliant blue-white. Above him green streaks of light expanded and contracted across the sky, Aruvel's children playing among the stars.

Clouds of condensed moisture formed with each exhale, causing tiny balls of ice to form on the ends of the hairs around his mouth. When he turned south, a jagged black line cut through the ice no more than four body lengths away.

Krnar proceeded slowly, probing ahead with his spear until he stood a body length from the crevasse. Lying on his stomach, he crawled forward. His head protruded over the edge, giving him a better view of the length and breadth of the fissure.

How will I get around this? He wondered.

A blue-white light rippled across the ice below. Krnar squinted and then blinked back his protective lens.

One of The People!

It had to be one of the other contestants.

A tentative push against the other mind was grasped with sudden intensity.

It's Krnar, he sent. *What happened?*

I fell. It was Tllomell. *My left arm is broken. My right ankle might be as well. If I don't make it back, tell them what happened.*

I'm coming down.

No! Krnar paused. *You will be disqualified! You must go without me. I will find a way on my own.*

It was true, the rules were clear. Any contestant who gave or received assistance during the trials would be eliminated. But he could not leave her here. He would never be able to live with himself if she did not return. Earning his place as the chosen was not worth sacrificing Tllomell's life. If he was willing to let her die for his own gain, would he truly be the savior that his people needed?

After fishing out the supplies he would need for the descent, he searched for the best location to lower himself into the crevasse. Finding a likely location, he drove two lizard claws into the snowpack. Long lengths of gut line trailed from the claws, secured through the holes he'd drilled through the bone and tied back onto itself. He tied the end of one line to his belt and gripped the second with his bare hands.

Needles of ice worked their way under his fur as he shimmied backward on his belly until all but his head and shoulders had been lowered into the fissure.

Hand-under-hand he lowered his body, searching blindly for the narrow ledge he'd seen from the top. Finally, toes connected with a horizontal surface. Another hand span down, he dug the lizard teeth on the bottom of his boots into the slick surface.

Krnar, don't do this. Don't risk your dream on me. This is your only chance. You'll be an elder by the next junction...

Tllomell, hush, I need to concentrate.

A deep inhalation expanded his ribcage.

He eased his torso out over the abyss.

Feet remained firmly planted until his entire body angled out over the fissure, nearly perpendicular to the wall of ice. With great care, he removed one foot from the ledge and dug the teeth into the vertical blue wall before him. He repeated the movement with his second foot and paused. With the caution of experience, he slid one hand, then the other, down the line which he gripped with all his strength.

The pattern continued step after agonizing step.

A slow fire began to burn through his shoulders. It spread toward his fingers and seared through his back. He dared not shift his weight to look down. Not being able to gauge how far he had left to go made the journey stretch for an eternity.

When he lowered his right foot for the thousandth time, his heel struck ice. He let himself look and hissed in relief. He'd reached the ledge upon which Tllomell had landed. She rested now two body lengths away.

Arms shaking and thighs trembling, he gripped the ledge with his lizard teeth boots and pulled his body upright. Once he felt stable, he cut the line on his belt, as close to the knot as he could manage. His body weight pulling on the line had tightened the knot to such an extent that he could not hope to untie it.

Not trusting his balance on the slippery ledge, Krnar lowered himself to his hands and knees and slid his way to Tllomell.

"Krnar, you shouldn't have come." Tllomell kept her eyes straight ahead. Her body looked rigid. Whether from pain or anger he could not tell...maybe both.

"You're welcome," he said.

A twitch at one corner of her mouth was all the reaction he got.

Krnar glanced around to the other side of the ledge.

"Where's your pack?"

Tllomell jutted her chin out toward the chasm.

All her supplies, her food, her hooks and lines, gone. She never would have made it out. She'd have starved down here, if she didn't freeze first.

"How long have you been down here?" he asked.

"Since the recent storm," she replied. "Maybe two sleeps? I'm not sure how much time passed the few times I did nod off."

Krnar shrugged off his pack and pulled out a ration of meat.

Tllomell shook her head when he held the food out to her. He could see the muscles in her jaw working, chewing on her pride no doubt.

"Tllomell, don't be ridiculous. I'm going to help you whether you like it or not. You can either eat and regain your strength or I can lash you to my back like a dead lizard and carry you home. What would you prefer?"

For a moment he thought she would still refuse.

Finally, she snatched the ration from his hand and shot him a look of annoyance through narrowed eyes.

He smiled and nodded.

"Next we'll need to tend your injuries." Tllomell's left arm rested in her lap. "Let's see the damage."

She tried not to wince as she lifted the arm.

Krnar hissed when he saw the sharp white point of her bone poking through the skin and fur of her forearm.

He retrieved the two lengths of bone he'd been carving, as well as a strip of hide and some line.

"I'm going to have to set this." He began to reach out, but stopped just short of touching her. "May I?"

Tllomell nodded her permission and closed her eyes.

Working as quickly as possible, Krnar gripped her arm at the elbow and just above the wrist. He pulled until he felt the bones slide back into place.

A half growl, half moan rumbled in Tllomell's chest, but she didn't move.

Krnar placed a length of bone along each side of her arm, wrapped the brace tightly in place with the strip of hide, and then secured it all with gut line woven up and back down the full length of the splint.

"You okay?" Krnar asked.

Tllomell nodded and swallowed. She did not speak.

"I have nothing for the pain. I'm sorry. Now I need to check your ankle." He took her lack of response for permission and gently probed her foot and ankle with his fingertips. "I don't feel a break. Maybe a pulled muscle? I'll wrap it but I don't think it needs a brace."

When he'd finished with her ankle, he chipped ice from the wall behind him, placed a few pieces on his tongue, and offered the rest to Tllomell.

She took them with her good hand.

The chips melted in his mouth and slid down his throat. Krnar gazed up at the sliver of visible sky above.

"Now, how are we going to get out of here?"

EMPYREAN

Chapter 9

Lukewarm water slipped from the mouth of the canteen and soothed Jahira's raw throat. Once she'd quenched her thirst she poured some water into one hand and scrubbed her eyes which felt swollen and gritty after a day full of crying followed by a fitful night's sleep. She twisted Zarya's cuff around her wrist a few times, then checked her breast pocket to make sure the three little chips were still there.

"Good, you're up. Are you ready to go?"

Jahira jumped at the sound of Magnar's voice behind her. She hadn't even heard him approach. She turned to face him and found him staring off at the horizon. Though his face looked haggard, his eyes were clear, not swollen or bloodshot like she knew hers must be. His jaw was set, the muscles there twitched as he clenched and unclenched his teeth.

"Sure, whenever you are," she replied.

"I'm ready now." With that he walked to the Eagle and released the platform.

"Oh good, he's back," Tala said, walking up to Jahira's right side. She and Leiko were preparing to take off as well. "Is he all right?"

"I don't think so," Jahira replied. She turned to Tala and raised her eyebrows.

"Are *you* going to be all right? I still think I should fly with Magnar and you go with Leiko," Tala said.

"No, thank you, but I think I need to be the one to be there for him," Jahira replied.

Tala's brow knit in concern. "All right, but keep your comm open and call me if you need anything. I'll stay close."

Jahira nodded.

Tala nodded and pulled Jahira into a quick hug. Jahira wasn't usually the hugging type, but today it felt good.

"Thanks, Tala, for coming out here." Jahira glanced back at the Eagle and saw that Magnar had already strapped into his seat. "See you back at the rendezvous."

Tala released her and blinked furiously, trying to hide her own tears before she turned and walked to the Falcon. Jahira took a deep breath and let it out slowly before heading toward the Eagle.

She had thought the flight out to the crash site had been bad; the flight back topped it a hundredfold. Jahira could barely focus. Tears kept springing to her eyes and she fought furiously to keep them at bay. She tried to study the landscape but all she could see was her sister's smiling face, her parent's faces pressed cheek to cheek the last time she'd spoken to them on video chat. She felt wrung out, drained, and just wanted to lie down and sleep. It seemed that nothing short of unconsciousness could stop her imagination from replaying the crash over and over in her mind.

Then there was Magnar.

He wouldn't look at her, didn't speak, and she could practically feel the anger rolling off of him. It filled the flight deck, threatening to smother her with its ferocity. It formed a wall between them that she could not hope to breach.

By the time they reached the landing point where the Falcon and the four remaining colony ships waited, her shoulders ached from hours spent in isometric tension.

She and Magnar rode the platform down together, and were greeted by a flood of people who had come to give their condolences and to ask what, or whom, they'd found.

Magnar didn't even pause. As soon as the platform dropped to within an inch of the ground he jumped off the back and walked away from the crowd, away from Jahira.

Part of her wanted to follow him, she really didn't think she could deal with people right now, but as she looked into their faces, haggard from lack of sleep, drawn with worry, she realized how selfish she'd been. Three thousand residents had escaped The Aquilo. Five hundred had been lost when the Messier went down. Everyone had lost someone, a friend, a family member, a coworker. They all grieved. Her loss was no greater than any of theirs, even though it felt like it should be.

Bracing herself for the onslaught, Jahira stepped off the platform and into the crowd. She gave and received hugs, tentatively at first, then with more feeling as she realized how much she needed the comfort. The flow of the crowd pulled her to the Kepler Colonizer where General Thayer waited to speak with her at the foot of the exit ramp. The crowd lingered as Jahira approached the General.

She expected a lecture at the least, and probably deserved a demotion, but General Thayer surprised her. He placed his hands gently on her shoulders and looked her in the eyes.

"Jahira, I'm so sorry."

Not what she'd expected. She bit her lower lip to keep herself from crying and simply nodded.

"If there's anything I can do to help, let me know." Jahira nodded again. The General removed his hands and straightened his shoulders, becoming once again the formal figure that she felt comfortable with. "We already received the data from the Falcon. We're finalizing the list of names of those we lost. We'll share them tonight. In the meantime, I think you've got a lot of people who want to talk to you."

The General turned and walked back into the Kepler Colonizer. Jahira faced the expectant crowd. She wished now that she'd gathered more of the ID chips. With one hand she pressed the three small bumps in her pocket against her heart. They were all that remained of her family, that and her own memories; memories she vowed never to forget.

EMPYREAN

Chapter 10

Okay, I'm ready.

Tllomell notified Krnar once she set her hand hook into the highest divot she could reach. Krnar had spent two suns carving hand-holds up the ice wall. Now he could finally get Tllomell out of this frozen prison.

Moving up, and, go.

Krnar braced himself before he pulled upward. The line he'd secured around his waist and under Tllomell's arms grew taught. He supported her weight as they climbed.

Without the use of her left arm, Tllomell had to release her right hand-hook, stretch, and set it each time Krnar paused. Then she moved her feet up, flexed her knees, and waited for him to pull upward again so that she could safely release her hand.

This slow dance continued until, finally, both climbers sprawled on the surface, shaking with exhaustion.

"We should build an ice cave," Krnar said.

Neither of them moved.

"It's not that cold," Tllomell said. "Let's just dig in."

Too tired to argue, Krnar scooped out a shallow bed and then helped Tllomell finish her side. He spread a hide down in the depression. They both rolled in and Krnar pulled another hide over them. He briefly registered Tllomell's presence, so close he could feel the fur of her arm tickle his, and then he slept.

Krnar woke before Tllomell. He tied the thirty-third knot in the gut line which dangled from the shoulder strap of his pack. A grimace contorted his features when he opened the flap and faced the meager supplies which remained.

Nine rations left, he thought. *If we each consume a half ration per day, we might have enough to make it back.*

Gnawing his half of a frozen cut of lizard, he waited for Tllomell to wake.

The hide cover shifted and a low moan sounded from the small pocket of warmth.

Krnar turned his back and busied himself with a carving, giving Tllomell what little privacy he could.

Once she joined him, he offered the other half of the lizard meat. He continued to work his own frozen portion between frozen teeth.

Tllomell accepted without comment.

"How is your arm?" he asked.

"Which one?" she replied with a chuckle. "I'm so sore; if it weren't for the splint I wouldn't be able to tell which one was broken."

Krnar smiled.

"I know what you mean. I'm sore in places I didn't even know I had muscles."

Tllomell trilled softly in agreement.

They washed down their meager breakfast with handfuls of light powder. Krnar's stomach growled in protest. His body clearly felt it deserved more after yesterday's effort.

"We'll have to go around," Tllomell said, nodding toward a place over his shoulder.

Krnar turned his head and looked toward the yawning crevasse which separated them from their destination.

"I wish we'd been able to climb out the other side," Krnar said.

"Me too, but I'm glad we made it out at all. Any guess as to which end is shorter?"

Krnar studied the length of the fissure first one way, then the other.

"No idea."

"I don't suppose you'd be willing to split up, check both directions?"

"Nope."

"Didn't think so."

"I say we head toward Mrkellan," Krnar said, nodding toward the glowing orb hanging low on the horizon.

"Works for me."

Krnar gestured for Tllomell to lead the way. He wanted her to be able to set the pace, given her injuries.

Tllomell hissed at him, but turned and took a step, gingerly placing her foot to protect her injured ankle. The tip of Krnar's spear, which he'd given to Tllomell, pierced the ice in front of her, retracted, and repeated.

"I really don't want to go through that again," she said.

The weather held for the three suns that it took to navigate around the crevasse and then point back toward home. That was all the help that Aruvel saw fit to provide.

On the morning that Krnar tied his thirty-seventh knot, the wind howled and pushed against him. It felt as if the wind itself were on a personal mission to prevent him from succeeding. He leaned into the gale and forced one foot in front of the other. Driving snow blinded him so that he lost sight of Tllomell a handful of times, though she walked no more than two arm lengths away.

Tllomell, wait. We need to tie a line between our belts or I'm going to lose you.

Tllomell paused.

She secured one end of the gut line which Krnar proffered to her belt while Krnar tied on the other end. He tested the line and then nodded.

They trudged through the raging blizzard, stopping only when they were too worn out to continue, waking under a blanket of fresh snow.

Though neither spoke of it aloud, Krnar felt the urgency of their situation. He desperately wished to stop and wait out the storm. He knew it wasn't safe to continue, but had no idea how long the storm would last. On the other hand, he knew exactly how long the food would last.

Tllomell never asked how much was left. She never asked for anything to eat until he offered. Krnar saved the last ration until hunger dug at his belly with claws sharper than a krska's.

With snow circling them like a frozen tornado, they consumed their last ration in silence.

Krnar chewed slowly, letting the morsels thaw so that warm blood mixed with saliva in his mouth. Fervently, he hoped this would not be his last meal.

Like a toddler whose fit had finally spent, the storm lifted.

In the dark of that brief but lengthening night, Tllomell stopped suddenly and trilled.

Krnar paused.

"What is it?" he asked.

Tllomell held up a hand to silence him. He waited.

"Open your mind," she finally said.

Krnar obeyed, and was rewarded with the faint tickle of many minds awaiting connection, the constant feeling Krnar had experienced since birth, strangely new after so many suns without.

Eyes wide, Krnar turned to lock gazes with Tllomell.

She grinned, a flash of white teeth in white fur.

In silent synchronization they moved forward, torn between the desire to run and the need to remain steady and focused.

With the lights of Aruvel's hearth fire dancing above their heads, Krnar and Tllomell stood at the top of the wall overlooking the community cavern; two glowing figures suspended in darkness.

"We did it," Krnar breathed.

Tllomell responded with a tight nod.

Ever since he'd found her in the crevasse, Krnar's focus had been on survival, on getting them both home safely. He'd never stopped to consider what it might be like for Tllomell once they arrived.

She'd fallen, been injured, and had required assistance to return. Her shame wound around her like bait on a hook.

A sudden trill from below interrupted his thoughts. A glowing hand waved from the shadows at the base of the ice and then a mind pushed against Krnar's. He opened to it.

Who is this? A child's voice spoke inside his skull.

Krnar, he replied.

Tllomell, he heard Tllomell's simultaneous response.

A pause as the child relayed the news to those inside the cavern.

Trills and ululating cries echoed across the rock. Light spilled from the cavern entrance in the form of three hundred glowing bodies. Luminescence moved toward them like a wave on the sea, coming to rest below their feet.

Krnar had already begun the climb down. He knew better than to offer to help Tllomell here where the whole world could see, but he watched her and matched her pace so he might be available if she needed him.

Once his feet touched the solid rock of home, a fire warmed hide enveloped him. Warmth soaked into his shoulders and arms, making him feel suddenly tired and heavy.

He and Tllomell were half carried back to the cave where bowls of hot food and steaming tea appeared like magic.

For a few blessed moments, Krnar's thoughts did not stray beyond the sensations of his own body.

Heat, a long forgotten companion, cradled him like a mother's arms. Warm, salty liquid coated his tongue and thawed him from the inside out as he closed his eyes and savored the most delicious tea he had ever tasted.

EMPYREAN

Chapter 11

Jahira spent the next several days transporting anyone who wished to go over to the crash site. Some asked to search, hoping to retrieve ID chips of friends and family members. Others just needed to see it for themselves, to have some closure, to say goodbye. She cried at some point every day, but the raw pain of her loss seemed to ease the more she helped others through their own grief.

Tryg and Brenna took turns flying with her. Veronica, the aircraft commander of the Messier, had been Tryg's wife, and Brenna's best friend. They seemed to find some comfort in helping as well, though the dark circles under Tryg's eyes let her know he didn't sleep any better than she did at night.

When she returned from what she expected to be her last flight west, she decided to look for Magnar.

Ever since he'd walked away from her the day after the accident, she hadn't seen more than a glimpse of him. It worried her that every time she saw him, or tried to talk to him, he seemed to deliberately avoid her. In fact, he seemed to be avoiding everyone.

Weaving through the ever-expanding sprawl of tents toward the silver trees, she paused by Magnar's tent. She gave it a cursory glance, though she didn't expect him to be there. The coals of a long-dead fire chilled within a circle of damp sand. No foot-prints or worn path to the door; like the lone dead branch on a thriving tree.

She continued toward the river. Skirting the southern edge of the silver grove, she couldn't resist plucking one of the bright red fruits from a low hanging limb. After extensive testing in the K.C.'s lab, not to mention hundreds of documented field tests at this point, the fruit had been declared not only edible, but delicious.

Tart juice filled Jahira's mouth as she bit into the firm flesh of the perfect orb. The initial tang was followed by a sweet aftertaste that coated her tongue, making her crave another bite. She happily succumbed to the desire.

With her free hand, she reached up and mindlessly slid her fingers along the soft surface of one yellow leaf. The silver filaments on the leaf's surface tickled her palm. Leaning in for a closer look, she brushed a finger back and forth, watching the fine hairs lift and then spring back into place. She pinched the leaf between her fingers and watched the indentation fill back in; within seconds the leaf looked once again pristine. Again she pinched the leaf between her fingers, but this time she pulled.

It didn't budge.

Jahira frowned and tugged harder, but the leaf held fast.

Determined now, she wrapped her whole hand around a cluster of the spade-shaped foliage and pulled with all her strength. The branch which housed the cluster flexed slightly, but did not give up its decoration.

Jahira released the leaves and watched them slowly expand to their original shape.

She looked back toward the settlement to see if anyone had witnessed her failure, and then continued on her way, casting side-long glances at the mysterious plants.

The land began to slope downward toward a rocky ravine which the river had carved on its journey to the ocean. On a whim, Jahira broke into a run. Her body immediately protested the effort. Muscles and joints were still adjusting to the forces of planetary gravity, not to mention navigating the uneven terrain.

Ignoring the minor aches and pains, she lengthened her stride and pumped her arms to see how fast she could push herself. She reveled in the burn that crept up from her lungs and into her throat, making her feel alive. When she finally pulled up to a stop at the bank of the river, sweat dripped from her brow. With her hands on her knees, she gasped in lungful's of air. The gurgling sound of the cold, clear water rushing southward sang its invitation.

Once she'd caught her breath, she pulled off her boots and shimmied out of her flight suit. Clad only in thin undergarments, goose bumps stood out on her arms as the breeze tickled her bare skin. With her arms crossed tight against her chest, she stepped into the current and gasped.

"Cold, isn't it."

Jahira whirled toward the voice to see Magnar standing a few feet away.

"Hey, what are you doing here?" Jahira asked.

"Same thing as you, it looks like," he replied, nodding toward the water. "You know it's past time for a bath when you can smell yourself."

"Oh yeah?" Jahira grinned and unfolded her arms. "Let me help you with that."

She reached down and formed a cup with her hand, then sent a spray of icy liquid in his direction.

Magnar took a step back, a near smile twitching the corners of his mouth. Then his eyes moved to the silver cuff around Jahira's wrist. His face clouded and Jahira cursed silently as the almost normal moment passed.

She watched his eyes wander toward the horizon and linger there.

"Come on in," she said, trying to coax the moment back to life.

Magnar didn't respond.

"Hey, are you all right?" Jahira asked. She knew he wasn't. She knew it was a stupid question, but she didn't know what else to say.

Magnar took a deep breath then, and finally looked at her.

"I'd better get going," he said, then turned abruptly and clambered up the rocky rise.

Jahira muttered a string of profanities under her breath as she stepped out of the water and pulled on her rank clothing. Magnar was already out of sight by the time she'd laced up her boots. After scurrying up the ravine, she scanned the field until she saw him duck into the shadows of the silver trees.

Jahira narrowed her eyes, and followed.

She tried to stay far enough behind that he wouldn't see or hear her, but close enough that she wouldn't lose him. She tailed him for at least half of a mile before she began to seriously consider catching up and asking him where the heck he was going.

Finally the canopy opened up, revealing a vast circular field capped by the bright turquoise sky. Jahira stood beneath the trees and took in the view before her. She stood at the edge of a field ringed by thousands of the silver trees. In the center of the circle stood five hills, graduating in size so that they looked like a staircase to the clouds. She had seen all of this from the air of course, but she hadn't really appreciated how big it all was until now.

She watched Magnar climb the hills. Once he'd reached the tallest rise he kneeled in the grass. When she saw him lean down in slow increments and then jerk his head back abruptly, she started forward.

He did it again, compelling Jahira to run. She called his name as she sprinted up the hills.

Lungs and heart threatened to burst inside her chest but she pushed herself faster. When she stopped beside him, he looked up at her, his expression one of annoyance.

"What are you doing here?" he asked. "Did you follow me?"

"Yes, I did," she gasped, still catching the last of her breath.

"Why?" he snapped.

"Why?" Jahira echoed, beginning to feel rather annoyed herself. "Because I am worried about you, that's why!"

"Don't be," Magnar turned his face back toward the pool in front of him and that's when Jahira realized that the liquid was actually silver.

She took a step back, frowned, and then stepped forward again. She leaned in toward the pool to get a closer look. She'd assumed the pools were filled with water when they'd flown over during their scouting mission; apparently she'd been wrong.

"What is it?" she asked.

"I don't know," Magnar replied.

"We should tell the General, or better yet, Ryan."

Magnar didn't respond.

"Have you already told them? Or taken a sample to them?"

Magnar shook his head.

Jahira knelt down beside him.

"Look, Magnar, I've know you my whole life. We've worked together for the last five years. I lost my family too. You can talk to me."

"I don't want to talk about it." His voice took on a hard edge as he continued. "I don't want to think about it, I don't want to remember it, I don't want to keep seeing her burning to a pile of ash with our baby inside of her every time I close my eyes."

A knot formed in Jahira's throat. She placed a hand on his forearm. He jerked his arm away and balled his hands into tight fists.

"Please, just leave me alone."

Jahira pulled her hand back and rose to her feet. She stood there a moment, wishing she could do something, wishing she knew what to say.

Magnar remained motionless with his head down, fists clenched; closed off.

"I'm going to let Ryan know about these pools," Jahira said. "I'm sure he'll want to run some tests. I'll be back in a bit."

Magnar didn't respond.

She sighed, turned, and walked away, leaving him there alone.

Chapter 12

Krnar slept for a full sun and woke at dusk the following night. At least, that's what his brother told him. He had no memory of the passage of time.

"Neither Allnall nor Brdar have returned," Arkan said. His brother sat cross-legged on the opposite side of the small fire. Steam rose from the krska-skull bowl and with it the scent of boiled meat.

Krnar's stomach growled in anticipation.

"How many suns until a search team is sent?" Krnar asked.

Ulletta watched Arkan as he responded, one hand resting on the small swell of her belly.

"Three, maybe four," Arkan replied. "Neither left with the number of rations you did, if they don't come back on their own soon, it could be too late."

A flicker of hope sparked in his chest. Perhaps there was still a chance he could be chosen. If Allnall and Brdar had to be rescued, maybe the elders would bend the rules, send him anyway.

The sound of jubilant celebration carried into the cavern on the sea breeze. Krnar opened his mind for the message. Dread began to edge out the brief glimpse of hope.

Allnall has returned!

The message registered and his heart dropped.

She'd outlasted him. How had she managed to outlast him? Her kill had been smaller. Had she waited nearby until she knew he'd returned? He wouldn't put it past Allnall. No matter how she'd accomplished it though, the truth could not be denied.

Forcing himself out into the clear, frozen night, he allowed the pull of the crowd to carry him to the base of the ice. A small glowing figure rappelled down the face to the same cheers and cries which had sounded for him such a short time ago.

Why did it have to be Allnall?

His only hope now was that, by some miracle, Brdar returned. Most had given up hope for the final contestants, but here came Allnall, defying the odds.

He kept his eyes lowered as she sauntered by.

Allkoll, Brdar's mate, did not follow the crowd into the cavern.

Krnar watched her resume her perch on the look-out rock beneath the wall of ice, wrapped in a krska hide with only her up-lifted face glowing in the night. Krnar saw the determination written in her posture, the hope alive in her countenance. He remembered feeling the same way when he'd waited for his father to return from the final trial. Every sun he'd volunteered for watch duty. Every sleep he'd curled up in a hide at the mouth of the cavern, alert to the slightest sound. His watch had not ended well.

Staring up at the field of stars, he sent up a prayer for Brdar and then lost track of time, remembering. His only clue as to the length of his musings came when his feet began to tingle with cold.

"Think he'll make it?"

Krnar started and turned toward the speaker. "Allnall! What are you doing out here?"

Her eyes shone a little too bright within deep sockets, a fever perhaps? Her ribs protruded beneath her fur. He couldn't help but be impressed but, damn it, why Allnall?

"After almost two moons on my own, it's a bit overwhelming in there," she said.

Krnar nodded.

"So, you think he'll make it?"

"I'm not sure," Krnar replied. "I hope he does."

"He has to be out of food, probably two handfuls of suns past."

Krnar hissed softly. He'd been thinking the same thing, remembering the modest size of Brdar's lizard.

"If he does make it back, he'll be chosen." Krnar watched Allnall for her reaction.

Her lips pursed and she nodded.

"Who knows, I may just decide to go anyway." Allnall flashed a smile his way, and then turned her attention back to the wall of ice.

A jolt of surprise ran through Krnar's mind.

Allnall's words seemed to shift his whole world. Could she do that? Simply choose to leave? Would the Elder's allow it? Could they stop her?

The rigid adherence to laws and customs which ruled The People's lives had apparently robbed him of his ability to think beyond the established boundaries. It proved difficult to conceive of any action which had not been sanctioned by the Elders or Ellall.

"Would you?" Krnar finally asked.

Allnall shrugged.

"Why not? Better to die out there on some great adventure than to rot away in the dark of these Aruvel-forsaken caves."

Krnar blinked in astonishment. He'd never heard anyone speak this way. It made him uncomfortable and also…excited.

"What if we all left? Like our ancestors who fled from The Marked. We could flee from the ice. We could all return to the warm land, together." Krnar's voice dropped to a whisper. He was thinking out loud, not really expecting an answer.

"I've thought about that," she admitted. "No doubt the elders have as well. Many would be lost, and we have few enough to spare as it is."

In the heavy silence following this statement, Krnar imagined what it might be like- infants and elders crowded on ice floes, praying for enough food and water to survive the journey. No one had ever returned. Maybe no one had ever made it to the warm land to begin with.

Krnar excused himself and returned to the cavern, but sleep did not come that night. He sat at his hearth, watching the flames of the vrmefur flicker, trying to imagine a life that did not include rock and ice and sea.

When light began to stream through the cavern entrance, a shadow fell across his hearth.

Krnar looked up to see Arkan in full ice-climbing gear complete with a pack strapped over his shoulders and around his waist.

"Krnar, a search party is forming and I'm joining them. We're going to look for Brdar."

Krnar absorbed the news, nodded, and began to rise.

Arkan's hiss stopped him.

"You cannot go. You are one of the candidates." Arkan paused and Krnar could see there was something more his brother wished to say. "I came to ask you to watch over Ulletta while I'm away. If anything should happen…"

Arkan's voice trailed off.

Normally Ulletta wouldn't need any watching. She was a capable fisher and hunter, even better than her spouse at fashioning tools and utensils. Krnar knew, though, that she carried a child, only a few moons in the womb. The couple had not yet made an official announcement, but everyone knew. There were no secrets in a small community, only the unspoken but collective consensus to feign ignorance until the right moment.

"Of course," Krnar replied.

Arkan nodded and then strode away to join the small group of men and women who gathered at the cavern entrance.

Krnar stole a glance at Ulletta, who bustled around her hearth and pointedly did not look at the search party.

For five suns Krnar kept one eye on the Great Ice, more anxious for his brother than he had ever been for himself. What would he do if Arkan did not return? What would he do if Arkan left behind a fatherless child, like his own father had done? But no, this child would have its mother. These things would be Ulletta's to decide.

Fortunately, Krnar did not have to face these questions. His brother returned alive and well, which was more than could be said for Brdar.

Every voice rose in a trill of sorrow when the search group returned with Brdar's lifeless body. With a heavy heart and a familiar tightness in his chest, Krnar watched Allkoll follow the bearers of her husband's body to the mouth of the cavern. They placed him gently on the rock. Allkoll fell to her knees.

Keening wails rose from Allkoll's very soul as she pressed her forehead against Brdar's. Her cries pulled at Krnar's heart.

Bodies parted for Ellall, who stepped into the inner circle and began a low, mournful song. Those nearest her joined in quickly. Krnar added his voice when the second stanza began.

He sang until his throat grew raw, stopping only when Ellall raised her arms to the sky.

Voices fell silent and minds opened.

One by one, Krnar linked with the minds of his people until he could feel them all. Allkoll's grief stabbed him like a knife in the heart.

Images appeared in Krnar's mind. Memories of Brdar as a youth, of his first hunt, his first dance with Allkoll; memories shared by all, to be remembered.

Grkar saved his tribute for last.

The old man knelt beside Brdar and took his hand.

"I'm sorry I wasn't there. I should have been there," he whispered.

Krnar could not remember a time when the two friends had not been together; hunting, fishing, telling stories by the fire late into the night. Grkar's grief was nearly overshadowed by his guilt.

"Remember him for me," Allkoll said. She rose. The crowd parted again as she walked to the cavern. She returned with Brdar's favorite belt, knife, and spear which he'd had to leave behind for this part of the competition.

"I am ready," she said to Ellall.

Ellall nodded.

Brdar and Allkoll's children, along with Grkar, carried Brdar's body down the stone steps to the shore of the sea. They waded out, stopping just before the drop-off, and placed his body on an ice-floe.

Krnar watched from above, along with all but Brdar's closest family.

The bearers placed their hands on the edge of the ice and prepared to push it out to sea. Then Allkoll placed a hand on her son's shoulder. She spoke some words which Krnar could not hear. Her son turned and appeared to be arguing with her.

Murmurs and soft hisses floated around Krnar, buffeted by the chill wind.

Eventually, all backed away from the floe save Allkoll. She lowered her body into the waves and began to push the floe out to sea alone.

More trills, the tingle of mind-to-mind conversations which buzzed around him but did not include him.

Allkoll's daughter placed her face in her hands. One of her brothers placed a hand on his sister's shoulder.

Krnar's throat burned and hot tears formed in the corners of his eyes. With the pad of his thumb he quickly brushed them away before the tears froze.

Ululating cries of sorrow rose from the cliff-top as those around him began to understand.

Like a current of electricity, minds connected and then reached out to Allkoll.

Please, don't go.

Allkoll, come back.

Krnar heard the cries in his mind but Allkoll did not respond.

Finally, realizing the futility of their pleas someone projected, *At least take some provisions.*

I have all I need. I have Brdar.

Clear, strong, determined; Allkoll's final words rang in his head.

He watched Allkoll slide her husband's body from the floe. She wrapped her arms around her mate and swam toward the horizon.

"May you find the warm land," a voice whispered from behind Krnar.

"May you find the warm land," Krnar repeated.

He remained motionless until the two glowing dots merged into one and then disappeared.

Chapter 13

When Jahira returned with Ryan and Medic, Magnar still sat at the edge of the pool. Ryan and Medic knelt on either side of Magnar and stared at the opaque liquid.

"Have either of you touched it?" Ryan asked.

"No," Jahira replied without hesitation, and then glanced at Magnar, waiting for his response.

Eventually he shook his head.

"Good, that's good." Ryan opened a small case he'd brought with him and pulled out a pair of gloves. After wiggling his long thin fingers down into the individual casings, he sealed the gloves to his shirt at the wrist. Next he retrieved a stylus and a small transparent ball.

Jahira watched with interest. Ryan held the stylus over the surface of the pool and pressed the end with his thumb. A thin beam of light projected from the pointed tip, disappearing into the pool below. Ryan removed his thumb from the end of the device, but the beam remained. Next, he slid his thumb upwards along the side of the black tube.

Jahira's eyes followed the thin stream of silver liquid as it rose up into the beam of light.

Ryan tapped the side of the tube, trapping the liquid inside the beam, and then he stood. The beam of light remained the same length that it had been when he'd tapped the side, complete with its extracted sample of liquid. He then held this beam over a hole in the glass ball. When he pressed his thumb to the end of the tube again, the beam of light, along with the silver liquid, fell into the ball.

Ryan held the transparent orb aloft with a smile.

A tiny sample of silver liquid hung suspended in the center of the container, surrounded by a field of light. Medic held up the case and Ryan placed the clear ball and the extractor back in the kit.

"Let's take this back to the ship," Ryan said. He turned and walked away without waiting for a response.

Jahira watched Medic as he paused and looked at Magnar.

"Magnar, let's go see what Ryan finds out," Jahira said.

Medic looked at her, his concern for Magnar clear on his face.

Jahira frowned and shrugged.

Finally Magnar nodded and then stood.

"Yeah, let's see."

Jahira let Medic go first, she fell in behind Magnar.

"Have you told anyone else about this?" Medic asked after pausing to wait for Magnar and Jahira to catch up to him.

"Only the General, and just today, right before I found the two of you," Jahira said. "Tala and Leiko saw the pools from the air, like we did. General Thayer saw the original images from our scouting trips as well, but we all thought it was water."

Medic nodded then glanced at Magnar, who shook his head

They stepped out from beneath the swaying yellow canopy of the grove into the vast field where the settlement continued to expand. The four colony ships dominated the skyline, flanked by the two much smaller jets.

Jahira, Magnar, and Medic followed Ryan on his circuitous route around the bustling community. Once they reached the Kepler Colonizer, Jahira led the way up the ramp and into the lower hold.

She felt a chill run down her spine and wrap cold fingers around her insides. She hadn't been in one of the big ships since they'd evacuated The Aquilo.

The smell of metal and chlorine made her homesick. As they rounded a corner on their way to the ship's lab, an image of Zarya jumping out to surprise her, like she had every time Jahira had returned from a flight, hit her like a punch to the gut. She had to stop for a moment and catch her breath.

"Are you all right?" Medic asked.

Jahira nodded and resumed walking.

"Memories," she replied.

Medic nodded and gave her a small sympathetic smile.

They must have had the same thought at the same moment, because Medic's head turned in sync with her own to look at Magnar.

"What," Magnar growled.

Ryan waited for them in the lab, rocking back and forth with impatience.

The data screens hovered in the air around the table, waiting to be filled with information from his sample. Ryan extracted the sample from the glass ball, still suspended in the beam of light, and moved it to a net of lights which flickered over a black rectangle he'd set out on the table.

The net caught the beam of light, which held the sample. Information scrolled across the screens.

"Well, that's interesting," Ryan muttered. His eyes shifted from one screen to another.

Jahira waited several minutes for him to explain what he'd found. Finally, she could no longer contain her curiosity.

"What is it?" she asked.

Ryan shook his head as his frown deepened.

"I have no idea," he replied.

Chapter 14

The morning of the junction dawned bright with promise. The cavern walls vibrated with excitement. Stone cisterns bubbled over every fire, filling the empty spaces with savory smells. A steady stream of traffic came and went from the outside. Those entering bore ice, fish, and glow weed by the armload.

Krnar watched the activity, heard the curious whispers, but felt like an air bubble suspended in ice, immersed yet separated.

He would not be chosen.

The training, the seasons of waiting, had all been for nothing. Even if he had not broken the rules, Allnall had outlasted him in the final contest. She would leave the third continent on a quest to fulfill the prophecy and he would remain behind. He would return to the tunnels deep within the rock and grow old.

Nothing else remained for him.

Perhaps, like Brdar, he could compete one last time at the next junction and die with honor.

Adorned in his finest hides, fur oiled and gleaming, Krnar joined the other candidates who had gathered at the back of the cavern. He stood when expected, bowed at the right moments, but the day held none of the joy he had anticipated.

When it came time to name the chosen, Krnar wished he could leave. With his mind tightly blocked, he endured Ellall's words and focused on keeping his expression passive.

"It is never easy, choosing one to be sent away, knowing the chosen one might never return. So few of us remain," Ellall paused and seemed to get lost in a memory. Finally, she shook herself and continued. "The trials help us find the strongest and most resourceful among us. They allow us to see character tested so that we many choose wisely. For with the chosen goes our greatest hope for the survival of our people."

Ellall met the eyes of each candidate in turn.

Krnar tightened his fists in an attempt to physically hold himself together.

"The results were close this season." Ellall paused and looked straight at Krnar.

Krnar's heart stuttered.

"In the end, though, it came down to the one who is best equipped to make the journey alone and, Aruvel willing, return to guide our people back to the land of our ancestors." Ellall inhaled and extended her arms. "The chosen one, this season's sacrifice, is Allnall."

Ice worms seemed to weave through Krnar's stomach before tightening around his torso, making it hard to breathe.

Allnall stood and walked to the center of the circle.

Krnar had never hated anyone more.

She glided over the stone, all grace and confidence. As she accepted her token of victory, a figurine of a woman boasting a pair of true wings, Krnar's back burned. Whether from shame or the acute awareness of his distance from that picture of ideal, he could not tell. Did it matter?

The ringing in his ears prevented him from hearing the remainder of the formal exchange, but Allnall clearly accepted, for she smiled and then held her token aloft.

The cavern erupted in cheers.

After the ceremony, people migrated outside, where the feast had been laid out around an open space designated for dancing. Music drifted on the breeze, luring more to celebrate.

Bitter disappointment nailed Krnar to the ground.

"Brother, are you coming?"

Krnar did not respond to Arkan's question.

His hearth-brother squatted on his heels so close their fur nearly brushed.

"You did the right thing. Everyone knows this. There is no dishonor in today's decision." Arkan paused. "Besides, I think someone is very, *very* grateful."

Krnar could hear the smile in Arkan's voice.

He looked up and followed his brother's line of regard to find Tllomell folding hides and carefully placing utensils about her hearth. She had not left with the others.

In one fluid movement, Arkan rose and turned. He left without a word.

Krnar straightened as Tllomell approached.

"Krnar, I'm sorry-," she began.

Krnar held up a hand to stop her.

"It's not your fault. I do not regret my decision."

"But you will regret not being the one to leave tomorrow."

It was not a question. Krnar did not respond.

Tllomell sniffed and her eyes shifted. She stared out the cavern entrance where the sound of drums and rattles reached for the stars. The rhythm made his feet twitch.

"Will you dance with me?"

A glance over his shoulder revealed bodies weaving around each other in complex patterns. He knew if he opened his mind he would feel the energy building like the wind before a storm. The dance circle was the one area where touch was permitted between any and all.

"Not right now," Krnar said. His attention returned to the rock in front of him. "Maybe later."

An uncomfortable silence stretched for many heartbeats before Tllomell stepped past him and walked out of the cavern.

Krnar forced himself to do the same, knowing he would draw more attention by attempting to isolate himself.

The only other person who seemed immune to the revelry was Grkar. Sitting alone by a small fire, the old man stared into the flames, periodically prodding the vrmefur at its center to release more oil.

Krnar gave the dance floor a wide berth and stopped beside Grkar.

"Mind if I join you?"

Grkar gestured to the adjacent rock without looking up.

They sat for a time in companionable silence until Grkar cleared his throat.

"You did well, Krnar," Grkar said. "Silly thing to be eliminated for saving someone."

Krnar dipped his head in acknowledgement.

"Sure wish I'd been there to save Brdar. No dishonor in that at all."

Krnar swallowed around the sudden lump in his throat.

"Grkar, I'm sorry..." Krnar's voice trailed off. He didn't know what else to say.

"Yeah, be sorry for me, not for him. He lived a good life, died a good death. Better than being fed to the lizards next season."

Krnar grunted in affirmation. None could deny the truth of that statement.

"Will you join the Circle of Elders now?" Krnar asked. Grkar and Brdar had declined their previous invitation in order to compete in the trials this season.

Grkar scoffed.

"And sit in councils all day long while my backside grows numb listening to people complain? Going soft because people feed me like a babe? No disrespect, but that's not the life for me." Grkar paused. "What about you? Finally gonna find yourself a mate and help us increase our numbers?"

The old man's teasing grin drew a smile from Krnar in spite of his mood.

"Not if I hope to compete again," Krnar replied.

"Bah, your children will be grown by the next junction. Get yourself a wife, make some babies. It's not good for a person to grow old alone."

The unspoken but obvious, *like me*, silenced Krnar. The truth was he had decided long ago never to become a father. What if his children looked like him? He could hardly expect to take a mate and not father children, so he would remain alone, included but not completely accepted. The two men stared as orange flames licked the air like lizard tongues. Perhaps they could smell his fear.

A new rhythm vibrated through the rock as the drummers struck up a lively song.

Krnar fed another vrmefur to the flames. Grkar excused himself.

People came to congratulate Krnar on his performance, despite his ultimate failure. A few joined him by the fire and asked for his story. He began reluctantly at first, but found that talking lifted his mood. The audience grew and Krnar became more animated, recounting his adventures which, until today, he'd not been permitted to discuss.

The brief interval of darkness came and went. With the arrival of the first morning light, feet tired from dancing shuffled to form two lines facing each other. The lines stretched from the mouth of the cavern to the top of the stairs.

Allnall emerged from the cavern donned in hides which had been elaborately decorated with bone beads. A large pack bulged from her back, loaded with food and supplies. Her spear protruded from its sheath on one side of the pack. The Circle of Elders followed behind, each carrying a line of ice-filled bladders and a pack of rations.

People spoke blessings as she passed. Allnall's face remained solemn.

Krnar watched from his vantage point at the top of the steps. Each of the elders deposited their offerings on the ice floe which had been pulled to shore for Allnall's departure. When they were done, Allnall placed her pack atop the floe. Thirteen pairs of hands pushed the ice into the sea. Once it floated just off shore, the elders returned to the rocks at the base of the steps.

With strong, sure movements and eyes focused on the horizon, Allnall began to maneuver her frozen vessel through the maze of bobbing ice.

The People gathered along the edge of the cliff and watched her grow smaller and smaller until they could no longer make out her form against the merging blue fields in the distance.

The crowd dispersed and with their departure the celebratory air of the Season of Sacrifice ended. Hearts and legs felt heavy as The People made their way to the cavern. This day would be spent in rest, recovering from a full sun and sleep of revelry, and recharging for the final moons of the season. Come morning, the days would be filled with hunting, fishing, eating, and preserving; an endless cycle of preparation for the next Season of Ice.

Krnar waited until everyone else had returned to their hearths, then he descended to the sea shore. After one last glance at the top of the cliff, he lowered his body into the salty darkness and began to swim.

Chapter 15

A faint ripping sound followed Jahira's huff of exertion. She drove the sharp tip of her small survival shovel into the ground, severing the grass roots. Three more times she repeated this until she'd formed a small rectangle in the topsoil. She worked the brick of dirt from the earth and then handed it off to Brenna, who placed it atop the slowly rising wall of sod that would soon be Gavin and Brenna's home.

"No, Bren, you have to turn it like this," Gavin turned the piece and then pointed to the row below it. "They have to be cross-wise, each row the opposite of the previous one; that makes the walls stronger."

Gavin turned to cut another brick of sod. Jahira smiled as Brenna stuck her tongue out at Gavin's back, then turned to Jahira and rolled her eyes.

Jahira handed Brenna the next piece which Brenna accepted, then paused to turn it over in her hands.

"Isn't a house supposed to keep the dirt out?" Brenna asked.

Jahira laughed. With one forearm resting in the upright handle of her shovel, she tried to wipe the sweat from her brow with an equally sweaty forearm, managing only to smear more dirt across her face.

"Maybe someday," Jahira replied. "But hey, this way you can grow your own food on your house, you won't even have to walk to the garden to harvest. How fun will that be?"

Brenna appeared to consider the idea and then raised one eyebrow.

"Not fun enough, I'm certain." She smiled though, and gave Jahira a wink.

Jahira gazed out across the settlement where several more sod houses raced for the finish line against the one she helped to build.

Ryan had encouraged people to start building more permanent shelters in order to be able to have fires inside their homes when the snows came, as opposed to the outdoor campfires currently being used by any tent-dwellers.

Snow, Jahira thought. *That will be a sight*.

Jahira remembered him saying that winter was still almost a year away but that, according to his orbital simulations, the cold season would also last about a year.

"Do you really think these houses will be warm enough?" Jahira asked before she resumed her chore of cutting bricks from the soil.

"I guess we'll find out," Brenna replied. "I can't wait to see snow though. The pictures Ryan showed us were so beautiful! Can you imagine all of this covered in white?"

Jahira looked around, trying to picture what it might look like in the winter.

"I'm sure it will be beautiful, but also cold. That's something we've never had to deal with before."

"Maybe you need to find someone who will keep you warm at night." Brenna grinned and then glanced over at Gavin, who gave her a wink.

Jahira smiled but didn't respond. That was one subject her mother had harped on for the last several months before her death, and neither memory was one she wanted to entertain at the moment. Instead she lost herself in the rhythm of manual labor and by evening the walls were complete.

"All she needs now is a roof," Gavin declared. He stood, gazing at his new home with a satisfied grin.

"Do we have a palette reserved?" Brenna asked.

"A palette?" Jahira asked.

"Yeah, for the roof," Brenna replied.

"The pieces of the silicone cargo palettes from the ships will make a nice sturdy roof. We'll put a tarp over the opening, cover it with the heavy pieces from the palette; it'll be perfect."

Gavin placed an arm around Brenna's shoulders and gave her a gentle squeeze. "Only the best for my family."

Brenna scoffed, but leaned into his embrace. She placed a hand on her distended belly, her face radiated joy.

Jahira felt a sudden pang of loneliness.

"Well, I guess my work here is done," Jahira announced. She leaned her shovel against the wall of the house.

"Thanks for your help today," Gavin said.

"Yes, thank you." Brenna stepped out from under Gavin's arm to give Jahira a hug.

"No problem," Jahira replied, returning the hug quickly and then stepping away before she got choked up.

She nodded and waved before she headed back to her tent. Brenna returned the wave for a second, but then she turned and wrapped her arms around Gavin's waist. She began to pull him toward their new house with a playful smile. Gavin smiled back at Brenna and didn't even bother to wave. Before she was out of sight the couple disappeared through the opening in the tall dirt and grass wall.

Jahira sighed and rolled her aching shoulders. Her back burned with fatigue and her arms felt like jelly. She pulled off the gloves she'd worn to dig and winced when she saw the big circles of raw skin where blisters had formed and broken. She desperately needed to wash, but she didn't think she had the energy to walk to the river. Maybe a shower on board the ship?

The water tanks had been refilled from the river, and there would be heat. Sweaty as she was, a hot shower still sounded better than an ice-cold bath.

Once she'd retrieved a change of clothes from her tent, she headed for the Colonizer.

Dots of light appeared in rhythm with her steps as she walked up the ramp and into the belly of the ship. She took the elevator to the communal showers and sighed with relief to see that she was alone. Complete privacy was a thing she'd really never experienced before, and had only just begun to value.

She stripped off her rank flight suit and turned on the shower. After a moment of waiting, a stream of hot water cascaded from the nozzle above her head, causing steam to rise into the air. Jahira placed one hand in the waterfall to test the temperature. Air hissed through her teeth when the water hit her damaged hands.

She stepped forward and let the water soak into her skin. Her hiss soon turned to a sigh of contentment. Like a hot rain, it cleansed her body and restored her energy. She scrubbed the grime and salt from her pores.

Squinting through the steam and spray, she squirted a dollop of soap into her hand from the dispenser attached to the central column below the showerhead. She worked the soap into a lather up her arms and over her shoulders.

I wonder how long it would take to make more.

They had the recipe, they should eventually have the necessary ingredients, but the soap had been manufactured aboard The Aquilo. Another thing she'd taken for granted, never fully realizing how much she would miss it when it was gone.

She rinsed quickly before her ration of water ran out, then toweled off and pulled on a blessedly clean outfit which she'd grabbed out of her tent along the way. The long-sleeved blue shirt and a pair of form-fitting blue pants were normally worn for physical training. The material wicked sweat and helped regulate body temperature. It would be great for the warm days and cool nights of the new settlement. She patted her hair dry and smiled, feeling the effects of humidity at work on the tight curls which sprung from her scalp.

As she exited the bathroom, her footsteps echoed down the long empty halls. The previously peaceful quiet became eerie and haunted, the empty ship suddenly felt like a tomb. Jahira broke into a run once her feet hit the top of the exit ramp and she didn't stop running until she could see the crowd which had gathered around a blazing bonfire.

Gulping air into her lungs, she slowed to a walk. As she approached the gathering, she noticed Trevor standing between the crowd and the flames. His waving arms cast eerie shadows across the crowd, his deep voice rose toward the stars. He told a story of Earth, the place where The Aquilo had been built so many generations ago, but which none of them had ever seen.

Jahira half listened, intent on scanning the crowd. A movement to the right of the listeners made her turn and squint into the darkness beyond the light of the fire. A figure crept from the shadows of a nearby tent. The hunched figure moved furtively from one hiding place to the next, away from the crowd, away from the settlement, and finally toward the silver trees.

Magnar.

Jahira narrowed her eyes and began to follow.

After she'd checked to make sure all eyes remained on Trevor, she too stole through the settlement in pursuit of her friend. The shadows cast by the light of the three moons made her feel as if she walked through a dream. Objects could seem larger or smaller than their actual size depending on the play of the light and multiple shadows.

About halfway through the grove Jahira encountered a wide stream. Birthed and fed by the multitude of springs erupting from the ground around the silver trees, the stream began in the north and flowed both east and west from its point of origin. The two branches continued through the grove, drinking and growing until they once again met in the south, where they merged together to become the fast and frigid river which cut through the field on its way to the sea.

Picking her way carefully over slick rocks, she crossed the shallow water and continued after Magnar. Moonlight filtered through the canopy at odd angles. Even where the pale light touched the trees, she could no longer discern the green from the yellow in the hue of the leaves. The red orbs which had not already been harvested seemed to be shrinking in on themselves. Her brow creased as she contemplated the disappearance of what had become a primary food source.

Jahira's mind worked over the possibilities until she stopped just shy of entering the inner field. Her dark skin and dark clothes absorbed the light of the moons. She blended into the surrounding shadows. Magnar climbed the hills in the center of the field and knelt at the edge of the largest pool.

He leaned forward, slowly, then jerked back almost as if he'd been bitten. One hand pushed away from the smooth silver trunk of the closest tree as Jahira stepped from the shadows.

Her steps quickened when Magnar leaned forward again, but this time he did not jerk away. He dipped his fingers down and into the pool.

Jahira's heart began to hammer against her chest.

Magnar raised his cupped hands to his mouth.

"Magnar, no!" Jahira yelled.

She ran toward the largest hill. Hurtling up the rise with her hand stretched out as if to stop him, she was too late.

She watched in horror as Magnar tipped his head back and drank.

EMPYREAN

Chapter 16

Swimming like his life depended on it, Krnar caught sight of Allnall before nightfall. He wondered if he could have closed the distance if she'd not been burdened by a well-stocked ice floe.

Long before he drew close enough to be seen or heard, Krnar signaled to her mind-to-mind. The last thing he needed was a spear through the eye for surprising her.

Shock registered through the link, quickly followed by a warm welcome.

"I wondered if you'd do it," Allnall said when Krnar surfaced beside her. "I didn't think you would, to be honest."

"I didn't bring any supplies," Krnar stated. "I left as soon as everyone returned to the cavern. I didn't want to risk being seen or questioned." He wanted to get this out of the way immediately. If Allnall rejected him, he could still make it back without raising suspicion.

"You can fish, right?" Allnall said, her tone teasing.

"As long as there are fish to catch."

"We'll figure it out. I'm actually glad to have some company."

Krnar wasn't so sure he wanted to spend what could be the rest of his life with Allnall, but at the moment it beat the alternatives. He wisely kept his mouth, and his mind, closed on that issue.

"With two of us pushing, maybe we'll get there faster," Krnar said.

"This won't last us the whole trip," Allnall said, patting the edge of the ice.

"What do you mean?"

"Ellall had a few extra memories to share with me before I left," Allnall said. Her tone indicated they were not all good memories.

"You mean memories the rest of us don't have?"

"Yep."

"Why wouldn't she have shared these with everyone?"

"I'm not sure," Allnall replied. "Maybe somewhere down the line the Akaruvel decided it would be best. Maybe no one would leave if they knew the truth."

Krnar frowned. That didn't sound good.

"So what's the truth? What are the other memories?"

"Well, for starters, as the air and water get warmer, our trusty little craft here will melt, long before we reach the warm land."

He could hardly imagine such warmth, but he supposed it made sense.

"So what do we do then? Swim the rest of the way?"

"Nope. Hopefully before it melts we'll cross paths with a laro.

"One of the living islands?"

"Yep."

"And that will take us to the warm land."

"It should get us pretty close, so long as we catch one floating on the right currents."

"What if we don't?"

Allnall shrugged.

"You're not making this sound very promising."

"You can always go back."

Krnar sighed.

"Okay, let's say we make it. How far is the allarra grove from there?"

"I'm not sure. The memories from the journey to the Great Ice come from our ancestors. They flew over the land, and most of the sea, just stopping to rest on the laros. Ellall showed me what it looked like from above, mountains, forests, but she didn't know the routes through."

"No wonder no one has ever made it back. Maybe no one had ever made it there."

They pushed in silence for a while, contemplating that depressing thought.

"What do you say we take shifts," Allnall said. "Even though it's faster to both push, we'd be less likely to stray off course if we're not also resting at the same time."

"Makes sense," Krnar replied. "I'll take the first shift."

Allnall smiled.

"See, you're coming in handy already."

Krnar hissed.

A shower of sparkling droplets rained over him as Allnall lifted herself from the water and onto the edge of the ice. Her full back, and therefore the triangles of flesh folded between arm and torso stared him in the face with his own inadequacy. He decided he was thankful that he'd left.

"Hungry?" she asked.

"A little," he replied. In truth his stomach felt as hollow as the final moons of the Season of Ice. He didn't dare admit this though. He felt guilty about consuming the rations meant for Allnall.

Allnall smirked and handed him a piece of salted fish.

With a nod and three frosty fingers, he accepted the offering. He chewed slowly, making the small amount last and hoping it would ease the cramp in his stomach enough to keep it from giving him away.

Allnall chipped some ice from inside one of the water bladders and placed shards on her tongue to melt. When she extended a large piece to Krnar, he shook his head.

"If you want to help, you have to maintain your strength. We'll either make it or we won't, but if you get too weak to keep up, I promise I will leave you behind."

Krnar had no reason to doubt her.

"When I take a break, I'll have some," he said.

Allnall sighed but tied the bag and secured the line to the ice.

"I'm going to sleep for a bit. Wake me if you need me."

With that she rolled herself into a dry hide and closed her eyes.

Krnar kicked until his entire body went numb with fatigue. An aching cold worked its way from his toes and fingertips inward, threatening to freeze his vital organs. Pride forced him to continue.

Fortunately, Allnall woke before he sank lifelessly into the sea.

Without a word she lowered her body into the water.

Stiff and numb, he could barely pull his weight onto the floe.

"Need a hand?" Allnall asked. He could hear the smile in her voice. It was just the incentive he needed.

He growled low in his throat and kicked until his torso flopped onto the ice.

"You can use the hide," Allnall said.

Too cold to argue, Krnar gratefully rolled himself into the blessed warmth which lingered from Allnall's recent contact. In a matter of heartbeats he became oblivious to the world.

"Krnar, wake up!"

Consciousness returned in increasing increments of awareness...

"Krnar!"

Why is Allnall at my hearth? he wondered.

That final leap to realization struck like a blast of icy wind. He sat upright and blinked until Allnall's face came into focus.

"An ice mountain, there." Allnall indicated the direction with a nod of her head.

The pointed tip of ice jutted from the sea like the nose of a great frozen beast.

"I need you to help me get us over there and hook on."

After unraveling from the sleeping hide, Krnar slid into the water. Cold seized him, jarring him into sudden, acute alertness.

Together they kicked and pushed their frozen raft through low swells.

"Why do we need to get to another piece of ice?" Krnar asked.

"Another of Ellall's memories," Allnall replied. "Our ice floe is salt water, like the sea. Can't drink it. The ice mountains are fresh water."

"Got it," Krnar said, then, "Wait, how's that possible?"

"Don't know, not concerned about the details at the moment. I have two empty strings of water bags in my pack. We'll fill those."

Clouds appeared in front of his face with every ragged exhale. Icicles formed and clung to the fur beneath his nose and chin. A glance at Allnall revealed similar adornment. Her eyes were also rimmed with frost.

Allnall lifted her body half out of the water in order to peer over the ice.

"Almost there. Keep pushing straight ahead. I'm going to grab some line and hooks."

Glistening fur retreated across the floe. Krnar continued with a steady kick. His throat burned like he'd lit a vrmefur and then swallowed it. Odd how opposite ends of the temperature spectrum could create such similar sensations.

"A little farther."

He pushed on until the familiar groan of ice meeting ice drowned out all other sound.

Krnar stopped kicking. He let his legs drift downward.

Allnall's face appeared above him.

"Okay, we're hooked up. Come on up and get a drink."

Mustering what strength remained, he hauled himself to the surface. Once settled, Allnall handed him a chunk of ice, which he accepted gratefully. The ice melted on his tongue and cold liquid spread through his mouth, teasing him with tiny swallows that he felt would never satisfy his thirst.

For a full sun they worked and drank, chipping away at the ice mountain until the water bags were full and a large pile of ice rested on an extra hide.

"Fold that up and secure it while I unhook us," Allnall said.

Krnar complied, though it rankled a bit to be taking orders from Allnall.

"Your turn to swim," Allnall said as she stowed the lines and hooks.

Any irritation he felt toward his sole companion faded with the last rays of light. Surrounded by ink-dark waves and covered by a midnight sky, Krnar felt as if he were one of the stars. The glow of his body attracted a school of medium-sized fish. He took advantage of the opportunity to grab a few which came to nibble at his fur. Eventually they moved on and, while thankful for the unexpected meal, he hoped he didn't attract anything larger.

Gazing upward he found the Great Spear and let the glittering arrow guide his path across the heavens.

Chapter 17

Jahira raced across the field and up the series of inclines to Magnar's side.

Reaching out, she gripped his shoulder as much to get his attention as to hold herself up. She gasped air into her lungs.

Magnar turned and jerked out of her grasp. Jahira stumbled but quickly righted herself.

"What do you think you are doing?!" She demanded.

Magnar regarded her with narrowed eyes.

"What are you talking about?" he asked.

"I saw you, I watched you drink that...that," she said, pointing to the pool which reflected the moonlight like a mirror, making the top of the hill glow like a beacon.

"Why would I do that?" Magnar asked. He looked so sincere that Jahira began to doubt. "I just wanted to touch it." His eyes darted to the pool's surface and back to hers.

"I don't know. Why would you?" Jahira challenged.

Magnar's eyes traveled in a circle, staring at her boots, then at the pool, up at the moon, and over to the trees.

She waited.

"Well, it's getting late and I'm pretty tired. I'm going to head back to my tent." Magnar began to walk away. Without looking back, he called over his shoulder, "G'night, Jahira."

"Night," she replied.

Magnar's form grew smaller and finally disappeared into the trees. Jahira sat by the shore of the pool.

I know what I saw, she thought, *and I'm certainly not going to let him try again.*

She decided she would guard the pool for the rest of the night, to make sure that Magnar didn't return.

Once the sun had risen high enough to touch Jahira over the top of the silver trees, the increasing warmth of her skin and clothing woke her from a deep sleep. The smell of warm grass invaded her senses. As she opened her eyes the events of the previous night rushed to the front of her mind. She sat up abruptly and searched the surrounding area.

Jahira jumped to her feet and headed toward the settlement. She needed to find out if Magnar was okay.

Halfway through the grove a knot of hunger twisted her stomach, encouraging her to pluck a few of the red fruits from the surrounding trees. She could almost wrap her fingers all the way around the orbs. They were definitely shrinking.

Overcome by hunger, she finished the first fruit in three bites and then hurried forward. There were bigger things to worry about.

The settlement hummed with activity. She passed through on her way to the colonizer waving to acknowledge those who looked up from their chores. She needed to speak to Ryan or Medic, preferably both, and she felt confident she would find them in the lab aboard the big ship.

When she entered the lab, she was shocked to find not only Ryan and Medic, but Magnar as well.

"Good morning, Jahira," Medic greeted her. "How are you today?"

Jahira watched Magnar watch her as she entered the room.

"I'm fine," Jahira responded without looking at Medic. "How are you?"

"Doing great." Jahira could hear the curiosity creep into his voice. "What can we do for you today?"

"Uh, nothing, I was actually looking for Magnar." Jahira narrowed her eyes as she addressed Magnar this time, "And how are *you* this morning?"

"Great," Magnar replied in a monotone voice. He pierced her with an intense glare.

Medic's eyes shifted back and forth between them.

"I came by for a routine physical and everything looks perfect, right Medic?" Magnar asked, never taking his eyes off Jahira.

"Riiight," Medic replied slowly.

Jahira felt a twinge of relief. Magnar had come to see Medic on his own, he must have realized the potential danger of what he'd done, maybe he hadn't gone crazy after all. He actually did look a lot better than he had last night.

"Well, I'm glad to hear that," Jahira replied. "What are your plans for the rest of the day?"

She cocked her head and smiled a tight-lipped smile. There was no way she would leave him alone. Apparently he got the message. She saw one corner of Magnar's mouth quirk ever so slightly.

"I thought I might try my hand at fishing. Care to join me?"

"I'd love to."

"Is there something I should know about here?" Medic asked.

Jahira raised one eyebrow at Magnar. Magnar moved his head a fraction to one side and then the other.

"No," Jahira replied. "I think we'll be o.k."

"All right," Medic responded, sounding less than certain. "Why don't you take the drama somewhere else then, I've got patients to see."

Magnar jumped down from the examining table and stopped in front of Jahira. She extended one arm in an invitation for him to lead the way.

Chapter 18

"Jahira, you can stop babysitting me. Medic told you, I'm fine."

"Believe me, you are far from fine," Jahira retorted.

For two weeks now she'd barely let him out of her sight. She hadn't seen him drink the silver liquid again, but she couldn't be with him every minute, and she had to sleep. She had a strong suspicion that Magnar had found several chances to return to the pools.

"You've gotten more irritable every day, that isn't like you," Jahira said, and then stopped suddenly as Magnar rounded on her. He leaned in until his face was only inches away from hers.

"Did you ever stop to think it might be because I've got you on my ass all day every day?"

Jahira narrowed her green eyes and pressed a finger into his chest, forcing him back a step as she spoke.

"Did you ever think you're the closest thing to family I've got left? I don't want to lose you, too." She dropped her finger and balled her hands into fists to stop them from shaking.

Magnar's jaw worked for a moment before he turned in a huff and stomped across the settlement.

With a growl of irritation, she followed the trail of dust stirred up by the pounding of Magnar's heavy boots. She stopped at the outer ring of silver trees and, like everyone else who'd gathered here today, she began to harvest the new fruit.

The red bulbs which had hung in the branches since their arrival were gone. They seemed to have been reabsorbed by the trees. Not a single one had fallen to the ground, and for about a week, not a single one remained anywhere in the grove. Jahira knew this for a fact. She had scoured every inch of the place, not able to believe the evidence right before her eyes. Then one day new fruits had begun to grow in the canopy of green leaves. The settlers had waited as long as they could. Today was time to harvest.

"Morning, Jahira!" Tala called to her from a branch about halfway up one of the silver trees. Her legs swung to either side of the branch. Reaching and dropping in a steady rhythm, she tossed fruit down to Leiko.

"Morning," Jahira replied with a wave. "Hi, Leiko," she added as she stopped beside her friend.

"Hey," Leiko responded. "Have you tried one yet?"

Jahira shook her head.

Leiko handed her a grape-like cluster of fruit, each tiny oval was wrapped in a deep blue peel. When Jahira bit through the firm flesh, a sweet explosion of juice raced across her tongue. Inside, hundreds of tiny pods clung to each other. Every time Jahira chewed another pod would burst and fill her mouth with sweet liquid.

"Amazing, huh," Leiko said.

"Yeah," Jahira replied around a mouthful of fruit, "a little weird, but delicious."

Leiko looked up and caught another cluster of fruit from Tala then said, "I'm starting to think everything about this place is a little weird."

Jahira smiled and nodded in agreement. "So how's-" Jahira stopped when Leiko gasped and pointed.

Jahira turned to see Magnar on top of a woman he'd apparently tackled to the ground. Magnar had succeeded in pinning the woman's arms with one hand and now pulled the other arm back as his hand formed a fist.

Jahira moved without thinking. With a few long strides she closed the distance, and then hooked one arm under and around Magnar's cocked shoulder. With her other hand, she grabbed a fistful of his flight suit. She hauled him off the wide-eyed woman who scrambled to her feet and backed away. Magnar struggled and snarled.

"Magnar, calm down!" Jahira fought to keep a hold on Magnar. He strained toward the woman he'd tackled. Jahira was shocked when she saw who it was he'd tackled. "Lusela? What happened?"

"Jahira, what's going on?" Gavin asked. He moved in to help her restrain Magnar.

"I have no idea," she replied. "I was just asking the same question." She kept her arm locked around Magnar's, struggling to maintain her footing.

"Ask her!" Spit flew from Magnar's mouth as he shouted and pointed at Lusela. The head of maintenance had regained her composure. She avoided eye contact by brushing the dirt from her rumpled clothes. "Ask her what she said!"

All heads turned toward Lusela, who glanced up casually. Her attempt at indifference was belied by the deep red blush which crept up her neck and colored her cheeks.

"Well?" Jahira asked, addressing Lusela.

When she did not speak up, Jahira looked to the crowd of spectators.

"Someone had better speak up," Jahira demanded in a low voice. She leveled an intense gaze at each one in turn, ending with Lusela, "or I let him finish what he started."

A woman stepped from the gathered crowd, her hands twisting the hem of her long shirt.

"They were talking about the crash," she stated. "Lusela," she nodded toward the accused and was greeted with an icy glare. "She was makin' jokes about the wreck. She said, 'It was Messier all right.', that's when Magnar came flyin' at her."

Silence reined for a full minute. All eyes watched Jahira, wondering how she would react.

She fought to keep her expression under control, thankful that no one could see the hot flush which spread across her own dark countenance. She debated whether or not to help Magnar pound Lusela into the dirt.

Finally, she cleared her throat and pierced the offender with her green eyes.

"Is that true?" she asked.

The fact that Lusela's gaze shifted to the ground answered the question, but she waited for her to nod.

"Look at me," Jahira commanded through clenched teeth.

Lusela slowly looked up, not a hint of remorse visible on her face. Jahira's blood boiled.

"Never. Again." She bit off each word and then turned away. She couldn't stand to look at the other woman anymore.

She heard footsteps retreat from the area, but didn't turn to watch.

She finally released Magnar, placing a hand on his back to guide him over toward Tala and Leiko.

"Can you believe that?" Jahira asked.

"I knew she wasn't the most popular person on the Aquilo," Gavin responded, "but she always did her job well. I had no idea she had an evil streak."

"Well, now we know," Jahira said.

Once she felt they were out of range of any more trouble, Jahira stopped and looked at Magnar.

"You okay?" she asked.

Magnar's nostrils flared. He didn't bother to answer the question, but did finally speak.

"I need to be alone for a while." He looked pointedly at Jahira as he said this.

She bit back her initial response and nodded.

She watched him go and was relieved to see him head toward the river. It took all her willpower not to follow him but he was right, she wasn't his babysitter. If he needed space, she would give it to him.

Chapter 19

An earsplitting trill startled Krnar out of a dreamless sleep. He bucked so violently, he almost tipped himself and the pack off the ice floe, which had grown considerably smaller than when their journey had begun.

Allnall stood at the front edge of the ice, pointing at the horizon and laughing.

Krnar's pulse quickened.

Had she spotted land? They'd been traveling for two handfuls of suns. The water had grown warmer, and the ice mountains had disappeared. Good signs for finding the warm land, bad news for the thirsty travelers.

"It's a laro!" Allnall exclaimed.

Krnar stood, careful to remain in the middle of the floe to maintain his balance.

Shading his eyes with one hand, he squinted out at the endless blue landscape. A dark line, barely visible, sliced between the sky and water on the horizon.

"Are you sure?" Krnar asked.

"It has to be." Allnall dove overboard, quickly resurfaced and shouted, "Come on!"

Habit made him brace for the cold impact of salt water. Instead, the temperature didn't change at all as he plunged beneath the surface of the sea. He swam to the point of the ice floe where Allnall had already begun to push and surfaced beside her.

"When we get close we have to find the back of the thing," Allnall said.

"How do we tell one end from the other?" Krnar asked.

"Look at it underwater. The back doesn't have tentacles. If we try to climb up the front, we're lunch."

"Back end, no tentacles, got it."

As they drew near, Krnar dove and swam ahead to scout the best location.

Hundreds of waving arms extended from the flat body of the laro and hung deep into the shadows of the sea. Myriad fish darted in and out of the translucent appendages but avoided being drawn upward to the mouth, which Allnall had said was located somewhere in the middle of all those arms. Perhaps the laro waited for bigger prey.

There didn't seem to be a safe place to board.

I think we'll have to go around it, Krnar projected. *I don't see a place without tentacles.*

All right, we'll get on top and paddle around.

Krnar returned to the floe and they coordinated their climb to the top on opposite sides of the ice, then pulled out the bone and hide paddles they'd fashioned from Allnall's supplies.

It took the better part of daylight, which had grown shorter the farther they'd traveled, to find a safe landing place and climb aboard.

Like stepping onto a wet pile of glow weed, Krnar's foot sank into the slick flesh of the creature's back. Once he'd gained his balance, he reached out to accept the pack, which Allnall extended toward him. He slung the pack over one shoulder and then provided a steadying hand for Allnall as she joined him on their new ride.

With knees bent and arms out for balance, Krnar led the way to the center of their living island.

"Well, we found one," Krnar said.

"You mean *I* found one," Allnall countered.

"Yeah, right." With one statement Allnall stole all the satisfaction Krnar had been feeling. Too many days together with no one and nothing to distract them had fueled the tension between them rather than dampened it. Krnar wondered what it would be like if someone else, anyone else, had won in Allnall's place. At this point even being alone seemed preferable.

"Now we just have to hope it's taking the most direct route to where we're headed."

"At least the fishing will improve. Did you see all of the fish darting through those arms?"

"Yeah. Pray for a little water from the sky and we might actually survive."

This prayer was not answered by the time they'd secured the pack to the laro using gut line and lizard claws. In fact, the skies remained clear for the next handful of suns.

Krnar had never thought he could be depressed by too much sun.

The next morning, he woke to the sound of drumbeats.

When he opened his eyes, he stared as slashes of light cut through the sky. Dark mountains grew on the horizon. He heard the distant rumble again.

"What in the name of Aruvel is that?"

Not drums. Not anything he'd ever heard before.

Allnall sat up.

"What is it?" she asked.

A boom like the very earth itself had ripped apart caused Krnar to stagger backwards.

"I have no idea."

Black clouds overtook them. The flashes of light continued to chase each other through the darkness.

Krnar and Allnall cowered together. He had never in his life felt so small.

Then the sky opened. Fat drops of water poured from above, pelting his fur in a hard staccato rhythm.

Allnall laughed and tilted her head back, mouth open to the sky.

Krnar reached for the water bags.

Head back, lips parted, he drank his fill while his hands held the neck of a water bag open.

They raced to keep up. Bags filled and overflowed. Unwieldy liquid tipped the bags and sloshed out. Water poured down in sheets so thick Krnar struggled to keep his eyes open.

"They're all full!" Allnall yelled.

"I should've brought more!"

"Yes, you should have!"

From the profile alone he couldn't tell if she was teasing or beginning to resent his presence.

A deafening crack made him startle and then stumble. The wind drove the rain sideways. Froth formed on the tips of the rolling waves.

"I think we'd better anchor them!" Krnar yelled, pointing toward the full bags.

Once they'd lashed all their belongings to the laro with gut line and lizard claws, Krnar began to secure himself. Waves washed across the creature's back, threatening to carry the hitch-hikers away.

Swells and valleys rolled beneath his feet. Krnar clung with all his strength to the line he'd tied to his belt. His stomach began to roll in rhythm with the sea.

Eyes shut and lips pursed against the rising nausea, he took deep breaths through his nose. He didn't want to lose any of the precious water he'd just consumed.

When he dared open his eyes, he saw Allnall's glowing arm move against the dark backdrop of the raging storm.

She unhooked the line at her belt.

What are you doing? he projected.

Her chin jutted toward the pack.

One of the hooks which secured their, or rather her, supplies to the laro had worked itself loose.

Allnall waited for a dip between the swells. She crawled to her pack, grabbed the errant claw, and forced it back through the laro's flesh.

Another wave rose beneath them.

Allnall's feet slipped. Her free hand reached for the line but her fingers slid across the wet tendon.

The world tipped as the wave passed. Water rushed across the surface.

Allnall rolled across the laro, scrabbling for purchase. There was none to be found. Allnall's mouth opened in an unheard scream before she disappeared into the sea.

Allnall! Krnar found her mind, felt her shock, her fear. *Hold on! I'm coming for you!*

No! Calm resolve replaced the fear. *You have to go.*

She projected an image of the alara grove, silver trees glinting in Allorkan's light, and then she closed her mind.

Allnall! He shouted with his mind and then at the top of his voice, "Allnall!"

Another wave knocked him to his stomach. Krnar searched for any sign of Allnall's light as the next wave crested beneath him.

No light. No signal.

Allnall was gone.

****

When the storm broke, Krnar lay on the back of the laro groaning, drained, and empty. The continuous rise and fall of the sea had proved too much for his constitution. He hadn't been able to hold down the belly full of water. Then there was Allnall.

He couldn't feel her anymore, couldn't find her with his eyes or his mind.

Fingers numb from loss of circulation began to tingle once Krnar released the line around his wrist. The ends dangled from the hook which dug into the laro's flesh. He cut the line from his belt and checked the supplies.

One line of water bags remained, along with Allnall's pack. She'd risked her life to save that pack and she had lost.

Reaching for one of the water bags, he sipped and immediately spat the liquid out. The bags had filled with salt water from the waves. A few bites of salted fish revived him physically, though he longed for water to wash away the lingering taste of bile. Mentally he struggled with unanswerable questions, and unexpected grief.

Why hadn't he been the one to fall? What other secrets had Ellall shared with Allnall that he would never know? Should he try to final Allnall? Try to wait once he reached shore? Continuing on without her seemed heartless.

Having nothing else to occupy his day, he nursed his guilt and stared at the endless sea. Every bite of fish reminded him that he had not been chosen for this task. He had not earned this honor. He should not be here.

He was utterly alone.

It didn't feel as good as he'd thought it would.

Over the course of the next moon the blue which surrounded him remained unbroken. The waters were warm and the few creatures he saw so foreign he had no names for them. He began to make up names of his own. The sky opened every few days to fill his water bags. Rather than worry over thirst or hunger, he began to fear he might die of sheer boredom.

Then, one morning, he woke to unfamiliar warmth soaking into the skin of his face. When he opened his eyes, tears formed. He blinked his protective lenses into place and still had to squint against the bright glare off the water.

A sliver of light hugged the horizon and danced across the waves. Even the narrow crescent proved vaster and far warmer than Mrkellan during its closest pass.

Not daring to move lest he find himself waking from an impossible dream, Krnar stared until tears streamed over the fur on his cheeks.

Like a seedling breaking through the snow, he soaked up his first glimpse of Allorkan, the sun of the warm land.

The vision would be forever burned into his memory.

EMPYREAN

Chapter 20

The load on his back felt far too light for the journey ahead. Krnar faced an unknown land, an unknown distance with unknown dangers. He had never been one to give in to fear, but a part of him longed to remain on the laro where he knew what to expect, and knew he could survive…but then his people might perish.

The gray smudge on the horizon had expanded over the last five suns. Doubt and hope had toyed with him. Now he could see peaks rising from the dark mass, capped with white as they speared the sky and killed his doubts.

He could wait no longer.

Tepid waves buoyed his weight when he dove off his laro and kicked for shore. The longing to feel solid ground beneath his feet pulled him forward.

The sea below him teemed with life. The very floor of the sea moved. Countless waving tendrils swayed in rhythm with the push and pull of the water. The weeds here did not glow but provided a perfect hiding place for the myriad creatures which he'd never heard of.

Ahead, the land rose in a display of vegetation and color the likes of which he'd never imagined possible. Green, brown, a red so dark it might be purple, and trunks as dark as night blended together and spread to the base of the great, jagged peaks which erupted in the distance.

The first contact of bare foot on solid rock sent a shiver of excitement through his entire body.

I made it.

He alone, rejected son, deformed child, stood now on the land of his ancestors.

Allnall had told him they must cross the mountains. Neither she nor Ellall had known the best route or exactly how long it would take. It was up to him now.

Warm sand shifted beneath his feet. He smiled at the sensation, like walking through warm snow. Allorkan blazed in the sky above, heat pulsed on the top of his head and shoulders.

He knew the white caps on the mountains were formed by snow, but it seemed impossible for liquid to freeze in this heat. He hadn't even begun and already sweat tickled through his fur.

Gurgling water drew him to an inland stream. Cool, refreshing moisture caressed his hands as he filled his string of water bags.

He hiked through squat brush, a tangle of reaching vines and slicing thorns pulled at his fur. Shadows engulfed him when he stepped into the trees.

They had looked small from the back of the laro, at least in comparison to the mountains, but standing beneath the shifting canopy, Krnar felt no bigger than a worm.

Trunks he could not stretch both arms around sprouted from spongy soil. Above him creatures chirped and squawked and flitted. His already heightened senses coiled with tension. Every movement made him jump. He constantly glanced over his shoulder and couldn't shake the feeling he was being watched.

When the sun began to set, Krnar found an old tree with roots high enough to hide in. He curled up and spent his first restless night in a whole new world.

****

Krnar woke, blinked a few times to set his lenses against the light, and then gazed around in awe. The whole world sparkled in the morning sun. Shafts of light from the sunrise shifted across the forest floor as they penetrated the moving canopy over his head. Each time the light touched a root, a bush, or a rock, the illuminated object reflected a dazzling array of color. The temperature felt comfortable to Krnar, for whom a hard frost was like a summer rain; he sat and enjoyed the show while he consumed his morning meal.

Krnar eagerly resumed his journey toward the mountains. The forest overwhelmed him with sights, sounds, and smells. Birds called and careened through the trees overhead. Vegetation surrounded him, leaves fell from the trees, his own feet scuffled through the carpet of the forest, and the occasional scurry of a local inhabitant disturbed by his passing combined to overstimulate him to the point that he had to stop and rest, covering both ears and eyes to regain some calm. His mind was used to an endless stretch of blue-white ice, a blank canvas which he had mastered. Here he felt insignificant and disoriented.

He feared that he would not be able to remember it all. But would it matter? If he failed, if he could not find the grove or did not return to his people, there would be no one for him to pass his memories on to.

No, do not think like that. Look how far you've come, he told himself; but the thought echoed in his lonely mind.

At the beginning of this journey he had been focused simply on reaching the warm land. It had seemed like a dream, like a mythical place he had heard stories about for so long that he only wanted it to be real. He'd never in his heart been convinced that he would make it; but here he was, hiking through the legendary living trees. Now it seemed that anything was possible. He must believe that he could reach the grove; that he could climb the silver mountain; and he must trust Aruvel to show him how to bring his people home.

Chapter 21

Rain poured from the clouds in torrents, soaking through tents, through walls; it seemed to soak through Jahira's skin and saturate her body, leaving her limbs feeling weighted down like water-filled logs. She, like many others, sought refuge aboard the ships.

Once she'd toweled off and changed into some dry clothes, she found her old bunk and pulled out her data screen and then her virtual reality equipment. It had been so long since she'd used it that it felt strange putting it on now.

First, she removed her virtual reality lenses from their case and, using a small mirror built into the wall, fit the contacts to her eyes. Next, she attached one wireless receiver to her forehead, ran her fingers along the wire until she felt the next wireless receiver, then attached that to the top of her scalp over her motor cortex. A third receiver attached to the back of her head to interface with her occipital lobe. Thin cords hung now from either side; she smoothed these until she held the ear buds at the end and rotated the plugs until they felt comfortable inside her ears.

Jahira activated her data screen and tapped the wireless connection icon that appeared in the air in front of her. She felt the familiar tingling sensation of the headset interfacing with her brain, allowing her to believe that she moved in response to the visual stimulus she received through the lenses. With enough practice she could even develop muscle memory.

Anything she'd ever wanted to learn had been at her fingertips since childhood. She'd chosen to fly.

That's what she started with today, a series of flight simulations to keep her skills sharp; and it was just fun. After an hour or so of flight drills, she switched to some survival skills training. Visual and auditory data compiled by the ship's main computer were downloaded to create a virtual environment exactly like the planet on which she now lived. To this she added the basic survival programs. Once she'd had enough of archery, rope tying, and fileting fish, she removed the v.r. equipment and lay supine on her bunk. With the light touch of two fingertips, she pulled the data screen through the air until it hovered above her face. A few chapters of a fictional novel followed by a comedy vid ate away the afternoon. Finally, her eyes could take no more and she was forced to turn the screen off.

With a sigh she rose and paced the room. Joints creaked and muscles ached from the extended period of inactivity. Unaccustomed to sitting for so long, she felt irritable and restless. Even aboard The Aquilo there had always been something to do, or Zarya to entertain her.

Jahira fidgeted with the cuff on her wrist and smiled, remembering her sister; so full of life but barely given a chance to live.

Hot tears pricked her eyes, making them burn where the hard lenses had irritated the cornea.

Time to get off the ship.

Rain continued to fall, but lighter now, more of a mist instead of the previous deluge. The last of the daylight had faded to a muted gray on the horizon. Wet mud sucked at her feet when she stepped off the ramp and worked her way slowly out into the saturated field. She began to shiver as the mist penetrated her flight suit and cold water seeped into the soles of her boots. Glancing to her right she saw the Eagle and decided to have a look inside. Those sims had her itching for the real thing.

She slogged her way over to the base of the jet and entered the code into the keypad on the leg which released the platform. Leaving muddy footprints on the smooth silver, she walked to the corner and stepped on the button which pulled the platform back up into the ship.

Once the seal around the platform hissed closed, she turned and headed for the flight deck. She stepped one foot into the control room and then jumped back in surprise. Someone was sitting in the left seat.

"Magnar, what are you doing here?"

His head swiveled at the sound of her voice. Jahira recoiled at the sight of him.

The skin of his face was drawn taut over protruding bones. New lines had formed around his mouth and along his forehead. Dark half circles stood out like bruises beneath eyes that seemed almost wild. He looked like he hadn't bathed or slept since he'd left her in the grove. This was bad.

"Jahira, good, sit down." He turned his attention back to the console and finished what she recognized as the end of the pre-flight checklist.

"Magnar, what do you think you're doing?" Jahira asked. "You are in no condition to fly. I doubt you even have clearance. Where-"

"Sit down," Magnar ordered. He rose and pushed Jahira in-to the command seat.

With both hands pressing on her shoulders, he leaned for-ward.

"I have to go and *you* are going to help me."

"Magnar, I-"

He placed a hand over her mouth and moved closer. His nose almost touched hers and she could smell his breath, a strange mix of sweet odors that seemed completely incongruous with his appearance.

"That was not a question." He waited until she nodded once, and then finally removed his hand.

Jahira took a steadying breath, her nostrils flared. Magnar slid into his usual place in the right seat and buckled in.

"So, where are we going?" Jahira asked as Magnar powered up the lights and activated the solar coil.

"North," Magnar replied.

"Can I ask why?"

"Sure, but I can't tell you the answer."

"What do you mean you can't tell me?"

"I'm not sure why, but I have to go."

Jahira frowned and stared at Magnar's profile.

"This is getting a bit scary, Magnar. What is going on?"

He didn't answer. Jahira noticed that his hands shook slightly as he engaged the engine.

"Ready?" he asked.

He didn't wait for a response.

Jahira grabbed the yoke as Magnar sent power to the bottom thrusters. The Eagle lifted and hovered. Jahira housed the landing gear.

"I did want to fly," she mumbled to herself, then responded to Magnar in a louder voice. "Ready."

EMPYREAN

Chapter 22

Dark clouds hid the light of the planet's three moons, making the world an inky blur as Jahira and Magnar flew north. An uncomfortable silence permeated the ride; Jahira tried to wait it out, tried to ignore it, but eventually she couldn't take it anymore.

"Are we there yet?" Jahira asked, grinning and glancing at Magnar out of the corner of her eyes.

Magnar didn't look at her and the question that she had meant to be playful hung there, unanswered.

"Seriously, Magnar, how do we know when we've gone far enough?"

"I'll know."

Jahira rolled her eyes.

"Well at least you finally answered me."

Though he was still a far cry from the man she knew, he seemed to be less twitchy the closer they got to, well, wherever it was he felt he needed to go.

"Did you drink from the pool again?" Jahira asked, glancing at him again to gauge his reaction.

White rings formed around his knuckles as he tightened his fingers around the yoke in a death grip.

"Yes," he finally answered.

Jahira let out a long, audible exhale. She chided herself for ever leaving him alone.

After that she gave up on having a conversation for a while. Instead she watched the forest thin until the land became scrub covered foothills. The foothills rolled into a vast mountain range which loomed on the horizon. Jahira checked the radar and noticed the storm they'd been following had slowed. They were catching up to it.

"Time to stop yet?" Jahira asked.

"No, we need to go into the mountains." Magnar leaned forward as he spoke. His voice had become bright, eager.

Jahira frowned but continued upward and forward.

The Eagle soared above snow-covered peaks and the temperature dropped rapidly. The rain, which had begun to fall more steadily as they approached the storm, hardened into sleet. The sound of it hitting the metal body of the Eagle reminded her of her mother's old rain stick which she had made for Jahira from a plant on one of the colony planets they'd stopped at when she was a child.

"We're close. We're very close." Magnar's eyes darted wildly as he scanned the dark.

"Magnar, the weather ahead does not look good. We're as far in as we can go before things start to get really bumpy. It's time to turn around."

"No, I can feel it," Magnar insisted.

Jahira glanced over and saw him squeeze his eyes closed. Pain etched deep lines in his face. He pressed the palms of his hands against his skull.

"That's it, we're done." Jahira began to turn, and then bucked in surprise. Magnar's hand shot out to grasp her own. He began to force the yoke forward.

"Magnar, let go!"

Magnar continued to push. Jahira fought to maintain their position. Finally, in desperation, she leaned forward and bit the back of Magnar's hand. The bite wasn't hard enough to break the skin, but proved effective in forcing him to loosen his grip. As soon as he stopped pushing, Jahira started to bank. He recovered too quickly.

Magnar jerked the yoke back and the nose of the jet dipped sharply.

Jahira cursed. The Eagle continued downward much too fast. They were caught in a downdraft.

"Magnar, let go or we are going to crash!"

That finally seemed to register.

Magnar looked up at Jahira, then out the window. He seemed surprised. He released her hand and shifted back to his seat.

Jahira worked to correct their position while Magnar sat and stared wide-eyed out the window. Before she could bring them out of the downdraft, the Eagle moved into the loss shear where the column of air contacted the ground, forcing it to gust outward at incredible speeds. The winds carried the Eagle along, parallel to the ground. Beads of sweat trickled past Jahira's temples. She fought to navigate around the base of the mountains. Her heart raced. A second, stronger gust caught them from behind and caused the jet to slow suddenly as the winds matched their flight speed.

"Shit," Jahira cursed. The Eagle's speed gauge dropped at an alarming rate.

The nose dipped again.

All that Jahira could do now was pray.

Chapter 23

Krnar trudged through the knee-deep snow. A mix of water and ice hammered him from above. Thus far he was not terribly impressed with the weather here in the warm land.

Visions of a warm fire began to creep into his thoughts. He could see the orange flames dancing, throwing shadows across the walls of a snug stone cave. He could practically smell the pungent combination of fish oil and salt filling the air and hear the soft sound of the vrmefur pop and hiss as it bubbled and melted in his mind's eye. He clung to this memory, forcing one foot in front of the other.

Slowly, over the sound of the howling wind and splattering rain, he heard something that sounded faintly like the scream of a dying lizard followed by the groan of the ice breaking on the distant sea. He stopped and cocked his head to listen. Another screech echoed through the canyon before the sounds ended with a crash that shook the very ground beneath his feet.

Krnar drew his knife and spear.

Wind, channeled into the gap between the steep rock walls, drove needles of ice into his skin. He paid it no mind as he pushed forward.

Finally, he stepped from the pass and immediately crouched into a fighting stance. Narrowing his eyes, he watched the great silver beast. He circled wide, keeping his movements slow and fluid. He worked his way around what he guessed was the tail, trying not to draw its attention.

It appeared to be some kind of giant bird. One great silver wing jutted up toward the sky. The other had been ripped away, but the creature did not bleed, nor did it seem to be breathing. He could detect no movement at all as he continued to circle toward the great clear eyes.

Once he stood facing the beast's head he stopped, breath held so that no part of him moved. The creature's eyes were still open.

Krnar peered through the dark and the rain, the lack of light did not impede his vision but the gusting precipitation made it difficult to even keep his eyes open, let alone focus.

He thought he saw something in those eyes.

Krnar approached with agonizingly slow movements, knife and spear at the ready, until he was close enough that he could reach out and touch the smooth silver hide. Fur covered fingers stretched forward a hairs-breadth at a time until, finally, his fingertips contacted the cold skin.

The body felt hard and lifeless. His confidence grew when the creature did not react to his touch. He drew closer, alert for any sudden movements.

Peering into the beast's great eyes, he trilled in surprise. Two beings were trapped inside the bird's head. His frown deepened as he examined the figures. They appeared to be tied with some sort of wide line. They did not move, and one bled from a wound to its head.

Krnar circled the beast more quickly now, prodding the body in search for a way inside, or a soft place to cut. The hide was like rock, hard and impenetrable. A strange screeching sound made him wince as the bone blade of his knife slid along the surface with no appreciable result.

No matter how he prodded and poked, the creature remained motionless. Krnar began to wonder if it was an animal at all. But if it was not an animal, then what could it be?

Finally, on the creature's belly, he found a section where the hide had already split. Krnar sheathed his spear and knife before he slipped his fingers into the gap. He pulled with all his strength. The split widened, encouraging him to continue until he managed to create a big enough space that he could slip through. One last pull resulted in a high-pitched screech. Krnar stumbled back. A large section of the bird's belly broke away from the body and fell into the snow. With a racing heart, Krnar stepped closer.

Krnar drew his knife again before he climbed into the belly of the beast. A soft trill of amazement escaped involuntarily when he saw that the creature was hollow inside.

His fingertips traveled along the silver walls as he approached the head. The walls were full of hooks and bumps jutting out from the hide; it was more like a cave than the inside of an animal.

Below the eyes of the beast, he saw a shelf of smooth silver covered with more bumps and many odd carvings. One more step and he stood between the two beings. They were shaped much like one of his own people. They had two arms, two legs, and an even distribution of features. They wore strange looking hides on their bodies. Likely due to the fact that, except for the hair on their heads, the parts of them that were exposed were as naked as a cave lizard.

One of the beings had skin as dark as the deepest caves. The other was pale, like the belly of a fish. The pale one bled in several places, but the cuts looked shallow. The dark one had a small cut over one closed eye; both were breathing.

Krnar moved to the pale one first, since it seemed to be the most injured, and cut the lines which held it in place. The pale one slipped forward. Krnar caught it, and then worked one arm under its legs before pushing its torso back and finally placing another arm behind its head. He carried the pale one to the cavernous belly and laid it carefully where it would be out of the direct line of blowing snow.

He returned for the dark one.

As he grasped the first line and pulled it away from the dark one's torso, he realized *it* was a *she*. Heat rose to his cheeks as the back of his hand brushed the swell of the dark one's breasts. He cut the line quickly, hopeful that she would not wake until he'd finished.

He placed the dark one's hands in her lap and noticed a silver cuff around her wrist. He scanned her hands quickly but saw no silver ring, no silver bracelet on the other wrist. Could she be an apprentice to an Akaruvel here in the warm land?

Curiosity, even deeper than before, overwhelmed his mind. *Who could these creatures be?*

He carried the dark one into the back and placed her carefully beside the pale one, which he now guessed was a male. He stared down at the two beings, wondering what to do next.

An image of a cave flashed through his mind. He'd passed an opening in the rock on his way to investigate the strange noise. The familiar sight of a cave in this foreign land had called to him, but he felt he needed to cover more ground before resting for the night. Now it seemed the perfect solution.

He nodded in agreement with his silent decision, and then scooped the dark one back into his arms. He slipped out through the crack in the silver belly and hurried toward the cave.

Chapter 24

Heavy, wet clumps of precipitation fell from thick clouds, creating a mess of slush on top of the rain-pocked snow. Krnar could feel the dark one growing cold against his chest, compelling him to move faster.

When he reached the cave, he continued to the back, out of the wind and snow. He laid the dark one down, and then removed the pack from his own back. As he rummaged through the contents, he was pleased to find that the lizard-skin hide had kept his supplies dry save for the bit of water which penetrated the cracks around the top flap. Finally, he found what he needed.

Krnar shook out the sleeping hide and stretched it over the cave floor. He moved the dark one onto the hide, and then wrapped her inside as best he could. What he really needed was a fire. He cast his eyes around the cavern for anything he might be able to burn, but found only rock.

With a hiss of frustration he rose and left the dark one and his pack in the cave. He returned to the silver bird to collect the pale one, who had started to turn a bit blue, especially around the lips. Krnar worried over his inability to keep the beings warm. He hurried back on the now well-packed path and tucked the pale one into the sleeping hide beside the dark one.

They would need each other's heat to stay alive, furless as they were.

Krnar piled what scant clothes and hides he could find atop the two sleeping forms, and then he paced. He kept glancing down at the two figures, trying to detect any movement, any sound. He knew he wouldn't sleep, but didn't know what else to do. Then he remembered objects strewn about the silver cave. They were foreign to him, but perhaps they would be of some use if the beings woke up. Perhaps they even had hides of their own that would help keep them warm. Krnar checked his wards one last time before leaving the cave.

Allorkan had decided to show its face this day, the golden rays warmed the rock above, but the fingers of light did not stretch down into the pass as Krnar followed his trail to the silver bird.

Krnar could only guess at the use of most of the items, but he did find two rolls of tightly bound material tied to one wall. They felt thin and slippery, but they might be of use.

Krnar stuffed the rolls into his pack, slid his arms through the shoulder straps, and then secured the waist band he'd fashioned. The pack had been made to fit Allnall, who was shorter and slimmer, not to mention blessed with a pair of water wings. He'd had to make some adjustments once he'd reached land. He stood, shifted the weight of his load until it rested comfortably, and returned to the cave.

His suspicions about the rolled material proved correct. Once unbound, they expanded into body-length cocoons. He guessed one must lie inside of them for warmth. He tucked each of the beings into a separate shell, and then wrapped his own hide around them again.

It was the best he could do.

A burbling rumble from his midsection reminded him that he hadn't eaten since the previous morning. He retrieved the last piece of semi-frozen fish from the pile of belongings he'd removed from his pack and realized that if the others woke, they would need food, and water.

He chewed on raw fish as he filled a string of water bags with snow and then tucked them along the edge of the hide which encased the two still sleeping forms. Their body heat would help speed the process of melting the snow into drinking water. After securing his spear to his back and lashing both knife and gut line to his belt, he left the cave again; this time to hunt.

Krnar returned to the cave just before sunset with two animals, one large and one smaller version of a four-legged creature with long, thick fur and hard, pointed toes at the end of rather spindly legs. He felt a pang of guilt, taking down a female and her suckling, but he and his charges would need the meat. The warm hides would also be useful for the hairless ones.

He deposited his kill at the mouth of the cave before checking on the ones he'd rescued. They still slept, and still breathed. The snow in the water bags had melted and he decided the two beings should have something to drink. Carefully placing one hand behind the dark one's head, he tipped her face up enough that he could dribble a few drops of water past her full lips. The reaction was delayed, but she did swallow, so he repeated this several times before he lay her head carefully back on the rock.

The pale one's swallow reflex took even longer to trigger. Krnar was more careful about giving him a small drop at a time. They both felt warm; that was something at least. He placed the pale one's head back down, wishing there was more he could do.

Food, he thought, *I can make sure there's food for them when they wake.*

He rose and returned to his animals.

They were already skinned and gutted. He'd left the parts he would not use, as well as a great deal of the blood, back near the stream where his prey had come to drink. The two hides, the organs he would use, as well as his own fur, had received a good scrubbing in the icy water. He didn't wish to attract unwanted guests to the cave.

With a section of gut line he strung the animals up in the back of the cave, looping the line over some jutting rocks to hold the meat aloft. He stepped back and examined the build and bone structure of these unfamiliar creatures. There were many possibilities for tools and utensils with all of those long, sturdy bones. Best of all they provided a good deal of meat.

He sliced a strip of the flesh and chewed, trilling at the unique but delicious flavor; not as good as fish, but it would be a welcome change in his diet regardless. He sliced off another piece and worked the tissue between his teeth before he returned to the two hides. He needed to finish cleaning the skins before they became too stiff to work with.

Using his belt knife, he scraped both skins clean, pausing now and then to scrub them with handfuls of snow. When all visible flesh had been cleaned away, Krnar rubbed a mixture of fat and ground brains into the hide with a smooth rock. He found himself wishing for some salt to add to the mixture. He wasn't certain how the hides would keep in the warmer climate. Shrugging, he continued his efforts. It would either work or it wouldn't, no use wishing for things that were beyond his control.

He stretched the finished hides across the cave floor, securing the edges with heavy rocks, and then stepped outside to clean himself.

Standing near the entrance to the cave, he inhaled deeply, cleansing his lungs with the crisp night air. One of the moons and hundreds of stars were visible in the narrow strip of sky above his head. He found the constellation his people called the silver mountains and trilled softly. A sudden swell of homesickness rose up in his chest and threatened to force tears from his eyes.

Krnar growled, scrubbed the moisture from his eyes, and stood. He returned to the cave and cut a few more strips of meat from the smaller, more tender, animal.

Darkness soon enveloped the cave, save for the blue-white glow around his own body. A soft scuffling sounded from the direction of his charges. Krnar quickly moved to the wrapped figures.

His own bioluminescence lit the dark one's face. He saw her eyelids flutter.

Krnar's heart raced as he grabbed a water bag and then returned to her side.

Chapter 25

When Jahira tried to move, everything from her hair to her toenails ached. An involuntary moan escaped her lips. When she tried to lift her arms, they would not move.

A flood of memories filled her mind, Magnar's hand on the yoke, the storm, the warning alarms blaring; she thought she must still be strapped to her seat in the Eagle, but then why wouldn't her arms move?

Her eyes felt gritty, and when she tried to open them the lids would not pull apart. Her heart began to hammer. Panic threatened to take over until she felt an arm behind her back.

Magnar, she thought. A flood of relief filled her chest.

She opened her mouth to speak and felt something cold against her lips. A thin stream of icy water trickled across her sticky tongue. All other thoughts fled as thirst consumed her. She drank greedily until the water stopped flowing and found herself wishing for more.

Finally, she managed to work one hand free from what she realized must be her sleeping bag. She could feel the slick, silky material against the back of her hand as she slid her arm out. She touched one eye with her fingertips and felt ice melt away from her lashes. Her eyes were frozen shut.

After she'd worked her other arm free, she cupped both hands so they covered her eyes and mouth, and then breathed warm air into the pocket until she could finally pull the thin membranes apart. She blinked a few times before removing her hands.

She pulled her hands away from her face and then turned toward what she'd thought was Magnar. She gasped and jerked back, but was unable to scramble away, caught inside her sleeping bag and held by the arm of some glowing beast.

Jahira's breath came in ragged gasps. She forced herself to hold very still, afraid of making any more sudden movements.

What is that thing?

Fear tightened around her throat as the creature reached down with its free hand and picked up a small bag of some kind. The bag began to glow when the creature held it in its hand.

It moved the bag toward Jahira's face and she slowly pulled back, shifting her wide eyes between the approaching hand and the creature's face. Her nose wrinkled as the thing's hand got close enough to smell the mix of blood and dead animal, then her eyes widened further when the bag was under her nose.

Water, she realized.

Fear gave way to physiological necessity; she leaned forward, allowing the creature to press the bladder to her lips. She gulped the frigid liquid as the glowing hand tipped the bag up to empty its contents into her mouth.

Once the water was gone, the creature reached down and exchanged the bladder for a strip of raw, red meat.

Bile rose in Jahira's throat. The tang of blood filled her nostrils, triggering her gag reflex. She shook her head as she pulled it back, holding one hand palm out in front of her face.

The creature seemed to understand. It placed the stringy red tissue back on the rock floor.

Rock?

Jahira looked more closely at the ground that was visible around her and realized she was definitely not in the Eagle.

Magnar, she thought, *where is Magnar?*

She twisted her head to the side and reached out, she sighed in relief when she felt a second sleeping bag beside her. A blue-white arm reached across and rested on the second sleeping bag. The creature trilled softly.

Her eyes had adjusted to the point that she could make out Magnar's form, his eyes were closed and there were a few scrapes on his face.

Asleep or knocked out? She asked herself, and then wondered how long she'd been out, and what had happened during that time so she now lay inside her sleeping bag somewhere other than inside the Eagle. *And where is the Eagle?*

Jahira's head began to hurt, and then she started to shiver. She wrapped her arms around her torso and hugged them to her body. Despite her efforts, the shivers turned to uncontrollable shaking.

The glowing creature pulled her sleeping bag back up around her body. With one hand supporting her back, it slowly lowered her back down to the hard ground. Then it growled at her, a low vibration of sound that made her breath catch. It paused and made the sound again, the same pattern of sounds actually, in a low rumble.

Jahira squirmed deeper into the warmth of her sleeping bag. She pulled the material up over her head so that only her face was exposed, then tightened the hood and hugged her arms around her body until she finally stopped shaking.

She felt weak, and a bit nauseated, but not at all tired.

Jahira watched the creature move around what she now realized was a cave.

She was in a cave, somewhere in the mountains, with a strange creature, and Magnar was unconscious.

She didn't think she'd be able to fall asleep for a long while.

Chapter 26

The snow on the ground sparkled like a field of jewels in the bright sunlight. Jahira ducked around the cave entrance to relieve herself, squinting against the glare. Cold air bit at her bare butt, and her head still throbbed, but she no longer felt nauseous. Instead her stomach growled and cramped with hunger. Her throat burned and her mouth felt sticky. She longed for more water and what was she going to do about food? The thought of that strip of raw meat made her shudder.

Once she'd finished, she moved slowly back along the wall of the cave. Her legs quivered and threatened to give out beneath her. The pounding in her head intensified until she thought she might pass out. Releasing the wall, she lowered herself to the ground and crawled across the floor to her sleeping bag, happy to snuggle down into its warmth. As if on cue, the creature from the night before moved to her side with a bladder of water and more raw meat.

It did not glow in the daylight, and Jahira could see now that every part of its body was covered by sleek white fur. Well, every visible part. It did wear a pair of shorts held up by a belt with some crude-looking tools tied to the wide strip of material. It also wore pieces of animal hide which were bound around its lower legs with some kind of twine.

Jahira sat up but kept the sleeping bag wrapped around as much of her as she could manage. She accepted the bladder of water with a nod. In spite of her intense desire to upend the bag and swallow the contents in one great gulp, she sipped slowly, conscious of her rumbling stomach. A wide strong-looking five-fingered hand proffered a piece of partially frozen raw meat; Jahira put a hand up and shook her head.

Her stomach growled in protest.

The creature growled in return.

Jahira narrowed her eyes, watching its face as it pointed to the meat, pointed to her, then growled again. Like the night before, she noticed the same patterns of sounds were repeated each time, and its lips moved as if it were speaking.

If its lips are moving, can it be called a growl?

Jahira concentrated as the creature repeated the sounds again, and again pointed to the meat. Whether or not she understood the words, the meaning was obvious.

What other choice do I have? she wondered.

Using one hand to rest the bladder of water on her outstretched thighs, she then extended her free hand toward the creature. Gingerly, she accepted the offering and drew it toward her face. She sniffed. It didn't smell too bad, having mostly frozen and all. Her stomach cramped again.

Jahira shrugged and placed the end of the strip between her teeth.

The creature nodded and made a gesture of encouragement as she worked a small piece of raw tissue loose. Her nostrils flared when the flesh hit her tongue and began to soften. She swallowed quickly before she could taste it and then paused to make sure she didn't throw it back up.

"Thank you," she said, nodding toward the meat and then toward the creature. "Thank you," she repeated, and was caught by a pair of intense blue eyes.

The lids around those blue eyes narrowed before it nodded back, and then it moved from her side. Jahira watched the creature gather another bladder and what looked like a spoon carved from bone.

It knelt before Magnar, dipped the spoon into the bladder, and then dribbled a small amount of water into Magnar's mouth.

Jahira placed her piece of meat on her lap beside the water bladder before she leaned over and helped hold Magnar's head up. The creature gave him small doses of liquid, taking great care to only allow a few drips at a time to pass Magnar's lips. It still seemed to take Magnar a long time to swallow, but maybe not as long as it had taken him last night when she'd watched the creature do the same thing.

She placed a warm palm against Magnar's cold cheek. The scrapes on his face had been cleaned and had already formed thin scabs. She hadn't been out too long then if the cuts were still fresh; perhaps a day, two at the most. After he had swallowed a few sips of water she gently laid him back down and pulled the hood of the sleeping bag up over his head. She tightened the drawstring so that it bunched around his face, keeping his body heat inside the shell.

His chest rose and fell in shallow breaths. She worried that he had not yet woken. What if he had a permanent head injury? What if he starved to death because she couldn't get enough fluid or calories into him?

The ship.

Emergency medical equipment was stored on the ship. If she could find out where the ship was, she might be able to save him.

Her stomach didn't seem to care about the seriousness of Magnar's plight. It cramped and gurgled, demanding to have its own needs met.

She could get protein powder for herself as well; if only she knew how to get to the ship.

Footprints, she thought. Their rescuer must have carried, or dragged, them here from the ship. If she'd only been out for a day, there should be footprints in the snow.

After wiggling her way out of her sleeping bag, Jahira stood and walked to the nearest wall. She had to pause there and put a hand against the cold stone for balance. The world began to spin. She closed her eyes against the movement, and then sank to her knees when it didn't stop.

With two fingers she pinched the bridge of her nose and took several rapid inhalations of cold air. She only opened her eyes again when she was sure she wouldn't vomit.

She would never make it to the ship.

A trilling sound caused her to look up. The creature stood by her side, its head cocked.

Despair filled her heart. She looked at the creature, unable to tell it what she needed, too weak to help Magnar; she felt completely helpless. It was a feeling she was not used to, and she didn't like it at all. She shifted her gaze to the dazzling light outside the cave entrance. Hot tears moistened her eyes.

How could I have been so stupid? she thought. *Why did I ever agree to join Magnar on this ridiculous trip?*

Then she remembered, she hadn't agreed to go, Magnar had forced her to go. She could have fought him, but fighting hadn't made sense at the time; maybe she would have if she'd known how this would turn out.

If it weren't for the alien, we'd be dead.

Jahira looked back at the fur-covered creature and smiled what she hoped it would interpret as a grateful smile. To Jahira's surprise, the creature smiled back.

Her smile faded as the silence stretched.

If only she could tell it to go to the ship. If only she could explain what she needed.

She decided to give it a shot.

"I need some supplies, tools," she corrected, pointing to the items hanging from the creature's belt, "but they're inside my ship. The ship," she made an airplane with her hand and flew it through the air in front of her, then sent it crashing to the ground, complete with sound effects. "The ship you took us out of, my things are there. A pack," she pointed to his pack, lying on the floor a few feet away, "some food," she envisioned the packets of protein powder which she could mix with melted snow and then she pantomimed eating. "I need your help."

She raised her eyebrows in a look of reserved expectation.

The creature trilled, picked up its pack, slung a spear on its back, and walked out of the cave.

She hugged herself as she began to shiver and decided it was time to return to her warm cocoon. It took forever but she finally managed to crawl back to her sleeping bag and wiggle down until she felt heat seep into her skin.

Had it understood? she wondered. *Would it really get what she needed?*

Jahira curled up inside the bag and tried to push down the panic that threatened to overwhelm her.

What if it didn't come back?

Chapter 27

Krnar stepped out into the sunlight and reveled in the warmth that instantly soaked into his fur.

It was a good day.

The dark one appeared to be recovering well, a bit weak still, but otherwise healthy. Her mind was another matter. She didn't seem to be able to focus her thoughts enough to project, or even stay with one image for very long. He had been able to pull a few pictures from her mind as she'd spoken to him in her fast, high-pitched tongue. She needed something from the silver bird.

He'd seen a pack, that one he was sure of since she'd simultaneously pointed to his own when she'd pictured the item. The other images were not objects he recognized, but he felt confident he would be able to find them. Most of all he was glad to have a task, it made him feel less helpless.

Krnar approached the downed bird with some caution, though after several trips in and out, he felt certain it posed no threat.

It took Krnar two handfuls of minutes to figure out how to open the shelves in the wall that he'd seen in the dark one's mind. He trilled in amazement when he finally did succeed, and found a startling variety of completely foreign objects. He pulled the pack she'd pictured off one wall and began to fill it with everything he could find. He opened all the shelves that had a similar closure and distributed the items between her pack and his own. When both packs bulged at the seams, he closed them and returned to the cave.

The dark one turned as he approached, then sat up when her eyes fell on the two full packs.

Krnar nodded in greeting and held both packs out to her. After she'd taken them, he knelt by her side.

She looked from the packs to him and smiled a radiant smile that made her vivid green eyes sparkle with delight.

"Open them," he said, gesturing toward the packs. "I brought everything I could find."

The dark one wriggled her arms out of her silky cocoon and opened her own pack first. The ripping sound as she pulled the material apart surprised Krnar as much as it had the first time, when he'd figured out how to open it himself. It did not seem to ruin the material though.

As her hands rested on the two sides of the pack, he noticed again the silver cuff on her arm. It looked like one of the bands Ellall wore. Was she Akaruvel?

The strangeness of it all made him wonder again who these creatures could be.

He was distracted from his thoughts when the dark one began to pull items from the bag, making small sounds of delight with each discovery. She laughed when she found the slippery white squares she'd pictured before he'd left. The she pulled out another, smaller pack and paused.

When she looked up at him this time, he saw her eyes had filled with tears.

Krnar worried he'd done something wrong, taken something that he shouldn't have touched, until she smiled and then reached out and grasped his hand.

He was so taken aback by the touch that he didn't even react. She squeezed his hand and laughed, and then she began to babble strings of words which he could not understand. She was happy with the find, and with him, that much was clear.

The dark one finally released his hand, leaving a tingle of sensation where her fingertips slid along his fur. She picked up a water bag and balanced it carefully on her lap, then tore a strip from one of the white squares. A powdery substance fell from the small square when she tipped it over the water. With the spoon he'd been using to give water to the pale one, she stirred the powder into the water. Krnar watched the mixture thicken into a sort of slush.

The dark one looked up at him, smiled, and then began to drink the viscous mixture. Her face was the picture of ecstasy.

Krnar frowned in confusion.

As soon as she'd finished, she reached for another water bag. This time she opened the small pack, the one she'd been so excited about, and took out a clear sac, a long tube, and a wicked looking silver needle. She hooked all three together so that the pieces formed something like a sea snake with a distended rear end.

The dark one poured water into the clear sac. Krnar hissed when she pulled out the pale one's arm and poked the needle into the vein on the inside of his elbow. She held the sac up high and Krnar could see the contents begin to drip into the tube, travel down its length, and then disappear into the pale one's bulging blue vein.

He stared in fascination. The dark one began to form a pile of rocks with one hand, while holding the sac aloft with the other. Krnar finally broke from his paralyzed astonishment and began to help with the pile of rocks.

The dark one nodded and waved him back when the task was done to her satisfaction. She secured one end of the clear sac between two rocks and stared at the tube for a moment. Nodding, she turned back to face him.

There was a moment of awkward silence, and then the dark one pointed to her chest.

Chapter 28

"Jahira," she said. "My name is Jahira."

The creature cocked its head but did not respond, so she tried again.

"Ja-hi-ra," she repeated, emphasizing the second syllable with a long /e/ sound. She looked expectantly at the creature and waited. She beamed when it pointed to itself.

"Krnar," it said. Its voice sounded deep and gravelly. It rolled the r sounds like a Spanish *erre*, to the point that they almost sounded like a purr.

"Krnar." Jahira's r pronunciation was flat, but it was the best she could do. She pointed to her chest again and said her own name.

"Lahira," Krnar didn't pronounce the j, which made Jahira feel a little better about her own errors, and it rolled the r in her name as well. She kind of liked it.

Jahira smiled and nodded.

Krnar smiled back.

Well, it's a start, she thought.

As she dug through the remaining items in the two packs, she spread them out across the ground beside her to take inventory of her supplies. With a gasp of delight she reached out and grasped a solar disc for starting fires. Her excitement waned as she eyed the cave for something to burn and found nothing. The disappointment didn't last too long though. After another minute she pulled out her knife, fastened securely in its sheath. This she laid carefully on her lap.

She scanned her stockpile and nodded with satisfaction. Most of the implements necessary for survival lay before her, she simply lacked the skills to use them effectively, but she could learn.

The first order of business must be to fashion some kind of coat which would keep her warm while she moved about the cave. She couldn't very well stay in her sleeping bag forever... or could she?

A slow smile spread across Jahira's face as she thought through her idea.

With a nod, she lifted the knife from her lap and pulled the blade from the sheath.

Krnar trilled, startling Jahira into temporary stillness. She wasn't sure what that sound meant. She glanced from the wicked looking blade to Krnar's wide eyes.

"It's okay, I'm not going to hurt you." She tried to use her most reassuring voice. She moved the knife very slowly back toward her lap. "See, I'm just going to cut some of this material."

Jahira's hands inched toward her feet. She inserted the tip of the knife into the bottom of the sleeping bag then paused and looked up at Krnar. He watched her closely, but didn't seem afraid. He seemed…curious.

"See," she said. She drew the knife along the seam creating a wide slit in the fabric. She pushed her booted feet through the hole and smiled up at Krnar. "Now for some arms."

Jahira loosened the hood and neck of the bag then carefully pulled her knife-wielding right hand inside while holding the left side of the bag out away from her body with her free hand. She cut a small slit in the left side, followed by the right, pushed her arms through and finally pulled the hood back up over her head.

Jahira decided to test her design. Once she'd sheathed her knife, she hiked the sleeping bag up high enough that she could get to her feet, and then let the material fall back down to the ground.

"It'll be a bit tricky walking around, but better than freezing my butt off, or lying here rotting." She looked at Krnar, her only audience. She raised her eyebrows and stretched her arms to the sides. "What do you think?"

He smiled and nodded.

"Okay then, next order of business, getting rescued."

Based on the length of time Krnar had been gone when he'd retrieved the supplies from the ship, she guessed the distance to the Eagle would be about two to three kilometers. She should be able to make that, maybe after another protein shake.

She mixed another pouch of powder into water and sipped it slowly. It tasted like sawdust someone had tried to mask with a zest of lemon, but failed miserably. No matter how it tasted, it filled her belly and kept the spins at bay.

After about thirty minutes she shuffled over to where Krnar sat cutting pieces from his animal hides. He looked up as she approached.

"I need to go to the Eagle," Jahira said. "I need to see if the tracking beacon is working, or if I can get it to work."

Krnar's head tilted slightly as he listened.

"The Eagle," Jahira repeated, then made an airplane with her hand and moved it through the air in imitation of a jet flying and then crashing to the ground. "I want to go to the Eagle." She punctuated her words with gestures, first pointing to herself, then scissoring the fingers of one hand to make them look like legs walking toward the crashed ship, played by her other hand.

A low, rumbling sound vibrated through Krnar's chest. He formed some unrecognizable words, and nodded, but then pointed to Magnar's still unconscious form.

"Yeah, I know," Jahira replied, followed by a long exhale. "That's one of the reasons I need go. I've got to call for some help or he might die. I need you to go with me, so that if I collapse in the snow *I* won't die. Hopefully we won't be gone long."

After hiking up the bottom of the sleeping bag, she walked over to Magnar to check his IV fluids. He still had enough liquid in the bag to last at least an hour. She began to walk toward the mouth of the cave, then looked back to see if Krnar understood, if he planned to join her.

Krnar stood and slid his spear into the strap on his back, and then he tied his knife to his belt.

"All right, let's do this." Jahira motioned for Krnar to lead the way, then slipped her arms inside her sleeping bag and held it up from the inside so that she could walk while also keeping her hands warm.

She followed Krnar's wide footprints through the shin-deep snow, praying the whole way that the beacon would work. She followed that with a prayer that Magnar would still be alive when she returned.

EMPYREAN

Chapter 29

Krnar's fascination with these new people grew exponentially. Everything from Jahira's strange eating habits to the language so foreign he could not even pick out similarities in the words fueled his curiosity until he burned with the need to know who they were and where they'd come from. It didn't seem possible that his ancestors could have changed quite so drastically.

Among the many things he didn't understand was why Jahira needed to go to what she called "the ship". She had conveyed her message well enough, primitive as her mental communication skills seemed to be. She seemed intelligent, and some of her tools were far more advanced than his, but her attempts at projection were those of a child. The pictures he could retrieve from her mind were hazy and fleeting instead of focused and sustained; yet another mystery he longed to solve.

Krnar led the way through the pass, at which point the ship became visible across the narrow opening. He heard Jahira gasp, and then groan. She caught up to him and they walked together to the open belly.

Krnar paused outside the opening. Jahira entered with confidence. She moved straight for the place where she'd been trapped when he'd found her.

Her dark fingers tapped and pressed in different places. She muttered softly to herself while she worked. Suddenly she whirled to face him, said something he did not understand, and walked past him close enough that her arm brushed against the fur of his chest.

He trilled as a jolt of sensation tingled through his torso.

Jahira stopped and turned her face so that her green eyes met his, a slight frown creased her brow; she seemed to be waiting.

Waiting for what?

Neither her expression nor her emotions seemed contrite, only curious. She apparently didn't realize she'd done anything wrong. He had no idea how to respond, or how to explain, so he simply gestured for her to continue.

Her eyebrows rose before she turned and continued into the larger section at the back. Krnar followed a few paces behind and watched her lift several of the silver flaps that lined the walls. From one of the holes behind one of the flaps, she pulled out several small, black, rectangular objects which were held together by a length of thick, flexible black line.

Jahira gathered these items and walked back out into the snow.

Krnar hissed in frustration at not being able to fully understand what happened, of not being able to communicate effectively, or even know if he correctly interpreted the emotions he could feel from her. To further complicate the matter, he watched Jahira stick the end of one of the lines into the belly of *the Eagle* before she began to unwind the line and free four black rectangles. She then unfolded the rectangles to make four larger squares. These she arranged in the snow so that the shiny surface of the square faced and reflected the light of Allorkan.

*****

Jahira completed her arrangement of the photovoltaic array and stepped back to assess her work. The solar panels on the Eagle's remaining wing were severely damaged. The other wing, along with its solar panels, had been completely torn off. The plug-in panels were necessary in order to charge the ship's back-up systems.

She had hoped she might find the Eagle in good enough condition that she could fly her back out of here, but that wish had died with the first sight of her beloved aircraft. The right wing was not only torn off, it was nowhere to be seen. It broke Jahira's heart to think that the Eagle might never fly again.

After she'd arranged the panels to her satisfaction, she returned to the flight deck to check the power. The narrow red bar on the console flashed, which meant the system was at least attempting to charge. Jahira willed it to creep up into the green. All she needed was enough power to send their location to the Falcon, or the Colonizer; even if she could turn on their local emergency pulse it might help someone find them if they got close enough. They had to have figured out by now that the Eagle was gone, and who had taken her.

What if they'd already come and gone?

She turned and began to pace through the belly of the ship. Krnar leaned against one wall with his arms crossed over his broad chest and watched her. She wondered what this Krnar must be thinking.

Why is he by himself anyway? Are there more like him wandering in the mountains? What is he doing here? And how did he find us?

She wished desperately for a way to communicate with him.

Him, she thought. Apparently at some point she had decided Krnar was male though she really didn't know for sure. Maybe it was the deep growly voice, or the lack of visible female anatomy. She had nothing to compare him to except humans, and he was obviously not human.

So what is he?

It had been the law aboard The Aquilo to never colonize a planet they knew to be inhabited by a sentient species, nor could they make contact no matter how tempting. They'd broken all the rules when they'd landed here.

After a few more turns in the belly, she checked the power bar again.

Still red.

The flashing red light made her think of the day they'd evacuated The Aquilo, which of course made her think of her family. Her chest began to tighten, as if someone were squeezing it with a vice to the point that she began to struggle for breath.

She whirled around and hurried out of the Eagle, into the bright sunlight. A deep inhalation filled her lungs with frigid, cleansing air. She turned to tell Krnar that she wanted to go back to the cave and nearly collided with him.

"Oh!" Jahira exclaimed, stumbling backwards. Her heel caught on the back of the sleeping bag and she began to fall.

Before she landed ungracefully in the snow, Krnar caught her and set her back on her feet. He kept one arm on her back and trilled with rising intonation.

"I'm okay, thanks," Jahira said. She also nodded.

Krnar released her and backed up a step. Jahira decided that the biggest difference in appearance between Krnar and a human was in the face. Since it was all fur-covered, like the rest of his body, she could not see his ears, or his nose, just two tufts of fur sticking out slightly from either side of his head, and a peak of sleek fur in the center of his face. He had a hint of eyebrows, a slightly off-white ridge above each eye, and she could see his lips, but under all that fur his facial expressions, if he had any, were impossible to interpret, except of course when he smiled.

Jahira cleared her throat and looked away, embarrassed to realize she'd been staring. She hiked up the bottom of the sleeping bag to keep herself from stumbling again and began to walk back toward the cave.

Her feet crossed the threshold, and a strong sense of foreboding gripped her heart. The IV bag was not visible against her small tower of rocks. As she hurried to the back of the cave her heart began to race. The hairs on the back of her neck tingled as she knelt beside the flat surface of the sleeping bag where Magnar's body should have been.

Magnar was gone.

Chapter 30

Krnar felt Jahira's confusion turn to panic. He joined her at the back of the cave and hissed when he saw her run a hand over the empty hide where the pale one had slept.

Immediately, he stood and walked back to the mouth of the cave to examine the surrounding snow.

"There are no tracks," he said, half-turning so that Jahira could see his gestures. "He didn't leave the cave. He must have gone deeper inside the mountain."

Jahira hurried to his side and looked out at the snow where he pointed to their tracks, and then to the unmarked snow around them.

"He didn't leave the cave unless he followed exactly in our footprints, and if he'd done that, we'd have seen him." Krnar was sure he would have noticed if there'd been a new set of tracks diverging from their path at any point, and until a person reached the mouth of the pass, there was very little room to diverge. He had to still be here somewhere.

He saw Jahira's brow furrow as she studied the snow. Allorkan peeked from behind a great wall of rock, as if spying on them. Already shadows dominated the landscape. He quested out with his mind, searching for an unfamiliar signal, a consciousness similar to Jahira's.

Krnar hissed when he encountered a mind full of pain.

"I think I found him," Krnar stated. "We'd better hurry."

Without looking to see if Jahira had understood, he strode across the stone floor and paused at the mouth of a tunnel which continued into the mountain from the back of the cave. He beckoned for Jahira and continued without looking at her, he could feel her near him.

The tunnel was tall and wide. Krnar could stand upright and, therefore, proceeded at a brisk pace. His glowing fur and dark-adapted vision allowed him to see his way clearly. After a few steps, he heard Jahira call his name.

Krnar turned and saw that she had stopped two body lengths behind him. He could feel her anxiety, tinged with annoyance, and he frowned.

"He went this way, we must hurry," he explained.

Jahira waved him toward her.

He approached slowly, wondering why she would delay the search for her friend. When he drew close, she reached out and grasped his arm.

Krnar trilled in shock, but did not pull away. Once she'd looped one arm through his, she began to move forward again. Her free hand lifted the cumbersome sleeping hide out of the way of her heavy boots.

She pulled him along as he tried to understand the situation. It became difficult to think with her hand and her arm constantly brushing against his fur, sending chills down his spine.

Jahira spoke, and Krnar could hear the admonishment in her tone. He had no idea what he'd done wrong but clearly her people did not have the same rules about uninvited touch. He sensed no embarrassment or shame from her at all, and for the first time he was thankful that she seemed unable to connect with his mind.

The tunnel continued deep into the mountain, becoming a vast system of tunnels and caves that made him feel at home. Jahira on the other hand gripped his arm more tightly the farther they went. He felt her anxiety begin to shift into panic, so he began to talk to her, about his home, about the caves, whatever came to his mind in an effort to distract her from whatever it was that caused her such fear. As he continued to talk, he could feel her relax, so he kept up his monologue until the thread of the pale one's mind led him, finally, to a small cavern. Two steps into the cavern, Krnar stopped and trilled in surprise.

An oranllo.

A pool of liquid silver reflected the blue-white glow of his body a mere two steps away from where he stood.

Krnar sensed Jahira's sudden relief. He looked at her, and then followed her gaze across the cavern to find the pale, almost glowing face of her companion.

The pale one knelt beside the pool. He cupped his hands and scooped some of the liquid, then turned. He moved slowly, careful not to spill the precious contents. After a few measured steps, he knelt again beside something lying on the ground that Krnar had not previously noticed. Something rested in the dark recess where its full form remained partially hidden by a jumble of rocks.

Krnar watched the pale one lower his hands behind those rocks and tip them, as if giving something, or someone, a drink.

A low growl vibrated through Krnar's chest. He shook off Jahira's hand and then drew his spear while simultaneously unsheathing his knife.

Jahira cried out in alarm. She positioned herself between him and the pale one on the narrow path around the pool.

Her eyes were so wide that he could see the white standing out around the green center. Her dark skin absorbed the light from his body as he moved a step closer. In desperation, Jahira placed both of her hands against his chest and spoke in an urgent voice. He responded to what he assumed was her concern for the pale one.

"I'm not going to hurt your friend. You must let me pass, he is in danger." Krnar tried to reassure her as he continued to press forward.

Finally she gave up trying to stop him and hurried ahead of him to stand beside the pale one. She stopped when she reached his side and Krnar heard her cry of alarm.

He arrived in time to glance over her shoulder. The pale one poured the last of the silver liquid past the parted lips of a wizened old man.

The low rumble of Krnar's growl increased in intensity. Coiled tight as a sea snake around its prey, he studied the inert form. Flesh hung from the jutting bones of the man's skeletal frame. The pale hide bore no more than a scattering of silver hairs.

The pale one licked the last of the liquid from his hands and then, reaching out with one tentative finger, he traced the pattern of scar tissue that formed three circles connected by a single horizontal line across the old man's wrinkled forehead.

The old man's eyelids fluttered. The paper-thin membranes peeled apart to reveal ice-blue eyes; eyes that matched his own.

Krnar hissed and then growled. He gripped the hilt of his knife with sweat-slick fingers. The old man met his gaze and then projected a thought into his mind.

I am Grollon, the first and the last of the Marked.

EMPYREAN

Chapter 31

Krnar lunged. Jahira blocked him just long enough to allow the pale one a chance to add his own body as a shield. The pale one spread his arms wide and curled his fingers into claws, baring his teeth at Krnar.

The Marked One's eyes never left him.

Jahira placed a hand on his spear and spoke in a commanding voice. Whether he understood the words or not, there was no mistaking her tone.

Krnar realized that in order to get to the Marked, he would most likely injure both his charges in these cramped quarters. Besides, the old man seemed barely able to move. That didn't mean that he wasn't a threat, but Krnar felt wrong about slaying a man who couldn't fight back, even if it was the enemy of his people.

After a long pause he nodded once and slowly sheathed his spear. He backed up, but kept his knife in his hand.

Jahira let out a sigh. She kept one hand on his chest and turned to the pale one. When she spoke her words were clipped and harsh.

The pale one gestured toward the Marked, and Krnar began to worry. *Were these the descendants of the Marked?* Perhaps those who had remained in the warm land had evolved even more dramatically than his own.

Jahira's voice rose in volume as she responded to the pale one's gestures. She pointed to the oranllo, then to her companion. He felt her worry harden into anger.

The pale one leaned toward Jahira and tensed as if preparing to strike.

Krnar instinctively wrapped an arm around Jahira and pulled her to his side. He tested his grip on his knife hilt and flexed his knees. The pale one narrowed his eyes, looking Krnar up and down, sizing him up.

Enough!

The mental shout caused Krnar to flinch. He noticed Jahira and the pale one react as well. Jahira watched the Marked with eyes that had gone wide with shock. Krnar felt her body tense at his side.

Jahira spoke aloud, addressing the Marked.

"Yes, I can understand you," Grollon spoke aloud in Krnar's own language, but must have also projected into the minds of the others for he saw Jahira's jaw drop. He wondered why the Marked included him in the conversation.

Jahira's eyes narrowed. She spoke again.

"My mind speaks to yours." Krnar wondered what kind of image the man used to project that idea.

Jahira frowned, and then asked the pale one a question. He nodded in response.

"Help me up," Grollon commanded.

Neither Krnar nor Jahira moved to assist him, but the pale one immediately moved to Grollon's side and slid an arm behind the old man's shoulders. The pale one helped Grollon into a sitting position.

Krnar heard Jahira's exclamation of surprise.

The pale one had hooked Grollon's arm around his own shoulder and helped him rise. Krnar stared open-mouthed at his ancestor.

Grollon looked up at them and smiled, revealing several missing teeth. The old man flexed his bony shoulders, causing two scaled wings to open and spread out behind him.

Krnar couldn't suppress his own trill of amazement. It was the first time he'd ever seen true wings.

EMPYREAN

Chapter 32

Jahira spent a few minutes wondering if she was really awake, or how hard she'd hit her head in that crash. She couldn't believe her eyes, or her mind for that matter. How could she see the pictures in her head so clearly? And how did she know they came from the old man? Were those really *wings*?

It wasn't until Magnar helped Grollon take his first few steps forward, which caused Krnar to growl and back away, that she found the will to move. She held on to Krnar's arm again as they returned to the tunnels. His phosphorescence created more of an aura of light around him than a projected beam like a flashlight would do so, in order to see where she stepped, she needed to stay close to him.

The irregular rhythm of Magnar's heavy boots followed by the soft shuffle of Grollon's bare feet followed her through in the dark. The sound faded as Krnar pushed their pace. Jahira wondered about the connection between him and the man Magnar had found. Krnar's reaction made it clear that he was not pleased about the discovery. This knowledge made her uneasy, even more so than all of the other troubling questions surrounding the situation, and also very curious.

More than anything, she wanted to know Magnar's place in all of this. He'd told her when she confronted him back in the cave that this old man, this *Grollon*, was the reason he'd come.

How could that be possible? How could Magnar have known where to find him? How could Magnar have even known the man existed?

She and Krnar stepped into the main cavern and Jahira began to shiver. The icy breeze from outside swept across the cavern floor and sought refuge in her warm sleeping bag. The cold seemed to curl around her ankles and move upwards like uninvited fingers, raising goose bumps on her flesh. She stopped by her pile of belongings and released the hem of her bag, as well as Krnar's arm, then pulled her own arms inside and rubbed them with the opposite hands to try to generate some heat.

While she attempted to warm herself, Krnar paced. He never took his eyes off the tunnel entrance. When Magnar and Grollon finally emerged, Krnar stopped pacing and stared at the pair, his body coiled with tension as if ready to spring.

Grollon never made eye contact, consumed with the apparent effort of walking that short distance. Magnar, however, glared back at Krnar with an expression she'd never seen on his face before. Anger seemed to pulse outward from him, creating tension in the air. Jahira felt certain that if Magnar had not been holding up the old man, he would have attacked Krnar. His reaction shocked her. Slivers of apprehension lodged in her gut and began to fester.

"Magnar, what is wrong with you?" Jahira hissed. He and Grollon stopped a few feet from her. "Krnar saved us."

Magnar didn't reply. He eased Grollon down onto his own sleeping bag. She noticed that he didn't seem bothered by the cold as he grabbed two packets of protein powder and a string of water bladders.

"You could at least ask," Jahira admonished in a low voice. "Those belong to Krnar."

Magnar continued to ignore her. A flush of anger crept up Jahira's neck. She sat across from the pair and glared at Magnar for a moment, then shifted her gaze to Grollon when Magnar remained oblivious to her emotions.

"Who are you?" Jahira asked, addressing Grollon.

Grollon took a small sip of water from the bladder which Magnar had offered him. Once he had swallowed he met her eyes with a cold blue stare that sent shivers down Jahira's spine.

"Grollon." He spoke aloud, using the same rolling speech pattern as Krnar, though Grollon's words seemed to have less growl and more purr.

"Yes, I got that part, but where did you come from? What are you doing here? How did Magnar find you?"

Jahira paused as Grollon took another sip of water. He coughed lightly a couple of times, clearing his throat, and then continued. Pictures appeared in her mind of the silver trees which ringed the five silver pools just north of the human settlement.

Jahira saw Krnar straighten, and then move closer until he crouched beside her.

"Then how did you end up here? And where are the rest of your people?"

An image of a large bird appeared in her mind's eye. As the image grew she realized it was not a bird, it was Grollon, flying. She saw him land at the shore of the sea and stare out at the waves, then turn and begin to walk back toward the mountains. Jahira didn't fully understand the significance, but she didn't interrupt. The pictures continued, playing a movie in her mind of the old man's journey through the mountains. He seemed to grow weaker until he finally reached a cave and lay down beside a silver pool where he drank, and then slept. The images stopped.

"Where are the rest of your people? We found no signs of sentient life on the entire second continent."

Grollon glanced at Krnar and then nodded in his direction.

Jahira heard a low, rumbling growl coming from Krnar. She looked back and forth, from the old man to Krnar and realization dawned.

"You went looking for him? His people? He doesn't seem too happy to see you."

Grollon met her gaze again.

Jahira's eyes narrowed and she asked, "What happened?"

Grollon did not respond. He turned his back to her and lay down on his side.

"Wait! Please! You didn't answer my question about Magnar. How did he find you? Why did he come looking for you? What happened to him?"

Grollon sighed, a long tired sigh.

Jahira saw a picture of the sun setting and, shortly thereafter, rising again.

Tomorrow, she thought.

Jahira didn't try to hide her frustration. She stood and began to pace, worrying over the scant information Grollon had provided. Fear over Magnar gnawed at her heart. Her friend, her co-pilot, sat cross-legged on the bare rock gnawing on a strip of raw meat. His gaze seemed vacant and his pupils were dilated; he didn't even seem aware of her presence. This was not the Magnar she knew. Something was terribly wrong.

As evening approached, wind began to howl through the narrow mountain pass pushing before it great gusts of swirling snow. The eerie symphony kept Jahira awake long past sunset.

Krnar didn't seem to be able to sleep either.

He had visibly relaxed after Grollon had fallen asleep, but she noticed him glancing over at the old man periodically, as if he didn't trust him even in a semi-conscious state.

Jahira finally gave up trying. She sat up and watched Krnar who gripped his knife in one hand and curled his body around something held firmly in the other hand. She moved a little closer to try to get a better look, and when she saw what he held she let out an involuntary exclamation of surprise.

"You're carving!"

Krnar looked up and tipped his head slightly in the way he did when he was trying to understand her. She pointed to the small piece of what looked like bone and he smiled. He held it out toward her and nodded. She reached out to touch it. Taking the piece carefully between two fingers, she examined it from every angle and then set it on her palm.

"It's the Eagle!" she cried. She made an airplane with one hand and flew it around briefly to clarify her message.

Krnar's grin widened and he nodded.

She studied the tiny replication of the jet, amazed by the detail. She ran a finger over the smooth contours which still held the warmth of Krnar's hand.

"Can I watch?" she asked. She handed the carving back to him, and then pointed to the ground beside him. He nodded again.

She settled herself on the hard ground and pulled her arms back inside her sleeping bag. Krnar set down his knife and the miniature Eagle, and then pulled a small hide-wrapped bundle from his pack. Holding the hide in the palm of one hand, he drew back the flaps with the other. Jahira leaned in and oohed over the contents.

The bundle was full of carvings, some things she recognized, others she couldn't even guess at.

"Laro," he said, pointing to one of the carvings. Jahira touched the one that was flat on top with many tiny threads hanging from the bottom. "Plinka," he said, touching one that looked like a fish.

Jahira pointed to another that looked a bit like a salamander.

"Krska," Krnar supplied the name, and then touched the hide on which the carvings rested. "Krska," he said again.

Jahira nodded, but her attention had already moved to the next piece. Krnar had carved a woman, covered in fur and with some kind of cape or something on her back, but clearly a female.

"I guess that confirms you're a man," she stated, not expecting a response.

Krnar picked up the figurine carefully and then held it out to her.

"Allnall," he said. His voice sounded a bit sad when he said this word. She wondered who this woman could be.

Suddenly an image of a stormy sea filled her mind's eye. A glowing figure rode atop the waves as the water swelled.

How is she standing on the waves?

Jahira could barely make out the face through the sheets of rain, then the figure turned slightly and she saw it was a female, *the* female. It must be the one he had carved. The woman began to move across a dark, slick surface.

So she wasn't standing on water.

A blue-white hand reached out as the woman was tossed into the raging sea.

Jahira gasped and the image stopped abruptly. She studied Krnar a moment before she was able to speak.

"That was you. How do you do that?"

"Allnall," he responded. He pointed again to the carving of the woman.

"Allnall," Jahira repeated, touching the tiny face of the carved image. It was the same face she'd seen in her mind. "Was this your wife?"

Krnar tilted his head and Jahira sighed, clearly it would be awhile until they were past the single word stage.

A scuffing sound behind her made Jahira turn her head. She saw Magnar rise from the ground where he'd been sleeping. Without a word or a glance her way, he walked to the back of the cave and then disappeared.

He'd gone into the tunnel.

Jahira stood, her mouth set in a firm line. She knew where he was going and she could not let him continue to do this.

After hiking her sleeping bag up around her knees, she set off with a determined stride across the cavern. She paused at the mouth of the tunnel. An arm's length away she could see nothing at all. The darkness was like a wall, preventing her from moving forward. She wondered how Magnar could see, or maybe he just didn't care. She placed one hand against the cold, slick rock and took a tentative step forward.

She had to help Magnar.

EMPYREAN

Chapter 33

Krnar wrapped his carvings, sheathed his knife, and followed Jahira. As wary as he was of Grollon, the old man did not prove much of a physical threat. The pale one on the other hand, this Magnar, made his hackles rise. The man's mind was a sea of pain and rage. He was all emotion and seemed barely lucid. He couldn't let Jahira go after him alone.

Catching up to her proved easy enough. She slid a hand along the wall and proceeded barely an arm length at a time with halting footsteps. He remained a step behind and to the side, instinctively allowing enough space that they would not accidentally touch. The pace became agonizing.

He did not understand the difficulty. He felt no fear from her. In fact, she was determined and anxious, yet her steps were as slow as Grollon's. She seemed agile enough within the main cavern, aside from her odd bulky covering, so what was the problem?

Finally, he offered his arm.

Jahira immediately switched the hand that held her covering and grasped his arm with a grateful sigh. She started forward at a much faster pace, though she occasionally stubbed the toe of her boot on the scattered rocks or stumbled over the uneven ground.

She cannot see in the dark, Krnar realized. The halting footsteps, the need to have him close, she produced no light of her own, she needed his.

He trilled with the pure satisfaction of having figured out at least one of the mysteries of this foreign woman. She glanced over in response to his sudden exclamation, and immediately stumbled forward when her toe hit a rise in the tunnel floor. Krnar caught her with his free hand and righted her.

Jahira growled in frustration and Krnar couldn't help but laugh. His laugh ended abruptly when she pierced him with a green-eyed glare.

"I apologize. I laugh because that is the first time you have sounded like one of The People."

Jahira's eyes narrowed briefly before she shrugged and continued forward, one hand still firmly gripping his forearm.

They stepped together into the smaller cavern where the oranllodi surfaced. Magnar knelt once again at the shore of the silver pool. His hands and chin glistened with the evidence of his recent consumption.

Jahira's body tensed. She released his arm and rushed forward. Krnar watched her place both hands on Magnar's shoulders and shake him lightly as she spoke to him in a firm voice.

Krnar was relieved to know that she disapproved of Magnar's actions.

Magnar pulled his graying lips back to reveal silver-coated teeth, like an animal warning another to back away. He did not speak to Jahira. Instead he brushed her hands away and retrieved a water bag from the ground beside him. He dipped the water bag into the oranllo.

One of my water bags, Krnar realized.

Jahira reached down and looked as if she intended to rip the water bag from the pale one's hands. Magnar lifted his free arm and before Krnar could get there, the pale one backhanded Jahira across the face.

Krnar launched himself across the gap and tackled Magnar to the ground. He drew his knife and pressed it against the pale one's throat. The bluish vein in Magnar's neck bulged against the pressure of Krnar's knife blade. Hate smoldered behind eyes the color of dirt. Krnar hissed in Magnar's face.

Jahira yelled and pulled on Krnar's arm. She radiated anxiety.

Krnar growled a low warning before he withdrew the knife. He kept the pale one pinned a moment longer before he stood and stepped back in one fluid movement.

The pale one scrambled backward until his head contacted the rock wall. Krnar flexed his knees. Magnar walked his hands up the wall, pulling himself into a crouch. The pale one pulled a knife from his own belt, and began to inch forward.

Krnar wondered when Magnar had retrieved the weapon. He'd never noticed him digging through the piles of supplies that Jahira had sorted. He stepped fully in front of Jahira now, assessing his opponent. He almost felt sorry for the man. The pale one's clothes hung from his bony frame, a wild tangle of hair surrounded sunken cheeks and dark-circled eyes. Krnar waited for Magnar to make the first move, and he was not disappointed.

Magnar lunged with his teeth bared and single-minded ferocity. Krnar easily deflected his attack with a side-step and managed to simultaneously plant a knee in Magnar's ribs. Magnar grunted in pain but turned to attack again, this time feinting left before striking to the right. He managed to gouge a bit of skin from Krnar's forearm before he had fully adjusted to the change in direction.

Magnar continued to attack in a frenzy, not seeming to care about injury to himself, intent only on taking Krnar down. Krnar managed to avoid any serious wounds, but could not get on the offensive. He parried Magnar's relentless and unpredictable attack, conscious of Jahira's voice yelling at them in the background.

Krnar studied his opponent, looking for any openings, and noticed that Magnar put all of his force behind every jab, whether it was likely to connect or not. Krnar continued to parry and step back, parry and step back, until he finally saw a way to get close. He allowed Magnar within arm's reach and, as anticipated, Magnar lunged with all his force toward Krnar's heart. Krnar shifted just enough that Magnar's knife hand slid between Krnar's arm and torso. Once the blade had passed, Krnar closed his arm against his body, trapping Magnar.

He ignored the pain of the knife slicing through the flesh of his upper arm. Magnar struggled and beat ineffectually against Krnar with his free hand.

Krnar brought his knife up.

"Krnar, no!" Krnar paused at the sound of the urgency in Jahira's voice.

Krnar growled. Magnar grinned up at him with a feral smile and twisted his trapped wrist so that the blade bit deeper into Krnar's arm. Krnar deftly cut a length of gut line free from his belt and tossed it to Jahira.

"Tie him," Krnar commanded, sending a visual as well.

Jahira's eyes narrowed, then she looked down at the line and back up at Magnar. She moved forward and twisted his flailing arm against his back. Magnar tried to kick, but Krnar pulled his weight forward, keeping him off balance while Jahira secured the line around one wrist.

Krnar sheathed his knife, using his free hand to grip Magnar's trapped forearm. He stepped, careful to avoid further contact with Magnar's blade. He twisted Magnar's arm behind him and forced the pale one to the ground. Taking the line from Jahira, he finished tying Magnar's hands before binding them to his feet.

His breath came in ragged gasps when he finally stood and then moved back, letting the pale one thrash and squirm until he wore himself out. Eventually the pale one stopped fighting and lay still, his face a mask of hatred.

He heard Jahira's long exhalation and looked to see her scrub a hand over her face before she kneeled down and peeled the pale one's fingers off the handle of the knife he still gripped. The blade had a small smear of blood. Jahira reached with one finger and touched the smear, then looked up at Krnar.

She stood and walked around Magnar's bound form. While speaking, she pointed to the knife and then to his forearm. He understood her meaning and lifted his arm to show her the wound.

Jahira gasped and reached out, but stopped a hand-length from touching the cut. A frown creased her brow as she looked up at him.

"It's fine," he said. "I am fortunate to be wounded so close to an oranllo." He pointed to the silver pool, and then walked around her and toward the silver liquid.

Warmth seeped beneath the fur that covered his toes as he stepped into the oranllo. He gestured for Jahira to come closer. Kneeling in the waters, he leaned so that he could dip the back of his arm into the opaque fluid while giving Jahira a good view of the wounded area. Jahira's frown deepened as she watched.

Krnar's arm began to pulse like it had a second heartbeat, and then the area around the wound began to burn. Closing his eyes, he forced long slow breaths between clenched teeth as the pain intensified. An instant before it became too much to stand, the pain disappeared, leaving only a tingling memory of the burning intensity.

Krnar stood and approached Jahira with one arm out-stretched. Jahira gasped and this time her fingertips brushed the place where the wound had been. Now a faint, furless scar was all the evidence that remained of the previous damage.

EMPYREAN

Chapter 34

Impossible, Jahira thought.

She could not believe her eyes. Her mouth hung open as her fingertips traced over the smooth scar. The fur was gone from the thin strip where the skin had formed back together, but otherwise it looked as if nothing had ever happened.

Krnar trilled softly and pointed to her face.

Jahira reluctantly pulled her fingers away from examining his healed wound and lifted them to the throbbing welt which had formed on her cheek. After pressing the painful lump, she winced and moved her hand away from her face. Her fingers came away sticky. Leaning into Krnar's light, she held her fingers out to examine them. Dark liquid covered the lighter skin on the underside of her fingers.

Krnar's voice purred out a series of soothing sounds. After gesturing for her to sit, he pulled gently on her sleeping bag until she responded to the pressure and dropped to her knees. Her mind reeled with all she had witnessed in the last few minutes. Magnar attacking Krnar, Krnar healing his own wound; the dark of the cave pressed in on her, making her feel like she was in a dream.

Krnar scooped a handful of the silver liquid with his left hand. With his right, he dipped a fingertip into the cupped palm of his left hand. Before drawing the finger out, Krnar looked into her eyes and then spoke again in calm purring tones. He paused and looked at her expectantly.

Jahira frowned.

He spoke again, but this time she saw in her mind an image of him brushing the silver liquid against her cheek. He seemed to be asking if this was okay.

Jahira glanced down at his healed wound and realized what he meant to do. She nodded but couldn't stop herself from flinching away as the silver liquid approached her face. What if it entered her bloodstream, would it affect her like it had Magnar?

Her pulse began to race though Krnar's finger moved forward at a snail's pace. She closed her eyes and then felt the pressure of Krnar's finger on her cheek. She felt the liquid cover her wound and then the cut seemed to grow hot. A second application of the liquid caused the area to burn as if a flame were being held too close to her skin. It took all her willpower not to reach up and brush it away. Krnar must have seen her hands twitch. He placed his hand on her own and continued to talk to her in a soft rumble.

The burning diminished to a mild tingle, and then it was gone.

Krnar released her hand and Jahira opened her eyes. He reached out and she felt his fingertips press against her cheek. She was surprised that it did not hurt. He nodded and spoke again. Lifting her own fingers, she pressed the cut, gingerly at first, then with more force when she realized that the wound wasn't there.

"It's gone!" she exclaimed. "It's healed!"

Krnar nodded in response, then took her hand in his and lowered it toward the pool. She stiffened. Instead of continuing to pull, Krnar scooped a bit more liquid and poured it on her bloody fingertips, and then scrubbed until the blood was gone. He released her hand and nodded again.

"Thanks," Jahira said.

Krnar proceeded to dip his own hands into the pool and then use handfuls of the liquid to wash away any remaining blood or dirt. As he scrubbed his fur clean, Jahira tentatively reached out with one finger and dipped the tip into the silver liquid. It felt warm; blessedly warm. She imagined herself soaking in that warmth, feeling it all the way to her bones. It would be nice to wash away several days' worth of sweat and stink.

Krnar trilled, bursting the bubble of Jahira's daydream. She looked up to find him standing. He pointed to her, then to the pool. He lifted Magnar and began to carry him toward the tunnel, all the while nodding at her and then the pool. He backed into the tunnel, out of the cavern, and Jahira was left in complete darkness.

"Krnar, wait!"

He returned after a few seconds and tilted his head in question. She motioned him closer so that she could see, and then felt heat rise to her face as she tried to figure out how to explain the situation. Finally, she took him by the shoulders and turned him around so that his back was to her.

"Stay," she commanded, then shook her head and added, "please."

Krnar crossed his arms over his chest and seemed to comprehend her meaning. He did remain standing with his back to her as she stepped to the edge of the pool and shimmied out of her sleeping bag.

Chapter 35

Krnar listened to the soft rustle of fabric as Jahira disrobed behind him. The tingle of her touch on his shoulders still lingered. It began to expand across his chest and downward when he heard the slosh of liquid that meant Jahira had entered the pool. He'd seen plenty of women without clothes, but none without fur.

Curiosity battled with propriety inside his mind until he finally had to focus on something else. He also blocked his mind for good measure. The images that kept surfacing were not ones he wished for anyone else to see, especially not Jahira. She didn't seem to be able to pull thoughts from his mind, but it didn't hurt to be cautious.

After an intensely uncomfortable stretch of time, he heard the rustle of fabric again. He jumped when he felt her touch on his arm, even though he'd heard her approach. Turning to face her, he watched as her full lips stretched slowly into a smile.

She spoke and simultaneously pointed to him and then to the pool. Her meaning was clear.

"No," Krnar responded. "I think I would much rather scrub down in the snow."

The lines of hair above her eyes pulled together in the small frown that meant she had not understood, a fact which he'd been counting on. He gestured toward the tunnel. Jahira nodded and then followed. About a meter from the opening, they stopped to retrieve Magnar who rested against the cavern wall with his eyes closed.

Krnar cut the length of line between Magnar's wrists and ankles so that the man could stand but not walk easily on his own. Krnar put a shoulder under Magnar's right arm and lifted. Jahira did the same on the left. They were nearly equal in height so it worked well to walk in sync and carry the now lethargic man back to the main cavern.

Krnar's eyes were immediately drawn to Grollon, who was awake and seated cross-legged atop Magnar's sleeping roll. The old man scooted to the edge of the slippery hide and gestured for them to lay Magnar down. Krnar nodded and looked at Jahira, tilting his head toward the mat. She nodded in response.

They laid Magnar down. Glazed eyes stared out from dark hollows.

What am I going to do? she wondered.

Outside, the blizzard continued to rage. Swirls of snow gusted through the cave's entrance. Drifts formed against the small rise in the rock floor just inside the cave mouth, preventing serious accumulation in the back of the shelter.

Jahira sat down a body length from Magnar and across from Grollon. The look on her face was determined. She spoke to the Marked, her voice even despite the emotion Krnar could feel building inside her.

"Your friend consumed too much of Aruvel's soul. He must be purged now, by Aruvel's blood." Grollon spoke aloud for Krnar's benefit, but Krnar could sense the link between the mind of the Marked and Jahira's. It made him uneasy, knowing the Marked was in her mind, but she did not seem distressed.

Jahira frowned and spoke again to Grollon.

Grollon sighed and then responded, "I will tell you my story, perhaps it will help you to understand." The Marked turned to Krnar and asked him, "Do you wish to share these Memories?"

Krnar hesitated. He wanted to hear the story, but sharing the memories meant opening his mind to one of the Marked; no, not just *one* of the Marked, *the* Marked. Grollon's images and emotions would heighten the telling, would help Krnar to remember, but at what cost?

Grollon raised one eyebrow.

Would he ask permission if he intended harm?

The stories Krnar had heard of the Marked said they could force a man's mind open, could change your Memories, steal them;

some said they could even steal your very soul. Krnar supposed if this were true, keeping his mind blocked wouldn't do him much good anyway.

Krnar nodded, and opened his mind.

Grollon's link gripped him with a strong and expert touch. Despite his misgivings, Krnar knew a moment of awe. He was the first of his people to touch the mind of one who had passed through the Gateway to Aruvel.

Krnar leaned in as Grollon began his story.

"Many seasons ago, I was young and strong, like you. At that time my name was Grdon. I served as apprentice to Illdar, my Akaruvel."

Krnar marveled at the crisp images and the strength of the memories. It was the first time he'd seen a true memory of Illdar, for Illdar had been the last Akaruvel to be filled with the Knowledge of Eternity. He glanced at Jahira whose eyes were closed and small furrows had formed between her eyes, she must be seeing the images as well.

"In my youth I was impatient," Grollon continued. "I had spent my life training, waiting for Illdar to declare that it was time for us to merge. I wanted to pass through the gateway; more than anything else I wanted to *experience* Aruvel. The second Junction in my lifetime came and went and yet I remained Grdon. As the season passed, my impatience turned to anger.

The Season of Deep Snow which followed that second Junction was harsh. Illness spread through The People; my mother, father, and sister all succumbed." Grollon paused and Krnar felt a wave of raw grief hit him. He focused on Grollon's link and realized the emotion did not come from the old man. Krnar turned to Jahira and saw that a tear had leaked from the corner of her eye. It rolled down her cheek before she lifted a hand and brushed it away. She did not open her eyes. Krnar turned back to Grollon and the old man continued.

"I never grew ill, and neither did Illdar. I watched my family die while I remained untouched. My heart hardened and my anger turned to a deep well of bitterness."

Krnar saw movement out of the corner of his eyes and glanced over to see that Jahira had opened her eyes. She stared at Magnar. Her lips were pressed together in a thin line.

"I drank from the pools, like your friend." Jahira's attention snapped back to Grollon as he continued. "Unlike your friend, I had consumed Aruvel's soul before, in very small quantities, and I knew the risks of taking in too much. The liquid in the sacred pools opens the mind; the greater the dose, the greater the visions, to a point.

I drank and I experienced Memories like I had never seen before. I grew to believe that Aruvel was showing me a new way, a life in which all The People could hear the voice of The One Who Knows All. So strong was this belief that I convinced others to drink. The People became divided.

Illdar tried to stop us. After searching the memories for the cure, Illdar sent followers to gather the blood of Aruvel from the south. Illdar's followers ambushed me in the night and purged my soul by pouring the liquid from the river of fire in this pattern you see on my forehead. It worked for a time, I even convinced others to be cured, but the temptation was too great. Eventually, I drank again."

Grollon paused and locked eyes with Krnar.

"Then I killed Illdar."

Krnar growled low in his throat. He felt his hackles rise when the Marked pierced him with his ice-blue eyes. He felt Jahira's hand on his arm and glanced over. Concern filled her green eyes. Krnar took a deep breath and got himself under control.

"Then, leaderless, my people fled rather than kill their own," Krnar's nostrils flared. He forced the words through clenched teeth.

Abruptly, he stood and walked to the cave entrance. Snow continued to fall in wet, heavy clumps but the wind no longer howled. In fact, the world seemed eerily silent. So quiet he could hear the sound of snowflakes hitting the ground with a faint plop. Krnar inhaled deeply and filled his lungs with crisp, clean air, hoping that it might help clear his head.

The trials had not prepared him for this.

He had known it was possible that descendants of the Marked still lived. He had been prepared to evade them, to fight them if necessary; he was not ready to face the man responsible for his people's exile.

The heavy footfalls of Jahira's booted feet approaching disrupted his thoughts. She did not touch him this time, or speak. She simply stood by his side and together they watched the snow fall.

EMPYREAN

Chapter 36

Panting with the effort of wading through the accumulation of wet snow, Jahira pulled frigid air into her lungs and exhaled clouds of steam in rapid succession. Even with Krnar breaking trail, her pant legs were soaked through in a matter of minutes. The skin on her shins burned and itched before both legs finally went numb with cold. Sweat rolled down her back and between her breasts. Every time she blinked her lashes stuck as they tried to freeze together.

She'd just started to wonder how long it took for a person to get frostbite when they reached the Eagle.

"Son of a..." Jahira muttered. The solar panels were buried beneath several inches of powder topped by a wet crust.

With the pair of hide mittens Krnar had sewn for her from the skin of one of the animals he'd taken down, Jahira brushed the snow away from the panels. Once the tops were clear, she began to dig out the legs. Krnar watched her for a moment before he began to help dig out the second and third panels. When they were done, Jahira stepped into the belly of the Eagle.

The tinny thud of her boots on the metal echoed through the ship as she stamped off as much of the snow as possible before entering the flight deck. Numb toes prickled with each footfall. She made a mental note to grab a dry pair of socks before they left the ship.

Green lights twinkled on the dashboard, welcoming Jahira and flooding her with relief. The backup system had power.

Jahira retrieved the coordinates of the ship's last impact point before losing function. She entered these coordinates into the radio beacon, flipped the switch, and said a prayer. The signal light began to pulse.

If anyone came close enough, they'd pick up the signal and be able to find the ship. From there, they should be able to track her and Magnar's ID chips to the cave.

"That's the best I can do," she whispered.

She and Krnar returned to the cave to find Grollon and Magnar sitting across from each other. Grollon passed a bladder to Magnar, and Jahira watched his unbound hands accept the offering. He tipped the bladder back and took a long draught, then wiped the silver residue from his mouth with the back of his hand.

All of the fear, worry, frustration, and anger that had been tumbling around inside of her for the last few days seemed to consolidate and burst in a volcano of fury. After yanking her sleeping bag off over her head, Jahira walked with a determined stride across the cavern. She snatched the bladder from Magnar's hand.

"This stops now." Jahira's voice was low and fierce as she ripped the bladder from Magnar's hands and shook it in his face. "I will not allow you to do this to yourself! And you!" she continued, rounding on Grollon. "You know what it does! You know the consequences, and yet you offer my friend more. Are you trying to kill him?"

Momentarily done with her rant, she overturned the bladder and dumped the contents of the bag on the floor. Fingers of thick silver spread across the dark rock at her feet. Her eyes were still on Grollon when she heard a snarl. She turned her head just in time to see Magnar lunge for her.

She tried to turn and meet his attack, but she was half a second too late. Magnar's weight knocked her to the ground.

With one elbow digging into her chest, Magnar raised his torso and reached across his body to try to retrieve the bladder she'd dropped when he'd attacked.

Jahira shifted her hips, using her weight and his momentum to send him sprawling across the floor. She grabbed the bag before she scrambled away and finally rose to her feet.

Magnar was up and lunging for her again, but this time, instead of going for the water bag, he went for her throat.

Cold fingers wrapped around Jahira's neck and began to squeeze her windpipe. She brought her arms up and through the gap between his arms, breaking the hold, and then quickly brought them down and around to grasp his wrists. Jahira had trained against Magnar more times than she could count, but this was different; this was not Magnar. He was not rational, or predictable. She stared at the face of the man she'd known all her life and barely recognized him. Rage contorted Magnar's features and blazed in his eyes.

She knew that he would not stop.

Flexing her knees, she tried to hold on as he struggled. A flash of white in the corner of her eye forced her to attention away from Magnar. Krnar moved slowly toward Magnar from behind. Jahira shifted her eyes to meet his and shook her head.

Her momentary distraction gave Magnar the opportunity he had been waiting for.

Pain exploded across Jahira's forehead as Magnar's head smashed into hers. She staggered backward and lost her grip on his wrists. Before her vision had time to clear she felt pressure on her neck once more.

Jahira went to her knees this time, pulling Magnar down with her. The bulge of a rock dug into her shin and without thinking, Jahira curled her fingers around the solid mass and pulled it out from beneath her.

"Magnar, stop," her voice rasped before the last of her air cut off and all rational thought fled. Her vision began to narrow.

The tendons in her neck strained beneath Magnar's grip as she fought to pull air into her burning lungs. Her arm flew up instinctively and the rock in her hand struck Magnar's temple with a solid thunk.

The pressure on her throat released. Magnar's body slumped to the ground. Jahira gasped and coughed. She shoved his weight off her legs and finally massaged her bruised throat. She let the rock fall from her hand and heard the soft clink as it struck the ground.

Once she could breathe normally, she rolled Magnar onto his back and pressed two fingers against the artery in his neck. A strong pulse beat beneath her fingertips.

Krnar knelt across from her. He trilled in what sounded like sympathy, but said no more.

A lump had already formed on Magnar's temple.

What have I done?

After hooking her arms under Magnar's armpits, she began to pull him toward his sleeping bag. Krnar moved around to lift Magnar's feet and helped her carry him. They finally got him into his sleeping bag and Jahira hooked up the last emergency IV She stared at his face for several minutes, wishing there was something else that she could do. She didn't think she could handle it if she lost Magnar, too.

Chapter 37

Jahira's head snapped up and her fingers, which had been attempting to sew with one of Krnar's bone needles and some gut line, stilled. Her ears strained to identify the faint sound she was sure she'd heard, a sound so familiar and yet so out of place in the barren, frozen mountains. After a breathless thirty seconds of silence, Jahira set aside her half-sewn snowpants and stood. Quick steps carried her to the mouth of the cave where she paused and cocked her head to listen again.

"Jahira! Magnar!" The voices were distant and faint, but they were definitely human voices, and they were calling her name.

Jahira turned to Krnar, grinning and laughing, unable to contain her excitement.

"It's them! They've found us!"

Krnar joined her at the cave entrance and together they took a step out into the snow. Jahira shielded her eyes with one hand, but still had to squint against the dazzling light of the sun reflecting off the fresh snowfall.

"Jahira! Magnar!" The voices were closer this time, and to the left.

"Right here! I'm over here!" Jahira called back. She turned to Krnar and gripped his hands, squeezed them tight. She laughed, and then forged out into the snow yelling at the top of her lungs.

When she caught the first glimpse of a person approaching down the pass, Jahira felt like she might weep with relief.

Four days had passed since she'd knocked Magnar unconscious and he still had not revived. After the protein powder ran out, she'd filled his IV bag with warmed water and watched him shrink down to a skeleton. Finally, she would have help. If they could get Magnar back to the ships, maybe he would be okay.

"Jahira!"

She recognized the three approaching figures now and waved as she called back to them.

"Gavin! Tala! Medic!"

Jahira cursed when she broke through the crust of the snow again and again in her effort to hurry out to meet her friends.

Their paths finally met and Medic tossed her a pair of snowshoes. She strapped them on one at a time and then stepped forward on the surface of the snow. She hugged each of her friends in a fierce embrace. Hot tears welled in the corners of her eyes.

"Jahira, what a relief!" Tala breathed as she hugged Jahira back. "We have been so worried about you."

"Where's Magnar?" Medic asked.

"He's in the cave," Jahira replied, pointing behind her toward the opening in the base of the mountain. "But there's something-"

"What's that?" Gavin pulled a gun from his belt and pointed it toward the cavern entrance.

"Gavin! Put it down!" Jahira reached out and placed a hand on top of Gavin's. She gently pushed the gun down before she explained. "That's Krnar. He's a native of this planet and a friend, he saved our lives."

Gavin let the gun rest at his side, but he watched Krnar with narrowed eyes.

"You have a lot to tell us," Medic said.

"You have no idea," Jahira replied. "First though, we need to get Magnar and get him to the ship. He's been hurt and, at the moment, he's unconscious."

Medic started forward as soon as he heard the word *hurt*. Jahira turned and quickly caught up to him. She wanted to stay ahead of Gavin so that he didn't do anything stupid. She held a hand up to stop her friends a few feet away from the cave entrance where Krnar stood waiting. The gesture proved unnecessary. They had all stopped and stared, allowing Jahira to approach first.

"Krnar, these are my friends, they brought another ship and they're going to take us back to the alara." Jahira made a ship with her hands and used Krnar's word for the silver trees.

They'd had a few days with nothing to do but figure out how to communicate. He seemed to understand.

"This is Gavin, Tala, and Medic," she said, pointing to each one in turn. Krnar nodded to each of them. Jahira wondered what he was thinking. "Guys, this is Krnar."

"Does it talk?" Gavin asked.

Jahira gave him a hard look.

"Yes, *he* does, but in his own language, obviously. He and I are able to communicate most of the time, and he is picking up our language pretty fast, but there's another one…" Jahira paused, not sure how to explain Grollon.

"Do they live here?" Tala asked.

"No," Jahira replied. "Well, the other one that's inside, Grollon, he has been living here for a while but came here from the place where we landed. Krnar came across the sea, I think. We all kind of found each other by accident."

She'd learned more of Krnar's story over the last few days and it seemed like he was on some kind of quest.

"We'll have plenty of time to talk about this on the way home," Medic stated. "Let's get Magnar out of here."

Jahira nodded and led them inside.

Everyone paused to remove their snowshoes. Jahira heard Tala gasp when she looked up and saw Grollon. Gavin's knuckles turned white as he tightened his grip on his weapon. Medic was the only one who seemed unphased by it all. He walked straight to Magnar and knelt by his side.

Jahira watched Medic prick the end of one of Magnar's fingers and squeeze out a small bead of blood. He scraped this off with a tiny plastic wand which he inserted into the end of a handheld analyzer. Medic watched the screen, nodding a few times, and then he frowned. He ran the scanner over Magnar's body, pausing over vital organs, until every part of the comatose man had been assessed.

"His vitals look stable and he's only slightly dehydrated. You've been doing a good job considering the circumstances," Medic nodded at Jahira. "But there's something in his system that's giving me an error message." Medic raised one eyebrow in question.

Jahira sighed.

"He's been drinking from those silver pools."

A moment of silence ensued before Tala and Gavin started firing questions. Medic just nodded slowly.

"How long?" Medic asked.

"A couple of months since his first drink," Jahira replied. "I'm not sure how much."

Medic's eyes widened slightly, and then he looked back down at Magnar.

"Has he been awake at all since the crash?"

"Yes, he woke a day or two after I did, but was acting very odd, and aggressive. He's been out for four days this time."

"What happened?" Medic asked.

Jahira looked down at Magnar. The lump and the broken skin on his temple had healed in a single day. There was no visible trace of any injury. She *could* lie.

"I knocked him out."

"What!?" Gavin exclaimed.

"Jahira!" Tala added.

"What happened," Medic repeated.

"He attacked me, twice actually," Jahira explained. "There's a pool of that silver liquid deeper in the mountain. I caught him drinking it and tried to stop him. He attacked me and choked me. I reacted."

Medic's eyebrows pulled together in a deep frown.

"Well, let's get him back to the Colonizer. Maybe once he wakes up we can get some more answers." Medic motioned for Gavin to get his snowshoes back on.

Jahira gathered her things and stuffed them in her back-pack. She pulled on her half-sewn snow pants and the top of her sleeping bag, which had become a separate coat. She strapped on her own pair of snowshoes. Once Medic and Gavin were ready, they walked awkwardly back to where Magnar lay. Medic placed an arm under Magnar's shoulders so that he cradled his head and Gavin pushed both arms under Magnar's legs. They turned and walked side by side, carrying Magnar in front of them, and began to shuffle across the cave floor, trying to balance their awkward burden.

"You're never going to make it to the ship without dropping him," Jahira said. "Not through this snow anyway."

"What do you suggest then?" Medic asked.

Jahira looked around, saw Grollon and Krnar watching her, and realized neither of them had said a word or made a move since her friends had arrived. She wondered what they were thinking. She wondered if Krnar understood what was happening.

"Grollon, you and Krnar, you should come with us," Jahira still didn't completely trust Grollon, but she couldn't leave him here to die. Besides, he seemed to be the only one with any idea about what had happened to Magnar. "Will you come with us?"

Jahira watched Krnar as Grollon turned to speak to him. He stood still as a statue, his face unreadable. Grollon spoke for longer than she thought it should take to ask the question. As she waited for Grollon to finish, her shoulders tightened into knots and she held her breath. She realized with surprise that she was anxious about what Krnar would say.

Grollon stopped speaking and Krnar looked at her, then back to Grollon.

Krnar spoke quickly, too fast for Jahira to pick out any individual words, and then Grollon responded.

Jahira jumped when Krnar trilled a long, loud ululation that echoed off the rocks.

"Uh, Jahira?"

Jahira turned and realized that Gavin and Medic were waiting for her. Tala's eyes were wide with shock as she watched Krnar.

"What's going on?" Medic asked.

Jahira turned to Grollon expectantly.

Grollon nodded.

"They're coming with us," Jahira stated. She let out a relieved exhale and a slow smile spread across her face.

Chapter 38

Krnar could not contain his excitement. He could feel that his effluvience made the strangers uneasy but at that moment, he did not care. They would take him to the alara grove.

Over the last few suns he'd discovered that Jahira and Magnar had come from the grove. Now, they would guide him there. He gathered his few belongings, including as much of the sectioned and wrapped meat as he could carry, and stuffed it all into his pack. Grollon waited by his side while Jahira and her people talked and gestured.

Impatience made him shift his weight from foot to foot. He tried to follow the conversation, but it was too fast.

"What is the problem?" Krnar finally asked Grollon.

"They debated the wisdom of taking us, but Jahira won that argument. Now they discuss the best way to carry Magnar."

Krnar watched the exchange for a moment before he hissed in frustration. He walked over to stand on the opposite side of Magnar and held out his arms.

"I will carry him," Krnar said nodding for the two men to place Magnar in his arms. One of the men, the one Jahira had called Gavin, scrutinized his every move with narrowed eyes. The other looked to Jahira.

Jahira nodded and spoke to the two men.

Medic turned back to Gavin and spoke. Gavin barked a response, to which Medic replied in a calm voice. Gavin finally sighed and nodded. The two men extended Magnar's limp form toward Krnar.

Krnar received their friend with a nod, turned, and took a step toward the mouth of the cave.

"Krnar!"

He stopped and turned at the sound of Jahira's voice. She held up a pair of the odd looking shoes that she and all of her people wore. He tipped his head in an unspoken question and she pointed to his feet. She wanted him to wear them.

"I do not need them," he protested, but Jahira moved forward and placed the elongated shoes on the ground in front of him. "We are wasting time."

She looked up with those vivid green eyes and raised one eyebrow. He knew she would not leave until he'd put on the shoes.

"You're as stubborn as Tllomell," he muttered, but lifted one hide-wrapped foot and placed it on the smooth surface in the center of the strange shoe.

Jahira pulled several straps over the front of his foot, tightening them down with several rather ingenious buckles, and then tightened one more in the back. Once she was done with the first foot she tapped his other foot and then the center of the shoe. He obliged and she secured his second foot.

"Are we ready now?" Krnar asked, his voice gruff to hide the tingling sensation coursing up his legs.

Jahira looked to her companions and nodded.

Krnar turned and almost fell. One of the shoes had overlapped the other and he'd tried to step before he had it completely shifted. Fortunately, he righted himself without dropping Magnar. Head held high, he proceeded, ignoring Gavin's muttering behind him which was followed by Jahira's hissed response.

Once he was on the snow, and had figured out how to widen his stance slightly, the shoes were amazing. They held him on top of the crust despite the additional weight.

The two men from Jahira's people caught up and flanked him. Gavin watched him like a predator eyed its prey. One of his hands hovered over the strange looking tool he'd pointed at Krnar upon their arrival. Krnar wondered what it was. It did not look dangerous; there were no sharp edges, only a short hollow tube that did not even look very heavy. He doubted the man could hurt him with such an ineffective weapon.

Jahira and the other female, Tala, helped Grollon, which mainly consisted of slowing their pace to match his and making sure he didn't stray from the well-packed path he walked as the last in line. The old man had grown much stronger in the last few suns, thanks to the meat Krnar had shared and the abundant source of fresh water on the ground, but he was still slow.

Krnar stepped from the pass and into the clearing where he'd first discovered Jahira and Magnar inside their silver bird. He trilled softly, a feeling of awe rooted his feet to the ground. He'd known the second ship would be there, from Grollon's explanation, yet he hadn't known exactly what it would look like. This one stood upright on four legs, its great silver wings extended out on either side, undamaged.

The great bird loomed over him as he waited for Medic and Gavin to gather the same kind of black rectangles which Jahira had set out around the broken bird. They met back at the rendezvous point under one of the silver wings and waited a moment for the last three to arrive. Finally, all were gathered. Medic pulled what looked like a polished stone from his pocket.

Krnar watched with interest as the man pushed on the top of the stone. A hissing sound issued from above. Krnar took a step back and stared open-mouthed. A section of the bird's belly broke away from the body and began to lower itself toward the ground. Jahira placed a hand on his arm and smiled a reassuring smile.

Gavin and Medic stepped onto the silver rectangle without hesitation once it touched the snow.

Medic spoke to Jahira, who helped Grollon up onto the platform and then nodded. Krnar watched Medic press the smooth stone in his hand and the silver rectangle began to rise. Krnar's breath caught in his throat when the three men disappeared and the silver rectangle sealed back into place.

As Krnar and Jahira stared up at the bird, the rectangle released with another hiss. Krnar glanced over at Jahira. Her expression was eager, her emotions a mixture of relief and anticipation, he sensed no fear, no hesitation. She stepped onto the smooth silver rectangle the moment it stopped and looked back at him expectantly. Krnar hesitated. He peered up into the belly of the bird. Grollon watched him.

"Krnar," Jahira said and waved him forward when he looked back down at her.

After a deep inhalation, he placed one shoe on the platform and tested his weight on the slick-looking surface before pulling his other shoe up and out of the snow. Jahira grasped his arm as he shifted his weight, helping him to balance. He settled on the rectangle and nodded his thanks, then tipped his head back and stared above him. The platform ascended into a cavernous opening nearly identical to the one in which he'd found Jahira and Magnar.

The platform stopped moving. Krnar heard another hiss of air. Jahira bent down and removed her long shoes with a few quick pulls on the straps. She secured the shoes against the wall, then returned and held her arms out.

"Give," she said, curling her fingers in and out a few times to emphasize her point.

Krnar handed Magnar to her and watched her ease him to the ground, onto a thick-looking hide that gave slightly under Magnar's weight. Jahira strapped Magnar's body down and then reached for Krnar's legs.

"I'll do it," he stated, holding one hand up to forestall her touch; he had grown far too accustomed to it and while it had started to seem normal when they were alone in the cave, he felt the shame of their observed contact in the presence of her people.

He caught a flash of a smile from Grollon before he bent to undo the straps. The first attempt caused a great deal of frustration before he finally pulled the right way and released the strap from the tiny tooth which inserted into a tiny hole. Once he'd discovered the secret, the rest were easy.

He handed the shoes to Jahira with a nod of thanks and then stood with his arms crossed.

"Sit," Jahira said and pointed to the opposite wall.

Krnar looked back. He understood her word, but saw no reason to comply with her request.

Jahira pointed again to Grollon, who sat with his back to a wall while Medic bound him with thick black straps. Krnar looked back at Jahira and tilted his head.

"It's all right," Grollon said. "The straps are to keep us safe during the flight."

"The flight?" Krnar asked.

"That's right," Grollon replied with a grin. "We're going to fly."

Krnar's pulse began to race. He glanced back and saw Gavin and Tala sitting behind the big clear eyes, in the same place he'd found Jahira and Magnar.

"We're going to fly," Krnar whispered.

"She wants you to sit down so that we can go."

Krnar walked over and slid down the wall Jahira had indicated. He let her fasten and tighten the straps which held him firmly against the smooth interior. He heard a muffled exchange of unrecognizable words between Gavin and Tala. Then he felt the bird rock slightly before his stomach seemed to drop down to the floor.

The next instant his body lurched to the right as the bird shot forward.

His people were never going to believe this.

EMPYREAN

Chapter 39

They'd barely been in the air long enough for Krnar's stomach to settle when Jahira unhooked herself from the wall, and then released him. She motioned for him to follow her into the front of the ship.

Krnar stood behind Tala and watched the snowcapped peaks of the mountains draw near and then disappear in waves of grey and white. Sooner than he would have thought possible, the mountains receded altogether and rolling hills of lush grass stretched to the horizon. He tried to imagine how many suns it would have taken him to walk this distance, but could not even estimate.

A soft trill escaped his lips when the deep purple canopy and dark trunks of the dancing trees became visible. He flew inside a silver bird over a forest so vast his mind could not comprehend its size. The bright orb of Allorkan traveled halfway across the sky while he remained there, silent and staring in disbelief.

The fur of his upper arm began to tingle. Krnar turned his head just before Jahira placed a hand on his bicep. She paused, dropped her hand, and then nodded toward the rear cavern where Magnar lay. Reluctantly, he followed.

"Sit," Jahira said, pointing to the straps she'd used to restrain him at the beginning of the flight.

Krnar glanced around and saw that Grollon and Medic were, again, secured. He complied, holding his breath when Jahira's hands brushed the fur on his sides as she fastened the straps.

Would you like me to explain to her how it affects you when she touches you? Grollon projected.

"No," Krnar growled his response out loud, causing the old man to chuckle.

Jahira looked up with wide eyes at his sudden outburst. He tried to give her a reassuring smile. She finished with his straps and then backed away, settled into her own seat and strapped herself in, watching him warily. Krnar shot a narrow-eyed glare at Grollon, who continued to smile.

Krnar closed his eyes and blocked his mind. He worked on remembering his journey thus far; picturing every detail of every significant event from the moment he dove into the sea to follow Allnall up to now.

The ship rocked and Krnar opened his eyes. The sound of Tala and Gavin speaking to each other drifted back and echoed off the smooth walls. He heard them say Jahira's name, but could not make out the rest of the words.

In response, Jahira and Medic unbuckled, then worked together to position Magnar in the center of the floor. Jahira motioned for Krnar and Grollon to wait.

Medic pulled the smooth stone from his pocket again. The floor beneath Jahira and Magnar began to drop away. As it descended, Krnar felt a wave of hot air rush into the silver cave.

"Are we stopping to rest?" Krnar asked, hoping Grollon could provide more insight into the situation.

"No," Grollon replied. "We have arrived."

The piece of the floor which had fallen away re-appeared, empty now. Tala and Gavin stepped on to the rectangle; Tala motioned for Krnar and Grollon to join them.

Krnar fumbled with the fasteners for a moment before he managed to release himself. He and Grollon stepped together onto either side of the foreigners. The floor beneath him began to move. No matter how many times he experienced it, he didn't think he could ever get used to that.

A hot breeze, which had flowed through the opening when Jahira descended, enveloped him like a fire-warmed hide. When he took a breath the air felt thick and tasted of dirt. He watched his feet, trying to maintain his balance, until the platform stopped. Eagerly, he stepped off the moving floor and into the grass beside Jahira.

Long blue-grey blades tickled his thighs as it swayed in a breeze heavy with scent. So many smells Krnar could not identify filled his nostrils until his head began to swim. His eyes watered from the intense light. He blinked his protective and tinted lenses into place. When he could see again, he looked past Jahira and discovered hundreds of people like her in form, though their flesh came in a startling array of colors. They emerged from different parts of their odd-looking settlement and congregated many body lengths away, waving and calling out to the ones around him. Tension coiled in his gut when the crowd moved as one toward the ship, toward him.

Krnar's gaze slid over the mass of unfamiliar people. Something to the left of the crowd caught his eye. His heart seemed to catch in his throat. On the horizon he could see many thin silver lines topped with vivid green leaves.

The sacred grove.

In less than one sun he'd completed his journey. He felt as if he were dreaming, a very hot and very loud dream. Turning slowly, he committed every detail to memory. A half-turn allowed him to look out across the field to his right.

The sight that awaited him made Krnar's heart pound against his ribs. Unable to contain himself, he threw back his head and trilled with unchecked volume, exulting in his good fortune.

To his right, far in the distance, rose four great silver peaks glinting in the light of Allorkan. They reached for the stars, appearing exactly the way the memories had captured them; the silver mountains of the prophecy.

Jahira touched his shoulder, sending a jolt through his body. He turned and saw the look of concern on her face.

Krnar grinned and embraced her. Lifting her off the ground, he laughed.

"Thank you," he said. "You were sent to me by Aruvel. I know now that I am going to succeed!" He twirled her in a full circle and then released her with another laugh. Jahira's expression was one of pure shock.

Krnar opened his mind to hers for the first time since her people had arrived at the cave to rescue them. He wanted to know how she felt and also to try to explain. Immediately he sensed her surprise, her confusion, and something- a wave of excitement, relief, curiosity, fear- too many emotions to sort out, hit him like a violent wave and threatened to drown him with their intensity. He realized the crowd had stopped a few body lengths away and the people watched him. He could sense all of their emotions. They filled him to overflowing. He was forced to block his mind against the onslaught. Jahira stepped forward to receive embrace after embrace from more people than he could count.

Tala, Medic, and Gavin joined her and the volume of high-pitched voices increased and overlapped until Krnar's head began to hurt.

In order to give himself a bit of breathing room, Krnar took a step back and saw Grollon out of the corner of his eyes.

"What do you plan to do now?" Grollon asked.

Krnar paused, watching the expressive faces, the unabashed contact between hundreds of bodies. He let his gaze wander again to the grove, then to the mountains.

"I have no idea," he replied.

Jahira pulled away from the crowd then and stopped by Magnar's side. Medic joined her and they spoke, too soft for him to hear their words, with their heads bent together.

The crowd parted and two individuals came forward holding either end of a long, flat piece of material bolstered by two long poles. Krnar watched as the two laid the material down on the ground behind Magnar. Jahira and Medic moved him, still on the thick hide, onto the long carrier. The same two individuals who'd brought the carrier lifted it again, now with Magnar atop it.

Jahira waved him forward.

She turned and shouted something to the crowd. Voices hushed and then all eyes turned to stare at him. Jahira spoke again and then motioned for the two carrying Magnar to proceed.

Krnar fell in behind Jahira and he could feel hundreds of eyes following him. He squared his shoulders, kept his eyes forward, and kept his mind blocked. He did not have to have his mind open to know what these people were feeling. The whisper of a thousand voices that he could not understand said enough. He'd never felt so self-conscious in his life.

His breath came a little easier once they'd passed the crowd, until Krnar realized that Jahira led him straight toward the silver mountains.

EMPYREAN

EMPYREAN

Chapter 40

Once they were in the lab aboard the Colonizer, Jahira hung back, trying to stay out of the way. Medic and his staff bustled around Magnar. Magnar's ribs protruded through his skin. The joints of his knees and elbows bulged from his stick-thin limbs. Jahira blinked rapidly to keep her tears at bay when she saw how emaciated he'd become.

Once he was clean and dry, they pulled on some loose pants, laid him on an elevated bed, and began sticking him with needles and probes. One of the nurses even trimmed his nails. When they were through grooming and poking, he looked much better, but also much more vulnerable. The anger and pain were temporarily erased from his features. He looked like the old Magnar; thinner and weaker, but peaceful. The sight of him broke her heart.

"Now what?" Jahira asked.

Gilana, Medic's head nurse, shuffled the rest of the staff out of the room.

"Now we wait," Medic replied.

"Shouldn't you try to wake him up?" Jahira asked.

"No, not yet; a coma is the body's way of forcing a person to rest so that it can heal," Medic glanced over at his data screen in response to a soft blip and a frown pulled his eyebrows together.

"What is it?" Jahira asked.

Medic paused, glanced at her, and then scanned the screen again.

"Well, the strange part is that all of his vitals look really good, much better than they should, in fact."

It was Jahira's turn to frown.

"What do you mean?"

"Well, his organs are all functioning at optimal levels, brain activity is actually above normal for a person in his state, and there is no physical evidence of trauma inside or out." Medic shook his head. "This is not the data I would expect from someone who's been in a plane crash, malnourished, and knocked unconscious by a blow to the head. Your numbers weren't even this good."

"What does that mean?"

"It means he shouldn't be in coma," Medic replied. He tapped on his screen and scrolled down. "There is no medical reason, at least not that I can see, for him to still be unconscious."

Jahira leaned in, trying to see whatever it was that Medic was seeing, and then she remembered Grollon.

After spinning on her heel, she walked across the room and paused for the movement sensor to open the frosted glass door which separated the lab and the waiting room. A few more steps and she stood in front of the old winged man who sat in a chair, looking so out of place aboard the ship. Krnar sat beside him, his eyes shifting about the room. He looked even less comfortable than Grollon.

"Why is he still unconscious?" she asked Grollon.

Grollon projected an image of himself lying on the ground while another winged individual traced the pattern which still remained on his forehead.

"Yes, you showed me that before, but how is that going to help Magnar?"

Grollon repeated the image, but this time the figure lying on the ground changed. She saw Magnar with his eyes closed, another figure poised over him.

Jahira sighed, she didn't have time to argue about the details right now, she needed answers.

"All right, how?"

Grollon paused and glanced over her shoulder. He nodded toward the lab and Jahira saw a picture of Medic in her mind.

"Medic? You want to tell Medic?" Jahira asked. "I guess we could try, but don't expect him to believe it. Wait here."

Jahira turned and entered the lab again, where Medic continued to study the screen, scrolling back and forth, perhaps searching for the error that would explain the odd readings.

Jahira cleared her throat and waited for Medic to look up.

When he saw her standing there, wringing her hands and shifting her weight from one foot to the next, he turned and gave her his full attention.

"Grollon has a theory, about what we need to do to wake Magnar up." Jahira cleared her throat again and Medic frowned. She wasn't sure how much of Grollon's story to tell. She wasn't sure how to explain Grollon at all. Now that she was back among "civilization", the whole experience in the cave seemed like a dream or like another life that didn't quite fit with the one she was living now.

"How do you know?" Medic finally asked.

"Uh, well, he's able to communicate telepathically." Jahira paused and watched Medic's reaction to her words. His eyebrows raised but he did not comment, he simply waited for her to continue. "They both can, to some extent, but Grollon, well, I can almost always understand what he means. I can see his thoughts like a movie in my mind."

Medic's raised eyebrows pulled down and together into a deep frown. Now that she'd gotten past the worst part, she continued quickly before she lost her nerve.

"He's experienced this before, what Magnar's going through. He drank the silver liquid and so did some of his people, a long time ago. I think they figured out how to cure it, sort of, but, well…" Jahira paused and caught her breath. "He can explain it better than I can, and he's willing to show you, if you're willing to let him."

"Let him; you mean, communicate with me…telepathically?"

Jahira nodded.

"You've done this?"

Again she nodded.

"All right, if it will help me figure out how to help Magnar." Medic glanced around the lab. "Let's do it in here though."

Jahira nodded before she returned to the waiting room and asked Grollon and Krnar to come into lab.

Medic stood watching Grollon enter the lab. Jahira noticed that Grollon's movements seemed less stiff than they had in the cave, and he stood straighter, with his shoulders pulled back. Her eyes shifted from Grollon to Medic.

"Are you ready?" she asked.

Medic nodded once.

A mild tingling sensation crept through her skull, a feeling she'd come to associate with one of them connecting with her mind. It was much like the feeling she experienced when activating her V.R. unit. When Grollon connected with her mind, the crawling feeling seemed more intense than when Krnar put pictures in her head. It also ended faster, almost like her brain itched for a second or two, and then it was gone.

Jahira saw the images she'd seen before, of Grollon drinking the silver liquid and becoming violent, a group of winged individuals flying south to a volcano and returning to place something on Grollon's forehead. Afterward, Grollon himself administered the "cure" to his followers.

Medic looked at Jahira.

Jahira shrugged.

"He drank and then was healed somehow, by what he showed you. He thinks we need to do this for Magnar."

"Can he show us where to go?"

When her attention returned to Grollon, he and Krnar were engaged in a conversation of their own. Jahira instinctively took a step back as their discussion grew more intense. She could actually see the fur on the back of Krnar's neck begin to rise.

"What is it? What's the problem?" Jahira asked.

Nicole L. Bates

Krnar looked at her, then back to Grollon and spoke. Grollon pointed to her and replied. Grollon must have interpreted her words because Krnar looked at her when he spoke again.

"Grollondi," he said, pointing to Grollon's forehead. Then he pointed to Magnar and repeated the word, "Grollondi."

Jahira frowned and shook her head. She felt that itching, crawling feeling again before an image formed in her mind's eye, an image of a lava flow, bright orange and oozing. After a few seconds, the image changed to a picture of Magnar's face. She gasped when she saw the livid burns across his forehead which slowly sealed to form scars, scars which matched the pattern on Grollon's forehead.

This time when she shook her head it was more out of denial than lack of comprehension.

"What is he saying?" Medic asked.

Jahira looked at Grollon.

"This is what you want me to do to Magnar? Pour burning lava on his head?"

Grollon repeated the image of himself, this time including the minor details which he'd previously left out, the flesh of his forehead blistering and then burning away before it sealed over again.

Jahira drew a long breath before she answered Medic.

"If we do this I think it will leave scars, like the ones Grollon has on his forehead."

"And he thinks we are going to do that to Magnar?"

"He says it's what has to be done, what was done to him."

"Well, did it work?"

Jahira turned to Grollon and waited for his answer.

Grollon's eyes shifted to the ceiling and he seemed to be contemplating his response.

Jahira saw a brief image of a peaceful community, some with marks, some without. Grollon showed her the trees of the silver grove and she saw the colors of the leaves and fruit change a dozen times before she saw Grollon kneel by the silver pool and drink again.

Jahira waited for him to continue. When he did not, she looked at Medic.

"Temporarily? Is that how you would interpret that?" Jahira asked. "What do you think we should do?"

"I think we should wait," Medic said.

All heads turned as the lab door opened and Ryan, red-faced and huffing, stepped into the lab.

"Jahira! Welcome back!" He nodded in Jahira's direction but his eyes, bright with eager anticipation, quickly shifted to Krnar and Grollon.

"Thanks," Jahira replied, her voice conveyed her amusement. One did not have to be telepathic to read Ryan's thoughts. "Ryan, I'd like you to meet Krnar, and Grollon." She held a hand out toward each man as she said his name.

"Yes, hello, it's a pleasure." Ryan half-waved, then half-bowed, and finally straightened. A blush crept up his neck and colored his cheeks.

"Krnar, Grollon, this is Ryan." Jahira gestured toward the thin, middle-aged man who had already started whispering into the voice recorder on his hand-held data screen as he circled the two men, looking them up and down. "He's a scientist, a, well, a person who seeks answers about the world."

Grollon nodded and relayed this information to Krnar, who also nodded and then bowed in Ryan's direction.

"We will talk," Grollon spoke aloud in his own language, Krnar's language, but Jahira saw a mental picture of Grollon and Ryan in deep discussion. Ryan must have seen it as well because Jahira saw him jump back slightly before the color drained from his face.

"Ryan, Grollon is telepathic, he'll be able to understand you, most of the time, and can respond with pictures inside your head. That should keep you both busy for a while," Jahira commented wryly.

Ryan nodded slowly, gaping at Grollon.

"I need a shower, and some clean clothes. I'll come back and check in when I'm done." Jahira began to walk toward the door, then glanced back and saw Krnar looking around the room. His hands fidgeted with the gut line looped around his belt. She was sure she'd never seen him look so uncomfortable.

"Krnar?" Once he'd focused on her, Jahira gestured for him to come with her.

He nodded and his shoulders actually dropped an inch. He must have been really tense, maybe anxious about being left there alone. She tried to imagine herself in Krnar's place, in a strange situation with strange-looking people who all spoke a different language. Her experience in the cave had been surreal enough and she'd at least had the comfort of having Magnar with her, even if he wasn't himself. What could she do to make him feel more comfortable?

She had an idea.

Chapter 41

Silver walls curved around Krnar, forming a bright, smooth tunnel which wove through the largest of the silver mountains. Hundreds of tiny lights glowed as if stars from the night sky had been captured and suspended inside the walls. His head hurt with the effort of trying to make sense of all that he saw, things for which he had no frame of reference. He felt overwhelmed with questions and frustrated by the lack of answers.

Lost in his own thoughts, he nearly collided with Jahira when she stopped suddenly in front of a large silver rectangle, slightly recessed in the wall of the tunnel. After reaching out with one dark hand, she touched the wall to the right of the rectangle. In less time than it took him to step back in surprise, the rectangle disappeared into the wall. Jahira stepped through the opening into a small room.

The room smelled strange, an unrecognizable odor that burned his nostrils. Only a faint hint of Jahira's scent lingered in what was apparently her hearth, for she made sounds of delight as she opened compartments and pulled belongings out to lay them on a smooth, waist-high shelf which extended out from one wall.

He watched her movements, so relaxed, so familiar in such strange surroundings. He released the block on his mind and felt how comfortable she was, how happy. It made him ache for his own hearth and his own people.

"Krnar," Jahira's voice interrupted his thoughts and he stepped forward in response to her beckoning gesture.

He allowed her to usher him into a seat, but frowned when he saw the small glowing circle on the shelf in front of him. Jahira touched the circle and a picture appeared in the air in front of his face.

Krnar hissed and stood, backing away from the image. Jahira's voice, startled and apologetic, made him pause. Her smile, and the excitement that he could feel pouring out of her, pulled him closer.

His attention shifted from Jahira to the picture and back. She jabbered away, pointing from the glowing disc to the image hanging in the air. With one finger she reached out and slid her finger horizontally above the picture. The picture changed to an image of a knife, very similar to Jahira's own.

"Knife," she said after she'd tapped the screen. She tapped the picture two times fast and Krnar heard her voice coming from the glowing disc, repeating the word she'd said. After tapping a tiny image above the picture of the knife she said, "Vrsat."

Vrsat, the Lerroni word for knife, was one vocabulary word they'd both learned and used with some frequency back in the mountain cave.

This time when Jahira tapped the picture twice he heard her voice emanate from the glowing circle saying, "Knife," pause, "Vrsat."

She slid the image sideways and the knife disappeared, replaced now by a picture of a snow-covered field.

"Snow," Jahira said after she'd tapped the same tiny square above the picture. She tapped again and said, "Ulok." She tapped the picture twice and Krnar heard the words echo from the disc.

Realization dawned.

Krnar reached out tentatively with one finger. He drew it back quickly when the tip pushed right through the solid-looking image. With a gentle grip, Jahira guided his hand back to the picture and helped him "tap" the air in the correct location, and with the right amount of force.

They continued through perhaps a hundred pictures, Jahira would say the name first in her language, then Krnar in his.

Finally, Jahira yawned and stretched, then rose and held up one finger. She retrieved a small stack of material from the shelf she'd placed it on earlier and then pointed to the wall to his left. She held her hand against the wall and another opening appeared.

"Be right back," she said.

Krnar nodded.

He returned his attention to the screen and became absorbed in reviewing and learning the new words. He knew it would be essential if he wished to make connections to these people. They might be able to help him find a way to bring his people back to this place.

It seemed as if no time at all had passed before Jahira returned and sat beside him. Moisture glistened on her tight, dark curls and her clothes were different. A thin blue shirt and matching pants hugged her body like a second skin. Krnar could feel his own body responding to her proximity even before she leaned toward the suspended picture and brushed against the fur of his arm.

Fortunately, she seemed oblivious to his discomfiture and drew him back into the tutorial.

When they finally stopped, and Jahira made the glowing disk quit glowing, Krnar's eyes felt strange and tired. His head felt like it might explode from the abundance of new information that he'd tried to fill it with in so short a time.

They returned to check on Magnar, whose condition appeared unchanged. Many tubes and threads trailed from various parts of his body. Krnar could see the steady rise and fall of his chest.

He waited by the door while Jahira moved to Magnar's side and placed a hand on his cheek. Next, she brushed his hair back from his brow and then let one finger trail across the unblemished skin of his forehead. A heavy sigh emphasized the worry he knew she felt.

In an adjacent room, surrounded by pictures hanging in the air like the one Jahira had shown him, he saw Grollon and Ryan. As Krnar watched, Ryan gestured and moved pictures around, pointing out details to Grollon. A thought occurred to him. Perhaps these people projected their thoughts out into the air around them instead of directly from one mind to another. Perhaps they stored their memories in those discs so that everyone could access the knowledge, rather than expecting one person to remember it all, and subsequently losing so much when they lost that person. It was an interesting thought. He would have to ask Grollon about his experience with the *scientist* when the two men were done. At the moment, Grollon was too absorbed to notice his presence.

When Jahira had finished, she left the room without stopping to talk to Ryan and Grollon. For this Krnar was thankful. He needed some distance from the Marked, and he needed some fresh air.

As they exited the mountain, Krnar blinked back the lenses which protected his eyes from the light. Night had descended on the warm land. Glancing back at the light spilling from the doorway of the ship, Krnar added another question to his growing list.

How could there be light inside the mountain with no fire, even when it was dark outside?

Jahira interrupted his thoughts with a gesture. She held one hand out from her body, palm-up, swept it in an arc, and then shrugged.

"Where do you want to go?" she asked.

"Alara," Krnar said, pointing to the silver trees in the distance, which glowed beneath the light of the three moons.

Jahira nodded and they walked side by side through the settlement. The variety and design of these people's shelters fascinated him. Some were made from very large hides, others were made with walls of dirt. No one slept out in the open, even on a night as warm as this one.

They walked in silence through the settlement until there were no more dwellings. Then, forgetting about the strange new inhabitants for time, he focused on his lifelong goal. Anticipation built inside of Krnar as he drew closer to the sacred grove. Tall, thick grass brushed against his body, sending waves of sensation rippling through him. Every detail of his surroundings filled his senses as he tried to drink it all in. The sounds and smells overwhelmed him. On the third continent nothing grew, and very little could survive. The days on the glacier were silent save for the wind, and there was nothing to smell but ice. Here, in this place, night birds hooted, tiny creatures scurried through the leaves overhead and in the grass around him. The air felt heavy with the scent of life.

Krnar reached out and let his fingertips trail down the smooth, warm surface of one of the silver trees. With one palm pressed against the trunk, he reached up with his other hand and rubbed one of the thick green leaves between his fingers. The thin silver filaments tickled him. He heard the barely perceptible tinkling of the threads as they were displaced and then snapped back.

Finally, he plucked one of the clusters of fruit from a low hanging branch. The flesh of each individual oval was firm to the touch and when he brought it near his face it smelled faintly of home; clean, crisp, and refreshing, like a cold breeze off the sea.

Home, he thought. *This is home now, and it's up to me to find a way to bring my people back.*

When he bit into one of the small ovals, tangy juice filled his mouth. Seeds crunched between his teeth. The pulp left his palate and tongue tingling as he pushed it back and forth. He swallowed and his mouth immediately began to water, begging for more.

Krnar closed his eyes and savored every mouthful. When the first was gone, he pulled a second oval from the cluster for himself, and gave another to Jahira. They ate and walked in companionable silence. As he approached the central field which held the five sacred pools, Krnar could feel the hum of power, the force of The One Who Knows All; he prayed Aruvel would provide an answer.

Chapter 42

The blue-white glow of Krnar's body guided Jahira through the irregular shadows that played beneath the canopy of the silver grove. She placed her feet carefully and even tried to slow her breathing. It seemed wrong somehow to make too much noise. Though she didn't fully understand his mission, she could sense Krnar's anticipation as they crossed the inner field and climbed the hills. Finally, they stood at the shore of the largest pool.

Unease crept into her heart and squeezed. She stood there, staring at her reflection. Three white orbs circled her head in the mirrored surface. Krnar's phosphorescence reflected off the pool beside her own image. Thoughts of Magnar filled her mind as she stood at the shore; Magnar kneeling at these shores and drinking, Magnar lying in the lab, unconscious, because of this liquid.

Could Grollon be right about the cure? She wondered. *No, it can't be true. It's a barbaric ritual used by a primitive people-*

She stopped herself and cast a sidelong glance at Krnar, wondering just how much of her thoughts he could read.

"Sorry," she said softly.

Krnar didn't respond immediately, but after a handful of seconds he reached out and took her hand.

The gesture startled her enough that she almost pulled away...almost. As she stood there, wondering how she was supposed to respond, it occurred to her that this was the first time he had initiated contact with her. No, make that the second. When the Falcon had landed and he saw where they were, he'd hugged her. That had shocked her as much as this.

She gave his hand a gentle squeeze and smiled.

He turned to face her, gently pulling her hand with his so that her body also turned toward his.

"Thank you," he said, in English.

Jahira's grin widened. He was a fast learner.

"I should be the one thanking you. Magnar and I would have died in those mountains if you hadn't found us." Jahira paused and frowned. "What's going to happen now? What will you do?"

He tipped his head and she tried again.

"Thank you," she said. "Now what?"

She saw a picture in her mind of a large crowd of people who all looked like Krnar. They stood on the edge of a steep cliff, surrounded by snow and ice. He'd shown her this image before, and she'd learned enough to know that these were his people, but it still didn't answer her question.

Before she could formulate a new question, Krnar lifted his free hand. With the tip of his index finger he traced a circle on her forehead; his touch sent a chill down her spine.

"Darno a tal," he said, making the circle again, smoothing the lines of her frown with his thumb.

Jahira felt her pulse quicken, even though she didn't understand the words. When he released her hand and sat cross-legged in the grass, goose bumps rose along her arms. Jahira hugged herself against the sudden cold. She sat beside him, confused about what had just happened. She wanted to ask, but Krnar had closed his eyes; he seemed to be meditating.

For what seemed like an eternity he did not speak, did not move; she began to wonder if he'd fallen asleep.

Sleep, she thought. It sounded lovely, and the more she thought about it, the heavier her eyelids seemed to get.

The ground flexed and conformed to her body as she lay upon the thick grass. The warm air covered her like a blanket. The open-air bed was much more comfortable than the cave floor she'd been sleeping on for the last two weeks. She curled into a ball and closed her eyes.

When she opened them again, her skin felt hot on one side, and comparatively cold on the other. She tipped her head back slightly and saw Krnar, still beside her but no longer meditating. His eyes were open and fixed on her.

With one arm she pushed herself up to a sitting position and then used both hands to rub the sleep from her eyes. Shivers traveled along her skin as her body tried to regulate her temperature upon waking.

"Morning," Krnar said, the r rolling off his tongue like a purr.

"Allorkan a tal," Jahira replied before she covered a yawn.

Krnar smiled and then offered her a piece of fruit, which she gladly accepted. The juice helped to rid her mouth of the sticky film which had formed in her sleep. When Jahira was done she looked around for something to wipe the juice from her hands. Beside her Krnar plunged his hands into the silver pool, pulled them out, and then rubbed them vigorously with a handful of grass. Jahira imitated the routine and nodded in satisfaction when she held her hands out to examine the results.

Her body stilled as Krnar reached out and touched the cuff on her right wrist, turning it slightly so that it glinted in the sunlight. He looked up at her and tilted his head.

"Gift?" he asked. He'd learned enough to know that Jahira, though she seemed well respected, was not the leader of her people.

"It was my sister's," she explained. "Zarya."

Just saying her name caused a flood of memories. Jahira's breath caught in her throat, straining against the lump which had suddenly formed there.

She tried to focus on one of those memories, one of the images she held of her sister and focused until it became a still, clear picture in her mind.

"Sister," Jahira said, then repeated her name, "Zarya."

Krnar trilled and nodded. The image in her mind of Zarya was replaced with one of Krnar. Jahira frowned before she realized it was not Krnar.

"Arkan," Krnar said. "Marnar."

Jahira searched her memory for the meaning of the words and finally made the connection.

"Brother," she said.

Krnar nodded.

"Arkan is your brother," she said. Krnar had a brother. *What had happened to him? Where was he now?*

Jahira focused on a picture of her whole family, then replayed the day of the crash. In her mind, she showed herself digging through the rubble and finding her sister's bracelet. Tears glistened in her eyes, but did not fall this time.

Krnar trilled softly and touched the silver cuff again.

"Zarya," he said.

Jahira nodded.

There was nothing else to say.

Chapter 43

"There is no chance that I will approve this ridiculous plan!" Lusela, head of maintenance for the Kepler Colonizer, as well as the ranking maintenance officer for all the crews, stood and pounded her fist on the table as she spoke.

"Lusela, I know it sounds crazy, but it's been two weeks," Jahira countered. Over the course of those two weeks Magnar's condition had started to decline. Jahira had become desperate; she would try anything.

"I said no." Lusela forced the words through clenched teeth. "There is nothing you can say that will change my mind."

Jahira searched the other faces at the table, General Thayer, Medic, Ryan, the other pilots. Silently, she pleaded for someone to speak in favor of her request.

No one did.

"Jahira, think about what you're asking." Even Tala, her closest friend, wouldn't give the idea a chance.

"Krnar and Grollon think it's the only way to save him," Jahira replied. "This is their world, and we've tried everything that we know how to do. Maybe it's time to take a chance."

"Jahira." General Thayer didn't even try to hide the condescending tone in his voice. "You want to take our only functioning jet to a volcano in order to gather lava which you will then use to burn Magnar, all based on the testimony of two aliens."

She had to admit, it sounded pretty bad when the General said it like that.

"I think it would be wise to remember that *we* are the aliens here," Ryan offered.

Jahira nodded her thanks for even that limited show of support.

"Something is seriously wrong with him, something that has happened to these people before-"

"What if it kills him?" Gavin interjected.

Jahira paused and all eyes turned to her, waiting for her response.

"He's already dying," Jahira replied. "And honestly, I think that's what he wanted to happen from the start."

Eyes shifted away and bodies shifted in their chairs.

Jahira balled her fists in frustration. This was going nowhere. Had she been in their place, she would probably feel the same way. She really did understand their hesitation, but she had seen the changes in Magnar before she'd knocked him unconscious and ultimately, she trusted Krnar.

That's the key to it all, she thought.

None of them knew Krnar like she did. They still saw an alien, one that looked more like an animal than a man, to them at least, but she saw past the exterior, she *knew* him. Then there was Grollon. Even she didn't trust Grollon completely, but he had been through whatever it was that Magnar suffered from and he seemed to genuinely want to help her friend. He was the only one who had any first-hand experience with the consequences of drinking the silver liquid. He was the only one offering a solution.

If Magnar did die, it wouldn't be because she'd sat here and done nothing to prevent it.

The metal legs of her chair squealed as they slid across the floor. Jahira stood and addressed the group.

"Thanks for your time," she said. She ignored the startled looks, nodded, and left.

Once the door had sealed behind her, Jahira let out a long breath and then went to find Krnar.

He and Grollon waited back at her tent. They had all agreed that the meeting might go better if the two men were not physically present, if it were only Jahira proposing the idea of taking Magnar south in the Falcon. Apparently, they'd been mistaken.

The set of Krnar's shoulders told her that he already knew the outcome.

"What now?" Grollon asked. He was picking up the language even faster than Krnar.

Jahira tipped her head back and felt the sun warm her cheeks. She inhaled, let the breath out slowly, and fixed them both with a determined look.

"A wise person once said, 'It's easier to ask for forgiveness than permission'."

Krnar cocked his head in confusion. His expression soon changed as she laid out the details of her plan.

Chapter 44

An hour past the third moon rise, Jahira alerted her accomplices. She walked through the moonlit settlement as casually as possible, forcing her pace to remain even and her expression neutral. Krnar and Grollon skirted the tents and dirt dwellings to either side of her, or they should be anyway. The plan was for them to meet her at the ship.

It was disconcerting not to be able to see Krnar's glow when she searched the shadows to her right. He and Grollon had both wrapped themselves in coverings so that no one would immediately recognize them. She didn't want anyone to see them stealing through the night and grow suspicious. It could ruin everything.

They converged as planned at the base of the Colonizer. Jahira nodded to Grollon, who would wait outside and alert them if anyone approached. She waved for Krnar to follow before she stole up the ramp and tip-toed through the half-lit hallways toward the lab.

As they approached the room where Magnar lay, Jahira forced herself upright, squared her shoulders, and finally pressed a palm to the wall to open the door to the lab. As the door opened she prepared herself to greet Medic or Ryan if they were there, to explain to them that she couldn't sleep and wanted to see if Magnar's condition had improved.

The waiting room was empty.

After crossing the room in four long steps, she keyed in the code to the main examining room.

The door opened and Jahira could see Magnar lying on the raised bed, pale and skeletal. Her heart clenched to see him like that, but it also hardened her resolve to do whatever it took to bring him back.

Before she could give it too much thought, Jahira turned off Magnar's monitor. Her heart raced when the monitor blipped one last time before going blank. She removed the sticky probes from his body, but left the IV in place. After lifting the clear bag down from the hook on the wall and handing it to Krnar, she hurried through the room, gathering the supplies she thought they would need.

When her pack was full, and Krnar had Magnar securely in his arms, Jahira nodded toward the door and started forward.

Krnar hissed a warning seconds before the door slid open. Jahira stopped short and stood face to face with Medic.

"Medic! I-" Jahira was actually relieved when he held up a hand to stop her. She had no chance of talking her way out of a full pack of stolen supplies and Magnar in Krnar's arms.

"I know what you're doing," Medic stated. "Magnar is my patient and I can't have him hours away from a medical facility-"

"But Medic," Jahira interrupted. "You've seen his decline. You've tracked the numbers-"

Medic held up a hand again.

"I can't allow him to leave," Medic stated. "Not without his doctor."

The words of protest died on Jahira's parted lips and her eyes widened.

"You're going to help us!"

"My bag's all packed," he said, nodding to a corner of the room where a hard case rested against one wall.

"Packed?" Jahira asked with a frown. "How did you know?"

Medic raised one eyebrow.

"Have I ever told you how transparent you are?"

Jahira smiled.

"What changed your mind then?"

Medic paused and glanced at Magnar, whose head lolled against Krnar's chest.

"I *have* watched the charts, and I think you're right; I think he wants to die. He's trying to give up." Medic met her eyes and Jahira's throat tightened painfully.

"I'm not going to let that happen."

Medic nodded and replied, "Neither am I."

"Thanks," Jahira whispered. "Shall we go then?"

Medic entered the room, grabbed his suitcase, and nodded for Jahira to proceed.

"After you," he said.

"Does anyone else know about this?" Jahira asked.

She led the way through the waiting room and down the winding tunnels.

"I'm sure others suspected you'd try something like this, just not so soon."

"I don't feel like we have much time," Jahira responded.

Medic glanced back at Magnar.

"I think you're right."

Jahira picked up the pace.

Chapter 45

"There," Grollon said. He pointed out the flight deck window toward a dark mound on the horizon which rose up from the blackened, uneven ground.

Jahira pushed the Falcon forward and then held a low pattern around the base of the volcano until an orange glow became visible in the enhanced viewing screen. A long river of bright orange liquid oozed toward the sea and a great plume of steam rose into the air where the molten lava met the significantly colder salt water.

She swallowed her misgivings and began to take readings from the surrounding area in order to find the most stable landing site. After a few minutes, a green blip appeared on her map, showing her the recommended touch-down location.

The Falcon took a moment to find her balance. Once she was cleared, Jahira unbuckled from the command seat and joined the others in the rear cabin.

"Are you ready?" she asked Grollon.

Grollon nodded.

Medic handed the old man some supplies as he, Jahira, and Krnar waited on the exit platform. Jahira pressed the release on the disc in her pocket and waved to Medic, who would remain behind with Magnar.

Jahira and Krnar flanked Grollon. They proceeded over the landscape of hardened lava. It took all of Jahira's concentration to navigate the jagged and uneven terrain. She could feel the heat soaking into the soles of her boots. Glancing over at Grollon and Krnar, she wondered how they could stand it in those thin animal-hide slippers.

A sulphuric smell wafted on the breeze, filling her nostrils with its hot stench. A faint hissing sound could be heard in the distance, from the place where the plume of steam rose into the sky in successive bursts like a signal fire.

It was only mid-morning, but between the heat rising up from the ground and the sun beating down from above, Jahira felt like the proverbial Thanksgiving turkey. Sweat rolled down her back and at one point Jahira found herself staring with longing at the white-capped waves crashing against the blackened shore.

A hand on her arm checked her forward movement. Jahira glanced over to see Krnar beside her now. They stopped and waited while Grollon continue the last few meters to the edge of the lava flow.

Grollon pulled on the fireproof gloves which Medic had provided, and then he withdrew the same type of extractor which Ryan had used to pull a sample of the silver liquid out of the pools.

That seemed like a lifetime ago.

Watching him prepare, Jahira realized she hadn't thought things through as well as she might have. Would she have thought to bring any medical supplies? Would she have known where to find them? She would be eternally grateful for Medic's help.

Despite the protection he wore, it made Jahira wince to see Grollon lean over the molten flow in order to pull the lava up into the narrow net of light.

He finished in a matter of minutes. When he returned, Jahira could actually see the reddened, blistered skin of his arms heal before her eyes.

"How is that possible?" Jahira asked.

"The soul of Aruvel runs in me, it heals."

The soul of Aruvel, the silver liquid; the liquid was in his system and he could heal himself.

"Can Magnar do that?"

"Yes," Grollon replied.

"That's why the knot on his head healed so quickly, and the reason he didn't suffer as much from the crash and lack of food. He can heal his own body," Jahira made these statements aloud, though she expected no response. She was simply voicing a few new pieces of the puzzle.

"But he cannot heal his soul," Grollon added.

Grollon's statement spurred Jahira into action. She turned and led the way back to the Falcon where Medic waited. Magnar lay on his stretcher, held down by straps which were pulled taught over his chest, hips, and legs. Grollon had requested that Magnar be bound. Seeing him lying there unconscious and helpless, he looked so vulnerable that Jahira began to second guess her decision.

She watched Grollon release the sample of lava into the receptacle which Medic provided, and then the old man pulled the gloves off of his hands. As he looked around for someplace to set them, Jahira held out a hand and Grollon placed the gloves in her open palm. She tightened her fingers around the gloves and twisted as Grollon began to chant.

Grollon's voice continued in a steady, soothing rhythm. He dipped a finger into the dish of molten liquid. Without hesitation, he pressed the lava against Magnar's forehead and then drew a large circle in the center of his brow.

Magnar began to stir. Though his eyes remained closed, his fist clenched and sweat beaded on his face.

A smell like charred meat roasting over a fire filled the cabin. Jahira had to bite her lip to keep from screaming at Grollon to stop.

The volume of Grollon's chant increased as he repeated the process, but this time he formed a smaller circle to the right of the first, followed by another to the left. Magnar began to pant. Jahira glanced at Medic, whose eyes were glued to a hand-held device which monitored Magnar, tracking his vitals during the procedure.

Grollon burned a line from the left most circle, through the center circle, and ended all the way to the right. The tendons in Magnar's neck bulged as he strained against the chest strap. When he couldn't free himself, he began to thrash. His head rolled from side to side, jerking away from Grollon's fingers.

"You must hold his head," Grollon instructed.

Jahira hesitated. She gasped as Magnar's features contorted. A shadow seemed to pass over his face, but it disappeared before Jahira could tell what she'd seen. Then Magnar began to scream.

"Hold him!" Grollon commanded.

The gloves fell to the floor as Jahira moved to a position behind Magnar's head. Tears streamed down her cheeks but she pressed a hand to either side of his face and held him still. He continued to fight, and continued to scream, as Grollon traced the pattern of three circles connected by a line across his brow once more.

Through her tears Jahira could see the flesh on Magnar's forehead knit back together, erasing the burns and leaving behind three pale white circles and a long white line.

Magnar's lower back arched off the mattress. He let out a final howl of pure anguish and then fell back to the palette, silent and limp.

"Is he dead?" she gasped. Her voice shook with emotion.

"No," Medic replied. "No, he's not dead."

She collapsed back against the wall. Her hands shook. Magnar's chest rose and fell in steady even breaths. With the heels of her palms she scrubbed the tears from her cheeks and then looked up at Grollon.

"Is it done?" Jahira asked.

Grollon nodded.

"Will he be all right?" She looked down at Magnar's flaccid limbs, his pale countenance. "Is he all right?"

Grollon shrugged and Jahira felt a sudden urge to shake the old man.

"Only time will tell," he replied. "I need to rest."

Jahira's anger flared as he moved past her to take a seat in the flight deck, then she saw him look down at his hand. The tip of his index finger had burned away. Flesh and bone completely gone to the first knuckle; it was the finger he'd used to save Magnar.

All of her energy and every trace of adrenaline drained from her system in a rush, leaving a tired, heavy feeling behind. She let her head fall back against the wall. Her eyes shifted from Medic, to Magnar, to Krnar.

"Why the three circles and the line?" she asked, loud enough that Grollon could hear, though she didn't know if he actually had to be able to hear her words to understand her.

Grollon didn't turn. His voice sounded as tired as she felt. She tipped her head so that she could see him. He traced the circle in the center of his forehead and said, "Leron." This was the name that he and Krnar used for the planet. He touched the circle to the right and said, "Allorkan." the sun. He touched the circle to the left and labeled it *Mrkellan*. Jahira remembered this was their name for the second sun, one she hadn't seen but Ryan had showed her in the simulation. Grollon had spent a great deal of time with Ryan and his planetary maps.

Finally, Grollon traced the line which connected all three circles and said, "When all three align, the gateway opens."

Jahira glanced at Medic and raised her eyebrows. Medic shrugged. He continued to scan Magnar's vitals.

A gasp, followed by a cough, drew Jahira's attention back to Magnar. His eyelids fluttered.

Jahira immediately stood and undid the straps which held his body down and then she leaned in close to his face, keeping one hand on his chest where she could feel the reassuring beat of his heart.

"Magnar, can you hear me?"

His eyes opened.

"Jahira," Magnar said. His voice was a ragged whisper, and he frowned in confusion.

A half-laugh, half-sob bubbled out unexpectedly as Jahira looked into the familiar brown eyes of her friend.

"My head hurts," Magnar said. He ran a sticky tongue over his dry, cracked lips. "And I'm thirsty as hell."

Jahira accepted a canteen from Medic. She helped Magnar sit up and supported his back while she held the canteen to his lips. Tipping it up, she allowed a small trickle to run into his mouth before righting the container.

"I need more."

"I know, but we need to go slow. You've been through a lot."

Krnar trilled softly and Magnar's head swiveled toward the sound. Jahira felt him react by pressing into her chest, away from Krnar.

"What is that?" Magnar asked.

"*He* is Krnar, a friend. He rescued us when we crashed in the mountains." Jahira paused, and then frowned. "Don't you remember?"

Magnar studied Krnar for a moment before he replied.

"I'm not sure." He turned his head to look around the cabin and stopped when he caught sight of Grollon.

"That's-" Jahira started.

"Grollon," Magnar finished.

"You do remember!"

Magnar shook his head slowly, not in denial, more like an expression of disbelief.

"It's like I watched it all happen from a distance, but wasn't actually there," he explained, turning his focus inward.

"You were kind of out of it for a while," Jahira replied. "What's the last thing you remember clearly?"

Magnar met her eyes and the pain she saw there caused her breath to catch.

"Amara," he stated. "Is she really…"

Jahira nodded and then answered his unfinished question.

"She's gone Magnar. I'm so sorry."

"And your family?"

Jahira swallowed the lump in her throat before she could answer, "They're gone too."

Tears began to flow over Magnar's hollow cheeks.

"I'm sorry, too." He paused and searched Jahira's face. "Are you all right?"

Jahira smiled and pulled Magnar into a quick hug. He hugged her back and then pushed her away gently so that he could see her face.

"Are you?" he asked earnestly.

Jahira nodded and then responded, "Yeah, I think we're both going to be all right."

Chapter 46

A very intimidating welcome party awaited their arrival when the Falcon returned to the settlement two days later. Jahira tried to reassure herself that it would all be all right once they saw Magnar, and she had Medic to back her up. She cringed to think of what would have happened if she'd come back with Magnar's corpse.

It had worked though, Magnar was awake and lucid; physically weak but most definitely alive and, most important of all, aware. He almost seemed like himself again, though the shadow of grief still clung to him. He leaned on Jahira for support as the platform lowered to the ground.

Most of the faces in that crowd relaxed when they saw Magnar standing on his own two feet, smiling and giving a half-hearted wave…most of the faces. Lusela seemed to literally bristle with rage.

"You've got a lot of explaining to do," General Thayer stated firmly. His eyes kept flitting to Magnar's scarred forehead and away again, like it might be a mirage and if he looked again maybe it would be gone.

Magnar cleared his throat and then spoke in a voice just loud enough to carry to the waiting crowd, "Don't be too hard on them General, they saved my life."

Lusela's nostrils flared before she turned on a heel and stormed away from the reunion.

General Thayer, on the other hand, stepped forward and gripped Magnar's pale, bony hand in his own strong brown one.

"She'll get over it," The General said with a wave of dismissal. "Come on and sit down. We picked our first big harvest of home-grown vegetables today. You can test them out while you tell us what happened."

Jahira helped Magnar to the commons room aboard the Kepler Colonizer, where he did his best to recount what he could remember. Jahira filled in the details.

"Magnar, I'd like you to stay aboard the Colonizer, just for a week or so, in order to keep you close to the lab and make sure you, well, keep getting better." Medic waited for Magnar's response.

Magnar nodded and let Jahira and Medic lead him to his temporary quarters.

"It's pretty quiet around here," Magnar said after they'd stepped into his new room.

"I'll visit every day, I promise." Jahira smiled and gave his arm a squeeze. "You can always come and see me too, just let Medic know where you're going first, okay?"

Magnar glanced from Jahira to Medic then smiled, a rather sad smile.

"Well, I guess you have reason to worry," he stated. "I promise to check in."

Jahira made sure he had everything he needed before she headed back to her own tent. Krnar joined her in the evening, insisting that he would be fine sleeping outside when she offered to give him the tent and sleep under the stars herself.

Sleep wouldn't come that first night. Grollon's images of himself drinking again, of killing one of his own people, haunted her memory.

Rest grew easier as the week passed without incident. Magnar remained in his room for the most part, sleeping and eating. Jahira and Krnar visited often. Surprisingly, she found Grollon there most days as well. The two seemed to have formed a tentative friendship. Jahira was relieved to see Magnar gaining weight and looking healthier every day.

The second week Jahira forced him to get outside and start taking walks. She was thrilled with his progress, that is, until the day he stopped at the edge of the silver grove and looked longingly through the trees.

"I need to go to the pools."

Jahira narrowed her eyes and stared at him intently.

"Why?" she asked.

"I need to," Magnar replied.

A shiver went through Jahira when she heard those words, the same words he'd said when she'd found him aboard the Eagle, preparing to fly on his own to the northern mountains. She could see the determination in his face and felt certain he wasn't waiting for her permission, but instead working up the courage to take that first step.

"All right," Jahira said. "Let's go."

She wished Krnar or Grollon were with her, to ask their advice. She had no idea if this was the right choice, but she knew that if he intended to go, he would eventually, and she sure wasn't going to let him go alone.

Sunlight filtered down through the bright green leaves and danced across Jahira's dark skin. Pausing for a moment, she jumped and plucked two blue fruits from the branches, handing one to Magnar and keeping one for herself.

"What happened to the red ones?" Magnar asked, accepting the fruit but examining it carefully before he took a bite.

Jahira was startled at first, Magnar kept doing that; asking questions now and then that she thought he should know the answer to. It made her uncomfortable to realize how little he'd been aware of during the past six months.

"They changed. The leaves changed color and the red fruits were, well, kind of sucked back into the trees. The blue ones grew in before we left for the mountains."

"Oh, right," Magnar replied. He took a bite and resumed his walk.

When they reached the shore of the largest pool, Magnar knelt in the grass. She stood beside him, poised to stop him from drinking if she needed to.

Instead of leaning toward the pool as she had expected, he reached into his chest pocket and pulled out a tiny ID chip.

Jahira's shoulders relaxed and she knelt down beside him.

"I think I'm ready to say goodbye," he said softly.

Jahira nodded and pulled out the three ID chips which had belonged to her mother, father, and younger sister. Her fingers curled around them a moment, pressing them into her palm.

Ripples in the mirror-like surface distorted their reflections as Magnar lowered his hand into the pool.

"Here?" Jahira asked.

Magnar nodded.

"It feels right," he replied. "Are you ready?"

She lowered her own hand into the pool and opened her palm beneath the surface. The tiny chips slid off her hand when she tipped her fingers down into the opaque depths.

They withdrew their hands simultaneously.

Jahira twisted Zarya's cuff on her wrist.

"Goodbye," she whispered.

"Goodbye," Magnar echoed her words.

They sat in silence for a long time before Magnar spoke again.

"The body heals, but the soul never forgets."

Chapter 47

A warm breeze swept across the field, bending the yellow heads of long stalks of grain until the entire prairie seemed to be pointing south. A herd of what Krnar called srlendi grazed in peaceful ignorance. The four-legged mammals ranged across the fields to the south and west of the settlement, having migrated north from the third continent shortly after the humans landed at the site they were now calling Empyrean.

The occasional snorts of a mother reigning in her young punctuated the constant crunch of hard, energy-rich grains being ground between large flat teeth. Jahira observed the peaceful scene from her hiding place on the leeward side of a small hillock, regretting the fact that she was about to seriously disrupt the tranquility.

The ears of her chosen prey twitched away the darting insects as it grazed. Jahira watched and waited in tense anticipation for Krnar's signal.

Ready. She heard Krnar's voice in her mind a heartbeat before shouts and whistles erupted from the grass on the opposite side of the herd beast.

The straggler lifted its head and looked toward the sound. Waving hands appeared above the grass. The sound grew steadily closer. The animal's ears turned outward, it snorted, and finally made its first long leap toward her.

Jahira's heart raced. She tested her grip on the long shaft of her newly-made spear. As the animal leapt closer, she drew back her right arm. She waited until she was sure she would be too late, and then rose to her feet, took a skip step like Krnar had taught her, and hurled her spear just before the animal saw her and began to turn.

The sharp blade of the knife she'd lashed to the shaft whistled through the air until it met its target with a soft thunk.

The animal bellowed a long, deep sound which alerted the other herd beasts to danger and sent them running. Jahira sprinted over the hillock in pursuit of her fleeing prey. Gavin, Tala, Magnar, and Krnar soon flanked her. Chaos reigned. Herd beasts fled, bellowing and pushing their young to the middle of the pack. The wounded animal tried to rejoin the herd, but its pursuers cut it off at every turn.

Blood flowed freely from the mortal wound in the animal's neck. After a quarter of a mile it began to falter, finally dropping to its knees and gasping for air. A cloud of dust puffed from the ground as the animal fell to its side. Jahira stopped and doubled over. With her hands on her thighs, she sucked air into her burning lungs. The others stopped beside her, spitting and wheezing. Once they'd caught their breath, they moved forward in unison and surrounded the thrashing animal.

The srlen's eyes rolled in panic. Krnar approached with slow, precise movements. As he drew his knife from his belt, he spoke to the animal in his native tongue, the low growls and rolled consonants accenting his soothing tone. With the swift efficiency of long practice, Krnar drew his blade across the animal's neck.

Jahira joined Krnar where he knelt beside the srlen's head. He stroked its neck a few times before he pulled the spear head, which the animal's body released with a long sucking noise. He nodded in acknowledgment as he handed the weapon back to Jahira. She accepted it with mixed emotions.

She felt a flush of pride at her success, yet she hated to see one of the peaceful animals dead by her own hand.

It's necessary, she reminded herself. *We have five months to store enough food for a year-long winter.*

The produce from the gardens was consumed as fast as it could grow. The fish were still plentiful, for now, but the protein powder was almost gone. They would all need protein during the long winter, not to mention warmer clothes.

"Let's get this back before the smell attracts one of those big cats." Tala glanced around at the tall grass which surrounded them on all sides.

"Mlkalo," Krnar replied with a nod.

A chill ran down Jahira's spine at the mention of the predators. She'd never managed to get a close look at one, thankfully, but she and Tala had witnessed one take down a herd-beast while they were tracking the animal's movements from the air.

The hunting party wasted no time after that. Jahira tied the srlen's front legs together at the knee, while Magnar tied the back. They left holes in the triple knots for one of the long stretcher poles to slide through. Once it was secured, everyone took their place: Magnar and Jahira in the front, Gavin and Tala in the back.

"On three, ready: one, two, three." Four grunts of effort followed the count as the pilots-turned-hunters shouldered the pole and lifted the heavy herd animal from the ground.

Krnar quickly looped a line around the neck and then stood and pulled the line taught over his shoulder. He would lead the way while keeping the srlen's head from dragging on the ground.

Jahira took prolonged blinks to keep the sweat from running into her eyes. Every part of her skin itched from the combination of dirt, heat, and salt-water; she wondered how Krnar could stand it, all covered in fur. He never complained though, about anything. It could be annoying really. Once in a while she found herself trying to goad him into whining about something, but he either lacked the language to do so or he was the most stoic individual she'd ever met. He amazed her.

In a half an hour they were back at the campsite situated along one of the small tributaries southwest of the settlement which cut across the second continent on its way to the Silver River. Sweat dripped from Jahira's face and burned her eyes. They entered camp and finally set the carrying pole into the mounts. Jahira winced when the weight of the animal lifted from her shoulder. She rubbed and rolled her arm in an effort to stimulate circulation in her limb, which had gone completely numb.

Adrenaline, which had filled her during the hunt, had burned away during the long trek back to the campsite. She shuffled to the cold stream and sank to her knees at its bank. Moisture began to soak into the knees of her pants. She welcomed the cold water against her skin and sighed with relief as she scrubbed the blood and dirt from her hands and face. The sound of heavy footfalls alerted her to someone's approach. Magnar knelt down beside her.

"Who would have thought getting food could be so exhausting," Magnar commented.

Jahira chuckled and then replied, "It's a far cry from mixing a cup of protein powder, that's for sure."

It filled her with joy to see how much healthier her friend looked. His cheekbones still protruded a bit too far, and she could see the outline of the bones in his shoulders, but he'd always had a wiry frame. At least he no longer looked starved. The skin covering those cheekbones had a pretty good tan going after a month of being up and active, all except the white scar tissue which stood out in stark relief on his brow.

"How are you holding up?" Jahira asked.

"Good," Magnar replied. "I'm good. Even better now that I'm away from those pools."

"Yeah? It's better here?" Jahira rocked back on her heels and listened with interest.

He nodded before he replied, "Yeah, a lot better. It's like the closer I get to them, the stronger the pull. Out here I barely think about it."

They sat in silence for a moment. Magnar splashed a handful of water on the back of his neck.

"What has Grollon said about it? Does it get easier?"

Magnar shook his head.

"According to him, it never gets easier, you just get stronger."

"I'm sorry."

Magnar shrugged.

"I'll live," he paused and bumped her with his shoulder before he added, "Thanks to you."

Jahira smiled. It was good to have her friend back.

"I'm actually thinking of taking a crew back to the mountains to salvage the Eagle." Magnar waited for her reaction.

"And…"

"Well, I thought I might use the parts to try to build a boat."

"A boat?"

"Yeah, I mean, most of this planet is covered by water. I figure I could spend a lifetime exploring the oceans without ever having to get close to another *oranllo*."

Jahira let this information sink in before she responded.

"It's a good idea," she admitted. "But what do you know about boats?"

"I've got all the information I need in the ship's database."

"Maybe on how to build one; what about driving one, or sailing, or navigating…whatever you call it."

"Come on," Magnar scoffed. "I'm a pilot. How hard could it be?"

EMPYREAN

Chapter 48

Bright orange and white tongues of fire leapt toward the night sky and licked at the circle of carefully placed stones which surrounded the cone of burning branches. Krnar stared into the flames, mesmerized by the flickering shapes that shifted before his eyes.

The soft scuff of boots alerted him to someone's approach. He looked up, surprised to see that Jahira was not asleep after the day's exertions.

She smiled as she stepped into the overlap of light where the fire competed with Krnar's own glow. Krnar returned the smile.

"Can't sleep?" Jahira asked.

She sat beside him on his hide blanket.

Krnar shook his head once to confirm her observation.

"Me neither," she stated. "Worried I guess."

"Worried?"

"Yeah, nervous, scared we won't have enough to keep everyone alive through the winter."

Krnar nodded, he understood this concern well.

Silence stretched as they watched the fire. Krnar let his thoughts carry him away until Jahira's next words brought him back with a jolt.

"Darno," she said. "Darno a tal. What does it mean?"

Krnar cleared his throat and shifted slightly. He remembered well the night he'd first spoken those words to her; the first night he'd walked through the alara grove and sat at the shore of the oranlodi. He was surprised she remembered.

"My soul to you," he replied. He kept his eyes fixed on the fire.

When Jahira neither moved nor responded, he turned his head to face her. Her green eyes danced and her full lips parted in a slow smile.

"My soul to you," she repeated. Krnar held his breath as she reached out. With the tip of one finger, she traced a circle in the center of his forehead. "Darno a tal."

He didn't bother to correct the male-female modifiers. Instead he tried to focus on something other than his physical response to her touch, not to mention her words.

"Darno a tal," he finally said. He worked up the nerve to trace a circle on her forehead. "Here the soul lives. Here one soul meets another."

Jahira pulled his hand away gently and moved closer, until her leg pressed against his. Krnar felt heat expand through his body, starting from that focal point. He dared not move. Jahira leaned forward and pressed her lips against his. The fur around his mouth tingled. He trilled softly when she placed a hand against his chest. After a handful of staccato heartbeats, he drew back slowly.

"Darno a tal," she said. Her voice had become lower, huskier, more like one of The People.

"What is that?" he asked.

"A kiss," Jahira replied.

Krnar nodded and said, "It is good."

Jahira laughed and nodded.

"It takes practice to get really good though." Her smile had turned playful and she raised her eyebrows.

"Practice?" Krnar asked.

"Doing a thing many times, to learn; practice."

Krnar nodded, "Practice is good."

Jahira leaned toward him again.

EMPYREAN

Chapter 49

The sun beat against the east facing wall of the tent, heating the inside to an unbearable temperature. Jahira forced her eyes open a mere slit and groaned. Her body ached from yesterday's hunt and she felt as if she'd slept no more than a handful of minutes.

She wiggled out of her sleeping bag and slid her feet into her boots. A ripping sound like Velcro broke the stillness of the morning when she opened the tent flap. A gentle breeze cooled the sheen of sweat on her forehead as she stepped through the opening, squinting against the daylight. Her eyes went straight to the fire, which was surrounded now by Tala, Gavin, and Magnar. They chatted over a breakfast of fruit and tea.

"Morning," Tala called a greeting as Jahira approached the fire.

"Morning," Jahira replied, joining the circle. "Where's Krnar?"

Magnar nodded toward the herd-beast hanging from the stretcher pole. Krnar had already skinned the animal and staked out the hide.

"Doesn't he sleep?" she asked, mostly to herself, but Magnar raised an eyebrow. One corner of his mouth quirked in a failed attempt to suppress his amusement. Jahira felt herself blush and avoided looking at him.

"I'm so ready to get back to the settlement," Tala announced, oblivious to the exchange between Jahira and Magnar. "It gives me the creeps being out here alone."

"You're not alone," Magnar replied sweeping an open palm around the circle.

"Yeah, but there's safety in numbers, right. Well, four is not a big enough number to make me feel safe."

"Five," Jahira corrected automatically, which earned her another look from Magnar.

"I can't wait to see Chava," Gavin declared.

"How is she doing?" Jahira asked.

"Fantastic," Gavin replied. "She's growing like a weed, and she looks just like Brenna."

"Lucky girl," Tala teased.

"Can't argue with that," Gavin responded.

"How old is she now?" Tala asked.

"She'll be six months tomorrow."

"Wow! That went by so fast! Before you know it she'll be walking." Tala paused and then added, "Can you believe it's been six months?"

As their conversation continued, Jahira watched Magnar. She could practically see him withdrawing into himself.

"Hey, want to go help Krnar?" She directed her question at Magnar, then without waiting for a response, she stood and walked away from the fire. She felt certain Magnar would follow. No doubt the last thing he wanted to discuss was Gavin's happy little family and new, healthy baby.

Magnar caught up with her in a matter of seconds.

"Thanks," he whispered.

"Not a problem," Jahira replied.

They stopped a few feet away from where Krnar kneeled, scraping flesh from the animal's hide.

"Can we help?" Jahira asked.

Krnar paused and looked up.

Jahira felt a blush rise to her cheeks, remembering their encounter last night. Then, realizing that Krnar could probably read her thoughts, she tried to change the image in her mind, and then felt awkward. He seemed unaware of her discomfiture and simply acknowledged them both with a nod before pointing to the hanging carcass.

"Cut the meat," he instructed. "Small," he added, showing the desired size with his hands, "Then salt, wrap." He demonstrated his meaning with gestures, but Jahira did not see any pictures in her mind, or feel that crawly sensation along her scalp, which meant he wasn't in her head.

She tried not to dwell on his business-like manner. Soon, all thoughts fled save the task at hand. Sore muscles heated up and loosened as she and Magnar carved sections of the herd-beast into manageable portions. It didn't take long before new aches began. Her skin itched from the mixture of blood and sweat. Her back began to burn from the bending and stooping required to cut and shift heavy pieces of the animal's considerable muscle.

Gavin and Tala finally came to help. They took the hunks of raw flesh to the stream where they rinsed them before rolling them in salt. The final step required vacuum sealing the pieces with the equipment they'd brought from the Colonizer.

Allorkan hung in the late afternoon sky by the time the work was done. Jahira arched her back and pulled her shoulder blades together in an attempt to ease the tension which had collected there.

"Let's clean up and get home!" Tala exclaimed. She led the way to the stream to wash.

The ice water infused Jahira with a renewed surge of energy. She threw herself into the packing and loading with single-minded determination, then finally took her seat in the flight deck of the Falcon. Light from the setting sun spread like the yolk of an egg breaking open and oozing across the horizon.

"KC, this is the Falcon, over." Jahira radioed the control room of the Kepler Colonizer, where someone remained on duty 24-7 every time the small jet left the settlement.

"Kato here." There was a pause followed by a loud yawn. "Go ahead, Falcon."

"Cargo is loaded and we're preparing for take-off. E.T.A. one hour and twenty seven minutes."

"Roger that. Fly safe."

"Will do. See you soon. Over." Jahira completed her pre-flight preparations and then switched the comm-link to project her voice over the internal speakers. "Everybody ready?"

Tala glanced back to the rear cabin, and then nodded from the right seat. Jahira initiated lift in the bottom thrusters.

The flight proved uneventful, to the point that Jahira fought to keep her eyes open. The viewing screen, which allowed her to monitor the passengers in the rear cabin, showed her that the rest of the crew had lost that fight. She and Tala flew in comfortable silence until the four big ships appeared on the forward E.V.S.

Jahira zoomed in on the settlement. Very little movement and only a few fires could be seen dotting the sprawling community. Most people had already retired for the evening.

"Rise and shine, sleepyheads," Jahira spoke softly over the intercom. "We're home."

Scraping and rustling sounds drifted from the rear cabin, letting her know that her passengers had received her message. Jahira lowered the Falcon until it hovered a few meters off the ground and then released the landing legs.

"Smooth," Tala commented.

Jahira winked in response, then unbuckled once the ship had stabilized. The crew worked together to unload the cargo onto a sled which Kato had brought over from the Colonizer. They accompanied Kato to make sure the meat and hides were all stored safely aboard the big ship before they gathered their packs and dispersed with tired waves.

Jahira waited for Krnar. They walked silently back to her tent where Krnar unrolled his sleeping hide outside by the fire pit.

"Do you want to come in?" Jahira asked, feeling even more embarrassed at having to ask.

"No," Krnar replied. "Is too hot."

Jahira nodded and tried to keep her disappointment from showing on her face.

"Goodnight then," she said before she ducked inside.

She didn't see Krnar touch two fingers to his forehead and extend them toward her.

Chapter 50

A light mist began to fall shortly after the third moonrise; a mist so soft that it made no sound as it coated the ground, and Krnar, in a layer of beaded moisture which hardened into frost when the temperature dropped. Krnar woke with the sun and began to carve a new spear from one of the long, straight leg bones he'd cleaned and saved from the srlen.

As he worked the tip to a sharp point, a memory of the humans planning to leave the bones behind made him hiss again in disbelief. What would his people think if they ever did return here and had to live side by side with these foreigners? What would his people think when they learned that one of the marked still lived? Perhaps they wouldn't need to know. Grollon kept to himself and only interacted voluntarily with Magnar, which suited Krnar just fine, but also made him a bit nervous.

A faint shuffling from inside the tent let him know that Jahira was awake. He looked up as the tent's door flap opened with that loud ripping noise that so many of the human's materials made. Krnar recognized its usefulness but still did not like it.

"Morning." Jahira greeted Krnar with a voice that sounded a bit deeper and scratchier than it would be later in the day.

"Morning," Krnar replied.

He smiled when Jahira joined him by the empty fire pit. She smiled back tentatively and Krnar wondered for the thousandth time if he'd done something to offend her that night after the hunt. She'd seemed more distant the next morning, and ever since. He'd not read her thoughts, at first because he kept his mind closed whenever other humans were around, their barrage of thoughts and emotions gave him a headache. This morning he did not for fear of what he might discover.

Jahira shivered in spite of the hide wrapped around her shoulders, so he set down his spear and helped build a fire. He collected pieces of the dancing trees from a nearby hide, as well as a bundle of small sticks and leaves which Jahira used to start her fires. She nodded her thanks and he watched her build a conical structure with the larger pieces before arranging a small pile of sticks and leaves inside. Finally, from one of many *pockets*, she pulled a small tool which Krnar had seen her use before but never tired of watching its magic.

He leaned in and stared. Jahira pointed the tip of the small cylinder toward the pile of tinder and then pressed a button. A beam of red light shot from the cylinder and the small sticks and leaves soon began to smoke. Before he could formulate a question to ask how such a thing could be possible, the smoke turned to flames and a cheery fire burned in Jahira's hearth.

They ate fruit and drank hot tea in what felt like a strained silence. Jahira finished her drink and then she sighed.

"It's not coffee," she lamented.

Krnar did not know exactly what coffee was, but Jahira spoke of it often. She'd even shown him the plant that it came from, one that her people had planted in the field surrounding their settlement.

"I don't think I can wait three years," she added.

Krnar just nodded. He understood her words well enough after nearly two moons of immersion in her language, but he still did not fully understand the hidden meanings, the labels and comments for which he had no frame of reference, not yet.

After the small fire had burned down to embers, Jahira stood and beckoned to him.

"Come on, I want to show you something."

Krnar glanced down at his half-finished spear and decided that it could wait. He stood and followed Jahira through the maze of tents and dirt structures that sheltered these people. Most of the residents still slept; a fact which surprised him. Hadn't Jahira said that they needed to prepare for the coming winter? Why were they not up fishing or gathering fruit?

His thoughts were interrupted by his own trill of anticipation, which sounded overloud in the prevailing silence, once he realized they were headed to the silver mountains. He had not yet discovered their secret, or what part they played in the prophecies. He did not know the right questions to ask and he grew more anxious every day. The Season of Ice approached while he waited for Aruvel to reveal the answer he so desperately needed.

Jahira led him to the same room they'd been in when she first showed him her *computer* and had begun to use it to teach him her language. When she pulled out the same circular disc he'd seen before, he assumed they were here for more lessons. Inwardly, he sighed. He didn't think he had the patience for a language lesson today.

"Hold still," Jahira instructed.

Krnar obeyed, but felt his heart-rate increase as she secured some sort of band around his head before positioning two clear circles in front of his eyes.

"What is this?" Krnar asked. She proceeded to wrap soft bands around each of his fingers, followed by each of his toes.

"I'll show you in just a minute," she replied.

Krnar stood motionless, afraid to move. Jahira covered herself with the same unfathomable accoutrements.

"Okay, you know the pictures I've shown you before?" Krnar nodded a single, careful nod in response to Jahira's question. "Well, now it's going to seem like we're *in* those pictures."

Krnar frowned and watched closely as Jahira tapped the screen which hung suspended in the air in front of her. She continued to tap and slide symbols through the air until, suddenly, the pictures appeared right in front of his eyes. He could no longer see Jahira, he could see nothing except a bright green field surrounded by tall, coarse-looking plants similar to the dancing trees, and yet very different.

A high-pitched and unfamiliar bird call startled Krnar. When he instinctively looked toward the sound, he was shocked to discover that he could *see* something flying through the pale blue sky.

"Amazing, isn't it?" Krnar looked toward Jahira's voice and saw her, but she looked different, almost like he stood in a dream looking at a memory of her. She no longer wore the band on her head, or the smaller ones on her fingers or toes. He cocked his head in confusion, and then looked down at his own hands and feet. He could not see the ones she'd placed on him either, even though he could feel that they were still there.

"What is it?" he asked again.

"It's called virtual reality," Jahira explained. "It lets you see and feel another place without having to go there."

Slowly, Krnar knelt down and moved his hand over the top of the bristling green shoots which surrounded him. He hissed when he felt them tickle his palm.

"Do you want to see more?"

Krnar nodded.

The world around him changed suddenly, leaving Krnar feeling a bit nauseated for a moment. The sensation was forgotten when he looked around and saw a forest of lush vegetation. A light mist fell through leaves as big as his body while bright colored creatures flitted through the shadows. A nearly deafening racket surrounded him. Unseen and unknown species screeched and chirped.

"This is a rainforest," Jahira stated. She pointed out some of the animals and named them for him. Too soon the rainforest faded and he found himself standing on the top of a mountain, looking out over a green valley. A river meandered in a series of long bends and curves, flashing here and there in the sunlight.

"Your home?" Krnar asked.

"Yes and no," Jahira replied. "These are sims, pictures, from Earth, the planet my people started from, but this," the surroundings changed again; Krnar hissed when he found himself suspended in darkness with nothing to see but Jahira floating beside him. Thousands of points of light appeared, illuminating a giant grey sphere which drifted toward them, growing larger and larger as it approached. "This is The Aquilo, a world we made that can travel from planet to planet."

Krnar shook his head, expressing his lack of comprehension, and waited to see more, but the picture did not change. Jahira remained silent for so long that Krnar began to wonder if something had gone wrong. He lifted his hands to his head, feeling for the band that he knew had to be there. Jahira finally moved. She placed a hand on his and said, "I have to show you what happened."

In response, Krnar paused. He watched as a small piece of the now distant sphere broke away, followed by another. Fire began to shoot from the hole which had formed, then disappeared just as fast. More pieces began to break off and drift away from the main body, then Krnar saw something, make that several somethings, shoot from one side with more speed than any of the other pieces. These objects came closer and he gasped when he recognized the silver mountains.

His attention was drawn back to the main sphere when he heard a terrible sound, like a tunnel of rock collapsing in on itself, a sound that was distant but final; then silence. The grey orb exploded into a thousand fragments. When he unblocked his mind, he felt a wave of intense sorrow rush at him. Reaching out, he took Jahira's hand in his own but continued to watch the silver mountains approach. There were five of them in the picture, not four, he turned his head and followed their progress toward a new sphere hanging against the dark back-drop.

"Leron," Jahira said, pointing to the globe which the silver mountains sped toward.

Finally, the pieces that he'd been collecting since he'd found Jahira and Magnar in the mountains clicked together. They came here in the silver mountains when their world died. The silver mountains were ships. Ships can fly.

"I see now." He paused and pointed to the silver mountains speeding toward his world, Leron. "I see how to save my people."

Chapter 51

"General, we can save these people, we can bring them home and then they can help us, they can teach us how to survive here." Jahira said. She repeated her argument for what felt like the dozenth time, growing more desperate with each telling. "They can hunt, they're more familiar with the plants and animals, and they know how to sew clothes. Our supplies are not going to last forever. They could help us."

"Didn't you say they were driven to the third continent during some kind of war?" General Thayer asked.

"Well, my understanding is that the ones who fled there didn't want to fight, that's why they left."

"It's *your understanding*." The General didn't bother to mask his skepticism. "Jahira, one of our laws is not to interfere with native inhabitants. We shouldn't even be allowing him to stay here, we wouldn't even *be* here-"

"Yes, we wouldn't be here if it weren't for our own world blowing up, but we are here, and somehow these people knew that we would come."

The General gave her a look that told her she'd just gone too far.

"We have no idea what the rest of them are like, what they're capable of; we don't even know how many there are. It is my job to insure the safety of my own people and I'm sorry, but I cannot consider this."

"What about a vote," Jahira suggested. "What if we opened it up for discussion, for the whole community to decide? We could give Krnar a chance to present his story and-"

"No, Jahira. That is asking too much. We have our own survival to worry about and I'm not going to waste time and resources saving someone else when it will inevitably mean more problems for us." General Thayer turned his attention back to the plant he'd been tending, silently dismissing Jahira and her request.

Her jaw clenched and released several times as she fought down her frustration. Finally, she turned and walked to where Krnar waited, a few meters away. The sag in his shoulders made her heart break; it was the first time she'd ever seen him look defeated.

This is not over, she decided. She waved for Krnar to follow so that they could talk somewhere away from the General, away from the curious eyes of those working in the surrounding gardens.

"You understood?" Jahira asked as they walked.

Krnar tilted his head from side to side then answered, "Enough."

"I'm sorry about the General, but we can talk to others. If many people support the idea, the General will have to listen." Krnar narrowed his eyes and leaned in, a gesture she recognized as meaning she'd been talking too fast, he hadn't caught the whole message. "We talk to others, get them to help."

Krnar leaned back and squared his shoulders. He nodded.

Jahira nodded back and started walking, planning out a course of action as they skirted the settlement. She decided to start with Magnar. Jahira found him by the river and started to explain what she knew about Krnar's people and their history. She was surprised to learn that Magnar already knew the whole story, and even some details she had not known, thanks to his apparent friendship with Grollon.

"So, when I showed him what happened to The Aquilo, he saw the big ships flying away, he realized then that they were *ships*, not *mountains*, and that we could fly them to the third continent to save his people. I think we would only need one based on the pictures he's shown me, but *I* finally realized that's why he's here, that's the reason he left, to find a way to bring all the rest of them back." Jahira finally paused to take a breath, imploring Magnar with a look before she continued. "Magnar, we've got to help them."

"Sure, I'm in, let's steal the K.C. and go get them."

Jahira laughed.

"I wish," she said. "It's going to take a few more people and a bit more planning than that, but thank you."

"Have you talked to Medic, or Ryan? They both seem to like Krnar and have been pretty open-minded all along. Maybe they would have some good arguments to help sway the General."

"Good idea," Jahira stated. "Want to join us?"

Magnar shrugged and then answered, "What else have I got to do?"

Jahira smiled and led the trio out on a mission to convince as many people as they could that saving the Lerroni was the right thing to do.

She should have known there would be some resistance.

The third day into their campaign, Jahira happened upon a small knot of people listening intently to a voice which rose and fell in passionate indignation from the center of the crowd. Jahira moved in closer in order to hear what was being said.

"It would mean taking you away from your families and away from your gardens at a time that we need to be preparing for winter, and then what? What if they bring these creatures back to our home? That's more mouths to feed, more resources used up by a species we know nothing about except that their own kind drove them away. Maybe they had a good reason for chasing them off."

Jahira's anger swelled with every word until she couldn't take it anymore. She pushed her way through the crowd and stood face to face with Lusela.

"Jahira, what a nice surprise." Lusela pulled her lips back in an expression more like a snarl than a smile.

"What do you think you're doing?" Jahira hissed in a fierce whisper.

"What am *I* doing?" Lusela retorted. "I am telling people the truth, not feeding them idealistic falsehoods planted in my brain by some mind-controlling alien."

Jahira narrowed her eyes and her nostrils flared as she responded, "My mind is, and has always been, my own. You aren't telling them the truth; you've never even bothered to learn the truth."

"By law we are not allowed to interfere with the progress of any sentient species on any of the worlds we encounter," Lusela retorted. "I'm pretty sure rescuing an entire race from exile with a spaceship would qualify as *interference* which would then make you subject to the law."

"By *law* we shouldn't have landed here, but we had no alternative. We're here now and we have no choice but to do what is right. There is no law that trumps being a decent human being."

Lusela leaned in until she was mere inches from Jahira's face and she whispered through clenched teeth, "You won't be going anywhere without my maintenance crews, and I would rather tear my ships apart piece by piece than allow a single one of *them* to set foot in our settlement."

"You should be careful what you say, Lusela. Some words don't taste so good going back down." Jahira spun on her heel and marched away without a backward glance.

"As much as I hate to admit it, she has some valid points," Magnar said.

Jahira narrowed her eyes and opened her mouth to speak, but Magnar held up a hand to stop her.

"I'm not saying I agree with her, but a lot of people will."

A heavy sigh allowed the anger to leak from her system. Jahira nodded slowly.

"We conquered the stars, but we can't seem to conquer human nature," she said.

Jahira and Lusela continued their separate campaigns until the General was forced to call a community meeting. The settlers decided to put the issue to a vote.

Chapter 52

"It's all my fault," Jahira declared. She closed her eyes and shook her head.

"Jahira, no matter what you said, Lusela is the one responsible for this." Magnar placed a hand on her shoulder in an apparent attempt to comfort her. A lump had formed in Jahira's throat; part of her wanted to cry, the other part wanted to scream.

"How could she do this?" Tala asked. Her friend walked a slow circle around the mess that was left of the engine room in the Kepler Colonizer. The solar coils, which stored solar energy and converted it for the ship's use, had been sliced to pieces, leaving behind a pile of useless fragments which glittered in the light of a dozen solar flashlights. The Kepler Colonizer would no longer have enough power to take off, let alone fly to the third continent. The back-up systems would allow function of the critical systems inside the ship only.

"Did you know this was what she planned to do?" General Thayer asked taking a step toward Dan, the ranking maintenance officer now that Lusela had disappeared, and one of the few maintenance workers left in the settlement. Dan had been the one who discovered the damage and alerted the General.

Dan stood his ground and shook his head as he replied, "No, sir. She spread the word to all that crews that she planned to leave, just temporarily, to protest Jahira's plan. She told us in order to make it work, we all needed to go with her. Obviously, not everyone agreed. She must have saved the rest of her plan for the ones that she knew wouldn't stop her."

"Or she came up with a new plan when not everyone joined her."

General Thayer sighed.

"Can you fix it?" he asked.

Dan turned his beam on the damage.

"I'm not sure, sir."

"Lieutenant, I don't want to hear 'I'm not sure', can you fix it or not?"

Before Dan could answer, they were interrupted by Ryan, Gavin, and Leiko who'd gone to check the other ships.

"Report," General Thayer commanded.

"It's worse than we thought, sir," Gavin replied.

Jahira held her breath. The General's eyes narrowed to slits.

"What do you mean?" he asked.

The three exchanged glances before Ryan turned to face the General.

"All the ships are the same, all except the Falcon."

"All of them?"

"Yes, and on top of that all the meat we had saved in cold storage, it's all gone."

"What do you mean, gone?" The General roared, causing Ryan to take in involuntary step back.

"Well, we saw a lot of muddy boot prints and followed them. The food is gone."

"She *stole* our *food*!" Tala exclaimed in horror.

"It would appear so," Ryan replied.

Jahira's stomach twisted into knots. She should never have confronted Lusela the way she did. She'd practically challenged the woman to follow through with her threats, but she'd never expected this.

"What are we going to do?" Tala breathed.

"First of all, we're going to remain calm," General Thayer stated. "Dan, you are going to fix these coils, all of them, starting with the Kepler Colonizer." The General paused and waited for Dan to nod before he continued. "Next I need a volunteer to go after Lusela."

"I want-" Jahira started to volunteer, but the General cut her off.

"No. I need someone to go that Lusela might actually listen to; we need that food."

Jahira pursed her lips and nodded.

"I'll go," Kato stated, taking a step forward.

"Then I'll go, too," Creed added.

The brothers glanced at each other and smiled.

General Thayer nodded.

"What if she won't come back? Or what if they can't find her?" Tala asked.

"We'll find her," Kato assured them.

"We have five months until winter starts. Five months to replace that food and no way to freeze it. She's using this as her bargaining chip." Jahira glanced around at the half-lit faces.

She was surprised when Krnar stepped forward. His blue-white glow created an aura of light around him and the air itself seemed to still as he bowed a short bow to the General before he spoke. "Lerroni have food, enough for Nall'Urok."

He glanced at Jahira and she felt a small seed of hope sprout in the darkness of her self-loathing.

"The Season of Ice," she supplied, growing more excited as her mind made the logical leaps toward Krnar's meaning. "Their Season of Ice lasts six years, right Ryan?" she barely waited for him to nod before she continued. "Their food, combined with whatever we can store between now and then, could feed both our people for at least a year." She looked at Krnar expectantly. He confirmed her words with a nod.

"Lerroni will feed you, as thanks."

Jahira practically vibrated with excitement. She almost laughed when she thought about the fact that Lusela's attempt to stop them might be the push that would force it to happen. The smile disappeared when she saw the General watching her.

"The ship has to be repaired first, and I will wait to hear from Kato and Creed before I will consider any alternatives." He spoke to the group, but looked at her. She nodded once to acknowledge his decision. She let out the breath she'd been holding when his gaze finally shifted to Dan. "Lieutenant, round up whoever's left from maintenance. The first thing you're going to do is take the Falcon and recover the solar coil from the Eagle. Jahira, Magnar, you will pilot the mission. Get it done."

Dan nodded and departed.

"Kato, Creed, good luck." The brothers saluted and took their leave as well. "I expect the rest of you to be hunting, fishing, or repairing these ships from sun-up to sun-down. We'll hold a community meeting once I've had some time to figure this out."

The General left, and most of those who'd been part of the meeting followed. Jahira, Krnar, and Magnar lagged behind.

"Do you think he'll approve it?" Magnar asked.

Jahira shrugged and then responded, "He might not have a choice."

Chapter 53

Allorkan bled across the horizon that night. Krnar laid on his back and watched the red tendrils spread, wondering if it would be enough to purge all that had been broken. Part of him mourned for Jahira's people, splitting apart as his own once had; a bigger part of him worried for his own. He understood enough to know that the silver mountains may not fly again and he agonized over an outcome that he could not control.

Have I done all that I can? he wondered.

Even after the last hint of red had vanished from the sky, sleep would not come. Krnar finally gave up the pretense of rest and stood, sheathed his knife and spear, then proceeded into the alara grove.

He had learned that what the Lerroni called a moon, these people called a month; they had five months until the snows came. His people had five moons until Mrkellan would leave them and they would be forced back underground until the next Season of Light.

There wasn't much time, for any of them.

As Krnar stepped from the shadows into the inner field, he stopped and hissed. Someone was already there, kneeling beside the largest of the five oranlodi, someone whose body glowed blue-white in the moonlight.

It cannot be, he thought. *It is not possible.*

He started across the field, drawn toward that form like a plinka to a baited hook.

There is no one else it could be, he told himself, and then he started to run.

When he reached the base of the hills, the figure stood and in one fluid movement turned and drew a spear.

Her spear.

"Allnall!" Krnar called her named, then trilled and laughed as he sprinted up the hills. "Allnall!"

She sheathed her spear and raced to meet him.

They both pulled up an instant before colliding in an embrace that would have sent them rolling down the hills.

"You're alive!" It felt strange and wonderful to speak his own language again. Opening his mind, he reached out. His smiled expanded when he felt Allnall's expert touch, her controlled emotions. "How?"

Allnall smirked and he could feel her relief and amusement. "It'll take more than one little storm to stop me."

"But how did you survive after the storm? And how did you find the grove?" He had so many questions and so much he needed to tell her. He forced himself to take a breath and let her respond.

"I hitched a ride on another laro, fished, used the fish stomachs to collect rain," she shrugged as if her ability to survive without supplies was hardly worth mentioning. "I finally made it to shore, a shore covered with snow I might add." Krnar smiled, remembering his own first impressions of "the warm land". "After that I crossed the mountains and kept going south, same as you I imagine."

Krnar laughed and shook his head.

"No, not even remotely similar to me," he admitted. He felt Allnall's curiosity, sensed her questions, though her face did not show them. He was amazed to discover how much he'd missed his own people. "I have so much to tell you."

"Before you start, what about the mountains? Did you find the silver mountains?"

"I did," Krnar replied. "And I know how to save our people."

"What do-"

Krnar held up a hand.

"It's complicated, and at this point it's out of our hands. There are others here, people from another world and they control the mountains. I've been trying to convince them to help us…"

"And?"

Krnar took a deep breath and then exhaled slowly, thinking about his response.

"And I believe that Aruvel chose well. I believe we are the ones who will return, but it will not be easy."

"Nothing ever is."

PART 2

EMPYREAN

Chapter 54

An icy gust of wind tore across the surface of the glacier, worked its way up the exit ramp, and filled the cavernous hold of the silver mountain. The cold air shifted the sleek fur which covered Krnar's unclothed arms and legs. He shivered as the wind-driven flakes of snow sought refuge against his warm flesh.

He'd donned the traditional gear of lizard-hide boots, short pants, belt, and pack for his journey across The Great Ice. Now, facing the elements, he realized how soft he'd become after only a few moons on Leron's temperate second continent.

What would his people think when he shared his memories of a land teeming with life, bathed in sunlight, and so warm that at times he'd been forced to rest in the shade simply to cool down?

The soft scuff of hide on metal alerted him to another's presence. He nodded to Allnall when she stopped beside him at the top of the ramp.

It's time, she projected.

Heart pounding with anticipation, he kept pace with Allnall. He descended from the silver mountain and took his first steps onto the barren, ice-covered world of his former home.

The journey from the ship's landing site to the community cavern should take two or three suns, depending on the weather and terrain. Initially, Krnar had been disappointed, frustrated even, when Ryan and Jahira had explained how far away they must land. Ryan explained that they needed to find the most stable landing point for a ship of this size, and it had to be far from any edges of the massive moving shelf of ice.

Now, as he bent his head against the biting chill, he felt grateful for the time he would have to re-acclimate. It would not do for The One to Return to huddle beneath a blanket shivering like a feeble child.

Though Mrkellan pulsed in the turquoise sky, the second sun of Leron, and the only sun that saw fit to shine on this remote part of the world, seemed small and insignificant now that he'd felt the heat of Allorkan in her glory.

"Frozen fish balls, it's cold!" Allnall cursed. She had one arm across her chest, fingers wrapped around the opposite strap of her pack, while the other stretched in front of her gripping the spear that she used to test the ice.

Krnar grinned and then trilled in agreement.

"Do you think everyone will be able to make the journey back to the ship? The elders? The children?" Krnar asked.

"They'll have to," Allnall replied.

The question had been eating at him ever since they'd developed thier plan.

Only the strongest and most capable of The People ever ventured far on The Great Ice, and even they did not all survive. His own father, Brdar, handfuls more over the course of many seasons of exile had been claimed by the ice. Now he and Allnall must ask families to risk their loved ones to follow them out at the end of the warmest season, the most dangerous time to cross the glacier.

"We will guide them. We will make it. Aruvel has forseen this," Allnall stated.

Krnar did not respond. He nodded slowly, more in thought than acquiescence.

The farther they traveled from the ship, the more surreal it all seemed. Krnar began to feel as if his time in the warm land had all been a dream.

Mrkellan had traveled so far from Leron at this point in its journey that it appeared more like a moon hanging in the sky at dusk though it was actually mid-day. Stars were visible though faint. The Season of Ice approached.

When the dome over their heads became more dark than light, they stopped to rest. Quickly and efficiently, they erected a small ice cave and then climbed inside. Krnar removed his pack before he sat cross-legged on the frozen surface. After a meal of dried srlen meat and a handful of snow, he took out his carvings to examine them one by one.

With the thumb of his right hand he brushed over the details of each piece, remembering the stories that went with them. When they arrived back at the community cavern, he would share his experiences. It felt critical that he not allow the memories to fade.

"Can I see them?" Allnall asked.

She sat across from him in the small ice cave. The interior walls glowed blue with the reflected light from their bioluminescent bodies.

Krnar nodded. Allnall extended her hand. He handed the carvings to her one at a time and watched as she examined each piece.

"You have a gift, Krnar. You bring life to the material."

Krnar shook his head and replied, "The life is already there, I simply have to shape it."

Allnall studied him in silence for a moment.

"I'm sorry, Krnar."

Krnar raised one eyebrow and tilted his head.

"Sorry for what?"

"For the way I treated you when we were young."

Krnar shifted his weight and cleared his throat. He busied himself with placing the carvings he still held into the pouch hanging from his belt.

"I mean it. I was cruel and selfish and I'm sorry."

"Uh, thanks, but, you know, that was a long time ago, no need to apologize." Intimate conversations made him uncomfortable; especially intimate conversations with Allnall.

"Well, I feel like there is. Just because my father was awful to me doesn't give me the right to be awful to other people. I regret my behavior."

Krnar lifted his eyes. This time it was Allnall's turn to shift her gaze.

Allnall's admission, as well as her apology, shocked him.

"Apology accepted," he said.

Allnall nodded and then extended her hand, palm open. Krnar retrieved the life-like miniature of Jahira.

"You may want to save that one for yourself," Allnall said, a hint of amusement coloring her voice. "I can think of a few people who may not be happy to learn how you feel about the human female."

Heat rose to Krnar's cheeks but he tried to keep his expression neutral.

"I'm more concerned about their reaction to hearing about Grollon, and Magnar," Krnar said, deftly shifting the conversation away from an even more uncomfortable conversation than the one he'd already endured.

"About that," Allnall began. "I'm not so sure we should mention the Marked just yet. Perhaps to Ellall in confidence, but not to the community as a whole, not yet."

"Are you suggesting that we deceive them?"

"No, not deceive, simply omit a few details until we've made it safely to the grove. How do you think people will react when they find out that the one who drove our ancestors from the warm land still lives?"

Krnar considered the fear, the anger, the confusion he'd felt when he'd faced his winged ancestor deep within the mountain cave. The revelation would cause panic in the community. Some may even refuse to return. The journey, and what they were asking of their people, was strange and difficult enough. Perhaps Allnall was right.

"I see your point, but won't it be harder to tell them later, once we've kept it from them? We can't very well let them discover him on their own."

"We'll have to tell Ellall, somehow. She can decide how much to reveal and when."

Krnar thought for a moment, and then trilled softly.

Allnall shifted her pack, pulled out her sleeping hide, and began to spread it across the frozen ground.

"Time to rest, Krnar, we have a big day ahead of us."

Krnar spread out his own hide and lay down, but he did not sleep. Between the cold outside and the anxiety inside, his body refused to relax.

Fulfilling a prophecy and saving his people was not as easy as he'd imagined it would be.

Chapter 55

Jahira stared out across the unbroken expanse of ice long after the two figures disappeared from view. She longed to join them, to see Krnar's people, to be doing something other than waiting and worrying for days on end, but that was impossible. She'd be a hindrance at best and at worst, the more likely scenario, a casualty.

The actual temperature could dip down to minus seventy, even when the sun was out. The wind-chill would freeze her into the most detailed ice-sculpture ever created. A lifesuit would protect her, but would make traveling difficult, not to mention she would probably scare the wits out of Krnar's people.

Best to stay behind.

I hate staying behind.

The fingers of her right hand twisted the silver cuff which she always wore around her left forearm.

What if Krnar didn't come back? What if his people refused to come? What if they tried but didn't make it? There was no way to communicate with him at this distance. Krnar and Allnall each had a tracking device in their pack, but the human watchers couldn't know any of the details based solely on the movement of the two tiny blips on the screen. What if they waited here for weeks and no one came?

"Hey, you alright?"

A jolt of surprise shot through Jahira's body. She sucked in a small gasp of air before turning to find Magnar climbing the steps to the observation deck.

"You startled me," Jahira said.

"Sorry," Magnar replied. "What are you worrying about?"

Magnar stopped beside her and leaned forward, resting his elbows on the railing. He stared out the clear wall at the blue-white landscape.

"Who says I'm worrying?" Jahira said.

Magnar glanced down at her arm.

"You always mess with that when you're worried," he replied.

Jahira dropped her right hand to her side then, feeling awkward, she lifted both hands and gripped the railing.

"I'm nervous about them making it safely across all that," she gestured at the view where a gust of wind whipped the light snow cover into a tiny white tornado before driving it off toward the horizon.

Magnar shrugged.

"This is their home. They'll be fine."

"What about the rest of them? The elderly, the children, all trying to make it back here…"

Her voice trailed off and Magnar placed a hand on her shoulder.

"We did the best we could. They've got a chance, which is a whole lot more than they had before. Besides, from what I've seen of Krnar and Allnall, I'm betting every one of their people is capable of survival in the worst conditions."

"Yeah, I suppose you're right." Before she realized what she was doing, her fingers returned to the silver cuff and began to twist.

"It wouldn't be that you're worried about losing Krnar, would it?" Magnar asked.

Jahira folded her arms across her chest and tucked her hands into the bends in her elbows.

"I can hardly blame you, he's a good man, and those eyes…"

Jahira untucked one hand long enough to form a fist and punch Magnar in the shoulder.

He smiled.

"Come on, let's have a drink. The second batch of fermented fruit juice is ready and waiting for its first victims." Magnar pushed back from the railing and cocked his head toward the exit.

"Let's hope it's better than the first batch."

"It could hardly get worse."

"And yet it was gone pretty fast," Jahira said with a loaded glance in Magnar's direction.

"There's no accounting for some people's taste." Magnar paused in front of the main door. The panels zipped apart and Magnar held a crooked elbow out to the side.

Jahira linked her arm through his and grinned.

"Maybe the Leroni have perfected a homebrew that they'd be willing to share," Jahira said.

"What would it be made from, fish oil?" Magnar wrinkled his nose and Jahira laughed.

"Did you see Krnar when he tried the wine?"

"Like a kid tasting his Dad's coffee," Magnar said, smiling at the memory. "He's going to be fine you know."

"Yeah, so you keep telling me. How about that drink?"

Chapter 56

Three suns spent skirting fissures, interspersed with brief periods of rest, finally brought Krnar and Allnall to the end of The Great Ice. The difference on the horizon was subtle, no more than a shadow between blue ice and blue sky, but within that shadow lay home.

Allnall glanced at Krnar and grinned. He gave a tight-lipped smile and raised his eyebrows.

"Are you ready for this?" she asked.

"Not really," Krnar replied.

He opened his mind and immediately felt the buzz of distant minds. Like a hive of insects calling the stray one home, the hum of energy pulled him forward. He hadn't realized until now how much he'd missed that connection, the ability to feel those around him without being overwhelmed by them.

Around the humans, he was usually forced to keep his mind blocked. He required a barrier between his thoughts and theirs in order to focus on the words they were saying, the unusual and not-so-subtle body language they employed without even realizing distracted him enough without having to filter through their thoughts as well. Their minds were so busy, their emotions so mercurial, he often wondered how they made it through a sun without collapsing in exhaustion.

Then there was Grollon, the Marked, ancient enemy of his people turned…what…not a friend exactly…tentative ally perhaps? Krnar still didn't trust the man completely, but he'd become more comfortable in his presence.

But how would they explain him to The People?

Allnall trilled.

Krnar stopped and looked where she pointed.

They'd reached the edge of the ice. He could see the swell of the community cavern bulging from the peninsula of rock beyond the sheer drop in front of him. Ahead and to the side a lone figure stood, arms stretched wide as if trying to embrace Mrkellan. Weak sunlight glinted off the silver bands which circled both biceps and forearms.

Krnar knew, though he could not see, a silver circle around the figure's right fourth finger completed the adornments of office for the One Who Remembers.

"Ellall," Allnall whispered.

As if she'd heard her name carried on the wind, the figure turned and stared at the wall of ice rising behind the community cavern. Her eyes locked with Allnall's and then shifted to Krnar's.

A trill ululated across the rock as Ellall broke into a run.

Krnar unslung his pack and dropped it on the ice. He quickly dug through the contents to find his hand-hooks, which he needed to climb down the face of the ice. After checking the lizard-tooth-lined soles of his boots, he readjusted his pack onto his back and began to climb down.

Allnall matched him step for step.

Soon the sound of trills and shouts rose up from below. Excitement warred with apprehension within his soul. Krnar wondered how The People would receive him, how they would react to his leaving even though he had not been chosen. What would Arkan say to him?

Finally, his feet rested on solid rock.

Krnar barely had a chance to turn around before he was pulled into a brief but crushing embrace.

"Krnar, you rotten pile of krska plat," Arkan said into his brother's ear. He held Krnar by the shoulders and pushed him out to arm's length, nodded once, and then finally released him. Arkan straightened and took a step back, giving them both their proper space. "I've been worried sick. You disappeared. You said nothing, told no one, not even me! How could you?" Arkan paused long enough to take a breath and shake his head in disbelief. "You did it, didn't you."

One corner of Krnar's mouth twitched, but he held back the smile. He nodded to Allnall and said, "We did it."

Arkan tilted his head back, raised his fists toward the sky, and trilled at the top of his lungs. The entire community joined in until Krnar thought the humans could hear the sound all the way back at the ship.

The noise of celebration faded to echoes. Ellall raised a hand and projected into the minds of The People.

Make way for the chosen! Make way for the Ones to Return! We will gather at the circle to share the memories of those who have crossed the world and returned to us, returned to take us home!

The crowd parted. Ellall led the way toward the community cavern. Krnar fell in behind Allnall. He felt awkward and self-conscious despite Ellall's efforts to deftly include him as an integral part of this momentous event. Head held high, shoulders back, he played the part but did not feel like he belonged in this place of honor.

What did you expect? he chided himself. *Did you think you could leave without a word, fulfill the prophecy, and then return to your hearth as though nothing had ever happened? Isn't this what you wanted?*

Krnar wasn't sure what he wanted anymore.

He could see already that things were going to be different. Not for him necessarily, he'd always felt different, set apart, clearly that would remain the same, just for different reasons. When The People returned to the warm land, to the sacred grove, what would his place be then?

Ellall led them to the back of the cavern. Krnar couldn't help but catalogue the differences from the human settlement. There were no walls here, no privacy, and no secrets. Only circles of rocks or bone to designate individual hearths. Within each larger circle rested a smaller stone-lined circle where vrmefur glowed and bubbled. Tendrils of smoke curled toward the ceiling filling the cave with the cloying scent of fish oil. Sleeping hides were neatly laid out on the rock. Individual belongings meticulously placed alongside each sleeping hide.

After his journey across the warm land and then his time with the humans, the home he'd always known seemed impossibly small. The walls seemed to draw in closer as the crush of people jockeyed for position without ever touching, even by accident.

Once they'd reached the circle, Ellall gestured for Krnar and Allnall to sit in the place of honor which she normally occupied.

Allnall bowed and sat in one fluid movement.

Krnar hesitated.

A tense silence filled the cavern. Everyone waited expectantly, a roomful of eyes watching him.

"Krnar, we would not be here without you. Sit," Allnall said.

After taking a deep breath, Krnar finally joined her.

The People did not yet know the story. They did not know he and Allnall had been separated, that he had rescued the two humans and fought to save his people. To them he was still an extra, an outsider, one who had left without being chosen.

He began to relax as Ellall and the elders served them bowls of fresh fish and hot glow-weed tea. The ceremony, the familiarity, it comforted him and reminded him that he would not be shouted down, he would not be thrown out until he'd had a chance to explain himself, that was not The People's way. Only Aruvel knew why things happened the way that they did.

The bowls of fish and tea were emptied and cleared away. The Leroni settled in for a long day of stories, a day they would remember forever.

Chapter 57

Tllomell's eyes never left Krnar from the moment she took her seat on one of the long stone benches carved into the back wall of the cavern.

She couldn't believe he had returned.

She'd first been heartbroken and then furious when they'd discovered him missing. The anger had turned to a gnawing worry when suns passed and he did not return. No one knew where'd he'd gone, not even Arkan. All of his tools, save for what he'd been wearing, were still lying on the stone floor of his hearth. People had whispered and projected, speculating about where he might have gone and why.

Now they knew.

Seeing him here, physically present in the same cave, she realized that deep down she'd believed him to be dead, lost forever. They all had, except for Arkan. He had refused to hold a ceremony to remember his lost brother. He'd believed all along that Krnar would return.

Once the bowls had been cleared away, Ellall began to tell the story of The People's flight from the warm land. Many of the Leroni had been lost on that long journey across the sea. Many more had perished during the first long Season of Ice when Mrkellan hid its light for an entire generation. The People had not been prepared for that first season. Their ancestors found the caves by chance, so they did not all freeze to death, but they had no light, no food. The krska snuck into the caverns and stole children until the Leroni began to set traps and feast on their subterranean predators. Somehow they had survived. Somehow, their ancestors had found the will to keep going, but they'd never forgotten their true home.

Tllomell had to force herself to remain still.

She knew this story word for word and only half listened to its retelling. She did not want to hear this story again. Krnar's story was the one she longed to hear.

What had happened to him? What was the warm land like? Had he and Allnall found a way to take their people back to the land of their ancestors?

Bowls of food passed by her untouched. Her stomach churned, threatening to force back up anything she might have tried to swallow.

He'd spent six moons alone with Allnall. Tllomell could see a familiarity between them that certainly hadn't been there before. She studied Krnar's every move, searching for clues to the questions that filled her mind.

What she noticed was how he had changed.

Despite his obvious discomfort at being the center of so much attention, he held himself with confidence. Less like the young man desperate to prove himself who'd competed in the trials only six moons ago and more like the leader she knew he could be.

Ellall finally ended her lengthy monologue. She gestured to Allnall.

Allnall did not rise. Instead she nodded to Krnar.

"Krnar should be the first to speak. He has the greater tale to tell and without him, we probably would not be here today. Though I was chosen, it was Krnar who first discovered the silver mountains, and he who found the answer that will allow us to return to our true home."

Krnar bowed his head in return and stood.

His fur glistened in the firelight. He had gained some weight in the warm land. He looked strong and healthy, a vision of what awaited The People when they returned to the sacred grove.

When he spoke, Tllomell drank in the sound of his voice. When his fingers caressed the curves of his many carvings, she imagined that touch against her own sensitive fur. Keeping her mind carefully blocked, she remained riveted through the entire agonizingly beautiful experience.

It came as a surprise, though a welcome one, to learn that Krnar and Allnall had been separated fairly early in their journey.

Then he told them about the humans.

The revelation that another people now inhabited the sacred grove shocked her out of her personal indulgence.

Heads turned and trills rose throughout the cavern. Though everyone quieted immediately when Krnar began to speak again, she knew that a hundred conversations buzzed between open minds.

Another group had settled around the grove, but they were not descendants of the Marked. This was a relief in some ways, even more frightening in others. A people they knew nothing about, supposedly come here from another world, far from Leron and its two suns. How could this be possible?

Ships he called them.

Tllomell studied the strange carving of the silver mountain when it came to her in passing.

These humans had ships that could fly through the sky, that could even fly through the space between worlds.

"And this, my people, is how we will return to the land of our ancestors. A ship waits for us on the Great Ice. Just as Aruvel once led our people over the sea to this land, we will enter the silver mountain and fly home."

Krnar's statement caused a furor of response.

Where is this ship?

How will we cross the Great Ice?

Will they wait for us?

Is it safe?

Can it carry us all?

How does it fly?

Krnar waited for the voices to die down before he continued.

"We will journey together across the Great Ice to the place where the ship waits for us. It will not leave until we all arrive. The silver mountain is powered by the light of Allorkan."

More questions, more whispers.

Tllomell had a hard time grasping the idea. She could see Krnar's images of the silver mountain, the grand scale and foreign details. She could not imagine being inside something that flew but was not alive.

What strange place did these people come from? How had they learned to trap the light of Allorkan? What other strange and amazing things could they do? How would the Leroni compete for resources with a species that could harness the energy of the sun?

One final question lurked in her mind, one that sent chills down her spine.

Why had they come?

EMPYREAN

Chapter 58

"Any sign of them yet?" Jahira asked. She stared at the 3-D image of the third continent which hovered over the table in Ryan's lab.

"No, no movement on the glacier yet."

"It's been six days. Are you sure they made it? What if their people won't come back with them? Maybe they're having trouble convincing people to come."

"It took them three days to get to that peninsula. The tracking devices show them moving around this little wedge of rock and down to the sea. I'm sure they're just catching up with friends and family, packing, that sort of thing. Relax, Jahira."

"Yeah, I'm sure they're fine. Just promise me you'll let me know as soon as they start heading this way."

"You'll be the first to hear the news, I promise."

"Thanks, Ryan."

With nothing else to see or do in the lab, Jahira turned and exited through the silver doors. A strip of light on either side of the corridor illuminated her way as she walked toward the commons in search of some breakfast.

The door to the commons stood open. Jahira could see Dan and Magnar seated together at a table near the small circular windows.

Both men looked up as she approached. Dan waved a greeting.

"Morning, Jahira," Dan said.

"Morning, Dan. How's the buffet this morning?"

"Mmmm, tasty as ever," Dan replied. He lifted a spoonful of cloudy, thickened liquid from his bowl and then tipped the spoon so the viscous mixture slipped off the spoon and fell back into the bowl with an audible plop.

"Can't wait," Jahira said. She nodded toward the empty table in front of Magnar. "You not eating today?"

"I'm on a strict no-snot diet," Magnar replied. "I had a piece of fruit."

"I'm tellin' ya, you're going to be hungry again in ten minutes," Dan said. "It may look gross but it fills you up."

"Threat of starvation or no, I will be really glad when the last packet of that stuff is gone," Magnar said.

Jahira smiled at their banter, grabbed a piece of fruit off the nearby counter, and then slid into a seat opposite the two men.

"Any news this morning?" Magnar asked.

Jahira shook her head. She finished chewing and swallowing the juicy pulp and then answered, "They're still at the cave. Even if they leave today it's going to be at least four more days before they get everyone to the ship." She sighed and then took another bite. "How are we doing on power?"

"Good," Dan replied. "Doesn't take much to maintain a crew this small. Even though the sun's not as strong here, we're storing up plenty of juice while we wait. From a power perspective, the longer they take the better."

"That's good I guess. It would be pretty embarrassing if Krnar's people arrived and we couldn't take off."

"Care to help the cause and join me for a run after breakfast?" Magnar asked.

"Sure," Jahira replied.

They both looked expectantly at Dan.

"Don't look at me," Dan said. "I don't intend to waste precious calories by running on some machine that doesn't actually get you anywhere."

Jahira smiled.

"Oh, come on, it was your idea to rig the equipment to the power system. We're performing a community service with every stride."

"Good, you do that. I invented the system, I think that's quite enough."

"It was a rather brilliant idea, I must say," Jahira tipped her head to Dan.

"Well, the replacement coil is much smaller than the original. I had to come up with some creative ways to conserve what we had."

"Speaking of replacement coils, what's the latest on Lusela?" Magnar asked.

"Last I heard the guys found her and her group, tried negotiating, but they refused to come back. They're headed for the southern continent, probably to avoid the worst of the winter." Dan swallowed his last bite of slush and stared mournfully at the bowl.

"I still can't believe she did that," Jahira said, shaking her head. "How could she destroy the coils, take the food…and how does she think they'll survive on their own?"

"Lusela may be crazy, but she's also crazy smart. Food's not all they stole."

"What do mean?"

"Looks like they took a portable analyzer for testing food and water, weapons, several emergency medical kits, some mobile solar panels," Dan paused. "Honestly, I don't think she ever intended to come back."

"But why?"

Dan shrugged, "I guess she's less afraid of taking her chances out there on her own than she is of the changes that living with another species will bring."

"Or she just wanted to be in charge," Magnar said.

"Kind of the same thing," Dan replied.

"What do you think the General will do?" Jahira asked.

"What can he do?" Magnar replied. "She made her choice. I say good riddance."

"Is it true they captured a baby herd animal?" Jahira asked.

"Far as I know," Dan replied. "I heard they had it pretty well tamed and were trying to get it to carry stuff for them."

Dan swiveled the seat of his bolted-to-the-floor chair and stood, bowl in hand.

"Well, it's back to work for me. Remember…save energy, save the world."

Jahira smiled at the ancient slogan, established on Earth and flashing on every wall of The Aquilo since it set out for the stars.

Dan deposited his bowl and spoon in the sanitizing unit. Jahira and Magnar waved goodbye before he turned and walked from the commons.

"Well, you ready for that run?" Magnar asked.

"Let's do it."

"Where should we go today?" Magnar asked as they crossed the threshold from the commons to the long curving corridor.

"Hmmm, I haven't been to KA-375 in a while," Jahira replied.

"Is that the jungle planet?" Magnar asked.

"Yeah, with all the cool birds."

"And the dinosaur-looking things…"

"It'll be good for you, make you run faster."

"I wonder what they ended up naming that place."

The steady whir of a VR cycling unit greeted her when Jahira entered the physical training facility. Scanning the wedge-shaped room, she spotted Cholie, a member of Dan's maintenance crew, pedaling her heart out in the back corner.

Cholie didn't glance over, probably didn't even realize they'd entered. The woman's white-knuckled grip on the handlebars and the alternating up/down and side-to-side motion of the bike made it obvious that Cholie was deep in a VR sim on what looked like an intense trail ride.

"I wonder which planet she's exploring," Magnar said.

"How about these two?" Jahira said, nodding toward the flat belt built into the floor.

"Looks good," Magnar replied.

They were both dressed in their PT gear which doubled as standard non-flight-duty uniform.

Jahira donned her VR equipment and linked her unit to Magnar's. Within seconds she could see his virtual body hovering beside her in the empty green background.

"KA-375, trail system seventeen, moderate predator activity," Jahira spoke into her wrist mic.

She heard Magnar groan and couldn't help but chuckle.

The empty field filled with towering trees, enormous ferns, and long looping vines. A dirt trail stretched out before her virtual feet. Jahira could already feel the influx of adrenaline.

"Tell me again why I run with you," Magnar said.

Jahira glanced over at the uncannily realistic image of Magnar.

"Because, even in the virtual world, misery loves company."

"Yeah, but what if I don't love misery?"

"Too late now," Jahira heard the rustle of the nearby fauna a second before Magnar. She was two steps into her stride when she heard the roar of one of the native predators behind her.

"What I really want to know," Magnar shouted as he settled into his pace alongside her. "Is who volunteered to colonize this planet?"

"Probably a bunch of paleontologist's great-great-grandchildren," Jahira replied.

"I wonder if any of them are still alive."

"You should be more worried about your own skin at the moment." Jahira ducked beneath what looked like a vine. The vine hissed and dropped to the ground when Magnar's hair brushed its belly.

"You know, that barren frozen glacier outside is looking better every minute."

Chapter 59

The deep blue wall of The Great Ice glistened in the early morning sunlight. Yesterday's melt-water had refrozen, creating a smooth, slick surface that would be a challenge to climb.

Krnar did his best to ignore the fear and doubt gnawing at his belly. He stood facing the line of people he would be responsible for guiding across the ice to the silver mountain.

Arkan nodded, ever confident. Ulletta wrapped an arm protectively around her distended belly. Orvan, the eldest male in the community and most respected elder among the circle of elders shy of Ellall herself, gazed at him steadily.

His heart quailed as the weight of responsibility settled on his shoulders.

The other group leaders stood facing their own lines, waiting for him to give the signal to begin the climb.

He nodded and lines began to shift.

Allnall, Erget, Grkar, Tllomell, Krag, and Plldoll had each been assigned a group. Having participated in the trials prior to Allnall and Krnar's departure, these individuals were the most familiar with the precautions needed to cross the ice. The elders had decided that several smaller groups would move faster, and hopefully more safely, across the surface of the glacier than the entire community en masse.

Though Krnar didn't like the idea of separating, he had to admit it would be safer. If the ice gave way, better to have some distance between the groups than for everyone go down together.

Only he and Allnall had the tracking devices that would allow the humans to see where they were. Krnar wished they'd had the foresight to bring more but at the time they hadn't anticipated splitting The People up into several groups. What if some of the groups didn't make it? How would they find them?

We'll go slow, we'll stay in contact mentally, and everyone will make it.

They had to.

It took the better part of a day to get everyone and their packs to the top of the ice.

Krnar sent his group members ahead of him, to ensure that all made it safely to the top before he began.

Cold ice bit his fingertips as he set his hand hooks into the first carved-out divots. After digging the lizard teeth which were sewn into the bottom of his boots into a knee-high foothold, he pushed upward. Impeccable timing, the result of countless hours of experience, allowed him to release one handhook as his body surged upward and set it again before he lost his momentum. A deep inhalation, and then he repeated the process with the opposite arm and leg.

Sunlight glinted off the ice. Silence surrounded him. He was the last to make the climb and for a moment he paused, glancing to his left and right. This would be the last time he scaled this wall. The enormity of this realization hit him like an avalanche.

Krnar, are you coming? Arkan projected into his mind.

Almost there, he replied.

Muscles he hadn't used in several moons stretched and strained until, finally, he set his hooks into the snowpack on the surface of the ice.

After pulling himself up and over, he rose to his knees and looked around. The members of his group waited. Some watched him expectantly, others gazed out over the peninsula of rock where the community cavern sat empty, abandoned.

For many this would be the first time they had ventured farther than the top of the wall; the first time they would lose sight of their home.

Say goodbye to the caves and the sea, Ellall projected. *This is the last time you will see this rocky shore.*

Krnar rose and took one last long look at the place of his birth.

When his attention returned to his group, he noticed the lines tied between belts. Arkan had not wasted time while waiting for Krnar to join them.

"Thank you," Krnar said, nodding to the safety lines.

Arkan nodded in response and then held the end of a line out to Krnar. The other end was secured to Arkan's belt.

Krnar brushed the snow from his fur and leggings, and then accepted the offering.

"We want to keep enough slack that you can cut yourself loose if I fall," Krnar said.

Arkan opened his mouth to speak. Before he could protest, Krnar leaned in and projected into his brother's mind.

If anything happens to me I need you to get them safely to the ship. Krnar's ice blue stare met an equally determined, and stubborn, countenance. Eventually Arkan pressed his lips together and nodded.

A light breeze ruffled the fur on Krnar's arms. He stepped back and addressed his group.

"Is everyone ready?" he asked.

Nods and trills were immediate, confident.

"Then let's get started."

He moved into position at the front of the line, a place he'd always hated. Squaring his shoulders, he tried not to feel paralyzed by the responsibility of all of these lives in his hands. With the tip of his spear he tested the ice. After piercing the snowpack, a shudder traveled up the shaft as the point hit the solid ice beneath. Krnar took two steps forward.

He had one last duty to perform before prophecy became memory.

Failure was not an option.

*****

"When is it going to hit?" Jahira asked, watching the blue blob move across the radar screen and cover the third continent.

"It will start early tomorrow morning and it looks like it could last all day," Ryan replied.

Jahira glanced from the weather radar to the tracking screen. The two orange blips had finally started to move across the glacier late yesterday.

"They're not going to make it by morning," she said.

"No, not at the rate they've been travelling."

A sense of helplessness consumed her. There was nothing she could do. She couldn't warn them, couldn't rescue them; all she could do was watch as the storm swept across the glacier straight into Krnar and his people.

"I'm sure they've dealt with situations like this before," Ryan said, never taking his eyes from the screens. "I'm sure they'll be okay."

She couldn't tell if he spoke for her benefit or his own.

The fact that he couldn't seem to stop wringing his hands only served to increase Jahira's anxiety.

Chapter 60

A subtle shift in the wind stirred the sensitive fur on Krnar's exposed forearms. He knew that the others would feel the change as well.

Any chance we could make it if we walk through the night? Arkan projected.

Krnar stopped, probed the ice immediately in front of him and then scanned the horizon.

Even if it were close enough, I don't think we can push through the night. Krnar glanced back at the line of people connected to him. Arkan was by far the strongest of the lot and even he bowed under the weight of his pack after two suns on the ice. *I think we all need some rest.*

After adjusting his mental range to include all those in his group he projected again, *We'll continue around this ridge and then we'll make a shelter for the night.*

He felt the responses more than heard them: acknowledgement, approval, relief.

Visibility decreased with every step. After another hundred paces, Krnar called a halt. The entire group worked together to build an ice cave large enough to shelter them all from the approaching storm.

When it was done, they crawled inside.

One by one their bioluminescent bodies encountered the dark interior of the shelter. The walls began to glow a soft blue-white as The People's light reflected off the snow and ice. Krnar, last to enter, paused halfway out of the tunnel to admire the sight.

Bodies shifted to make room for him. Krnar nodded his thanks and then moved to the open space and spread his sleeping hide.

The wind howled around the meager shelter, battering the walls like angry fists. Flakes of wind-driven snow pushed through cracks between the blocks causing random showers of sparkling dust. Krnar took in the wide eyes, the huddled forms. Most of these people had never spent a night outside the caves. The impenetrable walls of solid rock were a fortress compared to the quickly erected ice cave.

"Can you tell us a story?" one of the children asked once Krnar had settled on his sleeping hide. "A story about the warm land?"

The child's mother leaned in and spoke softly in the child's ear, presumably to shush the child, but she watched Krnar out of the corners of her eyes.

Krnar pulled a piece of smoked fish from his pack and smiled.

"I think a story is an excellent idea," he said.

The child clapped her hands and the mother smiled. Everyone else shifted to a comfortable position and directed their attention to Krnar.

"How about the first time I walked through the alara grove," he said.

Soft trills responded to this suggestion. Krnar waited for the sounds to escape through the cracks in the walls before he began.

"In the warm land, Allorkan shines so bright it hurts my eyes. At night the light of the three moons cast long shadows that stretch into crazy shapes. It was at night that I first walked beneath the leaves of the sacred trees. Moonlight reflected off their silver trunks and the silver fur which covers the foliage. It's like walking through a dream." He paused and projected an image into the minds of his listeners. Lips parted in wonder and children gasped.

As Krnar continued his story, the storm outside increased in intensity, as if the land had become a jealous lover, unwilling to see its people run to the arms of another.

Children fell asleep in parent's laps. Elders struggled to find a comfortable position on the ice but continued to listen. Krnar continued the story long into the night and then, unable to sleep, he lay awake and listened to the soft, even breathing of his companions.

Hours later, when bodies began to stir and children started to whisper questions to their sleeping parents, Krnar crawled through the exit tunnel, stopping once his head and shoulders were exposed to the elements.

Needles of ice drove into the flesh beneath his fur. Stretching one arm out before him, he nearly lost sight of his fingers in the gale of shifting white.

Frustrated and shivering, Krnar shimmied backward into the shelter.

Well? Arkan projected from the opposite side of the shelter.

Krnar shook his head.

Visibility is poor and the wind is too strong. We would risk losing our way, or some of our group freezing if we continue now.

How long do we wait?

Until we can travel safely.

How long will they *wait?*

Krnar knew his brother meant the humans on the ship, their only means of returning to the warm land.

I promise, they will not leave without us.

How can you be sure?

Trust me brother. Even as he projected, a seed of doubt sprouted roots in his mind. They'd been delayed longer than the humans expected already. He had no idea how long the storm might last. Though he knew Jahira would wait, the decision was not hers alone, and he could not vouch for the entire crew. What if they *did* decide to leave? Or what if the other groups made it before his group and the humans felt they'd done enough? They did have their own families to think of, waiting back at the grove and preparing for winter.

All around him mothers and fathers fed their children or whispered into their ears. Men and women sharpened knives or organized packs. Quietly efficient, always prepared, survivors…these were his people. He had never appreciated the good that surrounded him before. He had never had anything else to compare it to.

"It still sounds pretty bad out there." Orvan's voice interrupted the peaceful morning routine. Eyes focused on the revered elder as he continued. "What will we do, Krnar?"

Giving a slight nod, he acknowledged his elder before he replied.

"We will wait for now. It is too cold and too difficult to see the path ahead for us to proceed safely."

Orvan bowed briefly in return and said no more.

Though he appreciated the elder's show of respect for his appointed position, Krnar wished Orvan would express his own opinion on the matter. Contrary or consenting, at least Krnar could share some of the burden of the decision.

The day crawled by, incremental as the movement of the glacier on which they rested. Krnar struggled to remain outwardly calm. His frustration grew with every passing heartbeat. Even carving held no joy for him today. The task that kept his hands busy but allowed his mind wander until it cleared did not work as it usually did. His mind would not let go of the worry.

When he could not stand another second, he crawled out the single exit tunnel and stood in the snarling gale. Snow swirled around his legs and pushed against his torso with the strength of a high tide.

With fists clenched, Krnar roared into the wind, willing it to cease its fury.

Aruvel remained deaf to his needs this day.

When he returned to the interior of the ice cave, he could sense the unspoken question hanging in the air. With lips pressed together in a grim line, he shook his head.

"The storm continues. We will remain here for another sleep." He paused and measured each expression, the reactions so subtle they could be easily missed. So different from the humans, whose faces displayed every passing thought clearly enough that one rarely needed to see into their minds. After a deep breath he added, "We will leave at the next rising."

EMPYREAN

Chapter 61

The observation deck seemed unnaturally silent given the ferocity of the swirling gusting snow outside the clear walls. Jahira felt as if she were in a reverse snow globe, safe and calm inside her bubble while the rest of the world spun out of control.

Ryan had told her that one of the tracking devices approached, close enough that its bearer should reach the ship that morning. The other hadn't moved for almost two days. Did that mean it had fallen from the pack? Or had either Krnar or Allnall fallen into a hole in the ice, never to be seen again? Most importantly to Jahira, whose was it? She felt guilty when she caught herself hoping the missing device belonged to Allnall, but how could she wish otherwise?

Too restless to focus on any other task, she paced the narrow walkway that overlooked the glacier to the west. Not that it did her any good, she couldn't see a thing, couldn't do anything to help even if she could see what was happening, but at least she could keep moving. The movement gave her the illusion that she accomplished something.

Consumed by her own thoughts, she didn't hear the main door open, or the soft footsteps approach.

"Jahira." A hand came to rest on her shoulder at the same instant that her mind registered the voice. She jumped and half-turned. Her heart pounded against her ribcage.

"Magnar," she said the name on an exhaled breath of relief. "You scared the crap out of me."

"Sorry," he replied with a grin. "I thought you'd like to hear the good news."

"What? What is it?"

"About a hundred Leroni are in the processing of boarding into the cargo bay. The General wants you to be a part of the team that goes to greet them."

"Do you know who's with them?" She asked, already jogging toward the exit.

Though of course Magnar couldn't know all one hundred Leroni, she didn't have to explain her meaning...not to Magnar.

"It's Allnall," he said.

Jahira's shoulders sagged but once the main doors opened she continued to jog down the curving corridor.

Maybe Allnall would know where Krnar was, or what happened to the other tracker. Maybe she could contact Krnar mentally and provide some relief for her worry-laden brain.

Her rush to reach the hatch proved an unnecessary waste of energy. She, Medic, Ryan, and the General were forced to wait while heat pumped into the cargo bay in order to warm the area enough for the humans to greet the Leroni without dying of hypothermia.

Ryan's head remained bent over his hand-held data screen as his fingers tapped and moved icons.

The General kept straightening his jacket and running a finger over the multitude of striped bars which decorated the left chest portion of his uniform. This was probably only the third or fourth time Jahira had seen the General in his mess-dress.

Conscious now of her tell, she avoided fiddling with Zarya's bracelet and instead she rubbed her right thumb back and forth across the Velcro strip attached to the inside of her hip pocket.

Of the four-person team, only Medic stood without moving. Feet slightly apart, hands clasped behind his back, he gave Jahira a small smile.

How can he be so calm? she wondered.

She wished Magnar could come with them, he was better at the whole PR thing, or at least he used to be. Krnar and Allnall had felt it best if Magnar stayed out of sight, at least until their people had reached the grove and had a little time to acclimate. The General had agreed. No one wanted to deal with the mass hysteria that might ensue if the first encounter these people had with the humans included one who'd been marked.

For much the same reason Grollon had not been invited to join this mission. He had never mentioned it either, but everyone involved knew it would have been a lot easier to have an accomplished interpreter along. The situation seemed tenuous enough without adding any additional surprises.

"Okay, we're at twenty-five degrees. It's still a bit chilly for us but probably getting uncomfortably warm for the Leroni. Are we ready?" Ryan glanced up from his screen and scanned the faces of the welcome committee.

All three nodded in unison.

The General bent to open the hatch which sealed off the emergency ladder. Again, they'd felt the use of an elevator might be too alarming for their first encounter. To appear suddenly out of nowhere and walk through walls in front of a hundred strangers who'd been living in the most primitive of circumstances didn't seem like the best way to begin. Jahira marveled at Krnar's ability to adapt on his own. She'd given no thought to his background or experiences when they'd first met, she'd been focused on surviving, on getting herself and Magnar safely back to the colony.

The smell of ice and the bite of cold air surrounded Jahira once the hatch released.

Medic descended first, followed by the General. Jahira raised her eyebrows at Ryan, who gestured for her to proceed.

Freezing metal stung her palms as she descended the ladder through the narrow vertical shaft. Jahira wished she'd thought to bring some gloves, and a hat. A drip of moisture formed in the corner of her nose and hung there, tickling and teasing. Jahira sniffed to try to clear the cold-induced mucus and then had to wiggle her nose for several seconds in order to unstick her nostrils.

When the soles of her boots finally touched the deck of the cargo bay, Jahira released the last metal rung with a sigh of relief. She flexed her fingers in an effort to stimulate blood flow, then drew them together and blew warm air into the pocket of her joined hands.

Turning from the ladder, she faced the main room and stopped mid-stride.

A sea of snow-white faces and glacial blue eyes stretched before her. One of them stood and bowed.

It took Jahira several seconds to realize that it was Allnall.

Jahira bowed in return.

When she righted herself, Allnall gestured to another Leroni to her right. This figure stood. Jahira took in the long hide dress, the intricately carved bone spear held loosely in one hand. On her arms, four silver cuffs reflected the man-made light in the silver cavern.

"Ellall, may the light of Allorkan shine on you this day," Jahira spoke in English, trusting Allnall to translate the formal greeting appropriately, and she bowed again to the Akaruvel, the leader of the Leroni.

Once Allnall had conveyed her greeting, Ellall tipped her head to Jahira. Jahira thought she saw approval shine in the woman's eyes.

Ryan, Medic, and the General stood to either side but slightly behind Jahira. She couldn't help but scan the bystanders, searching for Krnar's familiar features among the crowd of expressionless faces. She desperately wanted to ask Allnall if she knew where Krnar was. Jahira noticed a few pairs of eyes shift away from her gaze. She realized with a flood of embarrassment that every one of these people might be reading her thoughts that very second. Returning her attention to Allnall, she noticed the woman staring at her expectantly.

"Sorry." Jahira cleared her throat and felt her face flush. She wasn't sure exactly what she was apologizing for, but it helped her clear her head and focus on the task at hand. When she spoke again she raised her voice so that she might be heard by all of the gathered Leroni. "We welcome you to our cave and we offer food and drink."

Allnall translated the greeting.

Jahira started back a step as the entire gathering responded in unison. They spoke in their own tongue of course and once the echoes had faded from the air Allnall translated, "We accept your hospitality."

Allnall and Ellall joined the rest of the Leroni who were sitting cross-legged on the floor.

Jahira smiled and sat as well.

Medic and the General joined her. Ryan stepped forward holding a crate brimming with fruit which they'd brought from the alara grove.

"Ryan, start with Ellall but let her take the fruit out. Don't, under any circumstances, touch her, even by accident."

Ryan nodded and moved forward. He set the crate down in front of Ellall, released it, and then stepped back, taking no chances.

Ellall's eyes widened.

She spoke to Allnall in soft purring tones. Allnall responded and nodded her head toward the fruit.

A subtle change rippled through the crowd of waiting Leroni. Jahira watched them with interest. They did not lean in and whisper to their neighbors as humans would have done. Instead there were small nods or subtle gestures of acknowledgment as mental messages were given and received.

Finally, Ellall lifted her free hand and reached for the crate. With slow, precise movements, she selected a single fruit and held it reverently with the pads of her fingertips. Turning her wrist, she inspected the fruit from every angle, and then leaned in to inhale its scent. Lips curled back to reveal perfect white teeth, Ellall opened her mouth and bit into the flesh of the orb with her eyes closed.

A silence so complete that Jahira could hear her heart beating filled with eager anticipation.

Ellall held the sample on her tongue. Finally, the muscles in her jaw flexed and released as she chewed the offering. A slow smile pulled her lips apart until a dribble of juice ran from one corner of her mouth and discolored the pristine fur of her chin. A soft trill vibrated through her chest.

Ellall swallowed and then spoke to Allnall, who reached into the crate and began plucking fruit and passing them to waiting crowd.

Soft trills and murmurs of delight washed through the room. Jahira tried to capture every detail of the scene and hold it in her mind the way Krnar had been teaching her. She wished he could be here to witness this.

Jahira twisted the silver cuff around her wrist, impatient for the Leroni to finish so that she might be able to learn more about the whereabouts of the rest of the groups.

Ellall's eyes followed her movements. When the Akaruvel caught sight of the silver bracelet, her eyes widened and then shot up to hold Jahira's gaze.

Tugging the sleeve of her shirt down to cover the bracelet, Jahira bowed her head- a sign of respect as well as an excuse to break eye contact.

After every last drip of juice had been consumed, Ellall nodded to the four humans. Her voice, though not overloud, carried easily through the room. Jahira kept her eyes respectfully fixed on Ellall until she'd stopped speaking, and then she looked to Allnall for an interpretation.

"She says thank you. That was beyond her expectations."

Four heads bowed in acknowledgment. When they lifted, Allnall spoke of her own accord.

"Perhaps it is time for introductions, if everyone is ready?"

The General nodded and then gestured for Ellall to begin.

After a brief exchange which Allnall did not interpret, the woman turned to face the four humans, bowed, and then began to speak with her right hand open toward Ellall.

"Ellall, Akaruvel of the Leroni. She speaks for The People through me." She paused and gestured to the man sitting to her left. "Frmar, he learns from Akaruvel and will be next to remember for our people."

Frmar bowed. The humans returned the gesture.

Allnall placed an open palm against her breastbone and said, "Allnall, chosen, and now one to return."

To either side of Ellall and Frmar sat three Leroni whom Allnall referred to as elders. The human representatives exchanged nods of the head with each elder in turn and then Allnall sat.

Jahira cleared her throat before she began the introductions for the humans.

Though Krnar had been teaching her his language, she primarily knew the names of plants and tools, not exactly helpful in the current situation. Having no desire to embarrass herself with fumbling attempts at the Leroni's formal language, she trusted Allnall to figure out the best way to convey her meaning.

Jahira began with the General and, once it was clear to Ellall that he was the leader of the humans, she shifted her position subtly in order to better orient herself toward him. The corner of Jahira's mouth twitched realizing Ellall had assumed she was in charge. Jahira wondered if the General noticed.

"Tell them they will be given rooms where they can stay until we land. They'll have to be buckled…uh, strapped in…at first, for their safety."

Allnall repeated the instruction in a series of purrs and hisses.

Ellall spoke and, though she appeared to be addressing the General, Allnall responded to what must have been a question without interpreting. Ellall trilled in surprise. The sound was echoed by a hundred Leroni as the unknown exchange spread through the crowd.

"What did she say?" Jahira asked.

"She asked how long," Allnall said, thought for a moment and then continued. "She asked how many suns to travel to the alara and oranlodi. I told her one."

Jahira smiled and then nodded when Ellall looked to her for confirmation.

Ellall spoke again.

"She asks how this is possible. The memories show her the warm land many sleeps from here. How can this mountain travel there in one sun?"

"We use the energy of Allorkan," Jahira replied, remembering that explanation was what had finally satisfied Krnar.

The Akaruvel's eyes narrowed.

"She asks how you trap Allorkan's energy," Allnall translated.

Apparently the explanation didn't satisfy Ellall.

"Tell her she can watch," The General said. "It's a bit more than we can explain right now, but she can have a seat in the control room and see the whole flight."

Once Allnall completed her translation, Ellall bowed her head to the General.

"Now, can we please get these people to their rooms before I freeze to death," The General said.

The four humans stood. Allnall must have projected a message to the waiting Leroni, for they stood as one.

"We'll go up first. Allnall, please send four or five at a time up the ladder. We'll meet them at the top and take them to their rooms." The General paused and turned to address Jahira. "Maybe once everyone is settled you and Allnall could go room to room and explain how everything works. We don't know when the rest will arrive so we'd better see that they're comfortable and know how to use the head."

"Yes, sir," Jahira replied.

Bodies shifted and lines formed. Jahira waited at the base of the ladder. Allnall stepped in behind her in order to direct the groups to the top.

The General and Ryan peered down through the opening above. Medic was more than halfway up the ladder when Jahira placed a hand on the first rung. Before she began to climb she leaned toward Allnall and whispered, "What about Krnar?"

Allnall's face didn't change, but her eyes clouded with worry.

"The storm is bad. We lost contact before coming inside the mountain. I hoped you could tell me."

"The other tracking device hasn't moved for two days."

Allnall nodded slowly.

"They wait out the storm. We cannot leave without them."

"I don't plan to."

The two women exchanged a long look. Finally, Jahira broke the connection and began to climb.

Neither had dared ask the question that she knew they were both thinking- how long would they wait?

The cold which had long since penetrated her skin seemed to settle now in the pit of her stomach.

Chapter 62

Morning arrived, or at least that's what Krnar's internal clock told him. Between the lengthening dark of the late season and the raging winds which blinded him even with the slatted eye covers, it proved impossible to tell the exact time of day.

His hands trembled as he secured the straps on the top of his pack. The combination of the pressure he felt, his anxiety over the poor conditions, and fatigue after a sleepless night conspired against him.

Gusts of wind swelled and died, allowing brief windows of visibility which Krnar prayed would be enough to keep them on course. Right now he and his group members used these moments to tie smooth and slightly stiff lengths of gut-line from one person's belt to the next in line.

"Perhaps we should separate into two groups," Arkan suggested. "We would make better time."

Krnar considered the idea. With a line this long, those at the end would not be able to see him, they would have to rely on mental signals and tugs on the line to move forward. Two shorter lines would definitely speed up their collective pace. Krnar knew one of the greatest fears of his group was arriving too late and finding the ship had left without them.

"All right, let's split up. Arkan, you will lead the second group. Stay in sight on my left."

Arkan nodded and the brothers set to the task of dividing the members as equally as possible. Ulletta, Arkan's wife, tied her line to Arkan's belt, taking an extra moment to adjust and tighten her own belt below the swell of her pregnant belly.

Ulletta's nephew, Mrkon, tied on behind her. Both of Mrkon's parents had succumbed to illness during the last Season of Ice. Ulletta and Arkan had taken the boy into their hearth.

Ulletta reached as if to help with the knot but Mrkon shook his head and took a step back, frowning in concentration, his cold fingers working with deliberate precision.

Ulletta smiled and straightened. She exchanged a wink with Orvan, the elder who waited patiently behind Mrkon.

Mrkon finished and handed the free end of the line back to Orvan, who accepted with a small bow.

Spirits were high despite the weather. Krnar allowed himself to feel a whisper of optimism. Wind ruffled his fur and, though he'd wrapped it well, the patch of bare skin on his leg from his encounter with a cave lizard during the trials already ached from the cold.

The general feeling of sanguinity soon gave way to monotony as the two groups moved across the ice with agonizing slowness. Krnar couldn't see more than a body length ahead most of the time. With the tip of his spear, he probed the ice before each step. Tension gathered in his shoulders and up the back of his neck.

How's your group doing? he projected to Arkan.

They're holding up. Any guess on the distance?

Lifting his chin to the sky in an automatic gesture, Krnar hissed at the white barrier which obscured any clues he may have gleaned about where they were or how far they still had to go.

My best guess is another full sun, especially at this pace.

Arkan didn't respond but Krnar could feel his brother's restlessness, like and insect crawling through his fur the emotion tickled his mind.

The important thing is that we all get there. The words were for himself as much as Arkan. *Another hundred paces and we'll stop to rest.*

Okay.

The tingling sensation retreated from Krnar's mind, giving him a chance to get control of his own emotions.

Whenever the wind ceased long enough to give him a clear view of the line behind him, Krnar would glance back and assess the well-being of his group. Heads remained bowed against the storm, eyes focused on shuffling feet. A few prodded the ground around them with the tip of a spear but for the most part, they followed him blindly. He prayed he did not let them down.

True to his word, Krnar counted out a hundred paces and then called for a halt.

There wouldn't be time to build a shelter, but if they formed a tight circle, they might block the wind enough to get a brief respite from snow driving into their faces.

Krnar shrugged one shoulder out from under the strap of his bulging pack. Before he had a chance to pull the other arm free, a deep groan sounded beneath his feet. The sound seemed to originate from the very core of the planet.

Stumbling backwards, Krnar caused a chain reaction of shuffling, faltering movement.

A sickening crack echoed above the howl of the wind. Krnar's stomach heaved as the ground fell away before him.

The opening yawned like the hungry jaws of a giant lizard, waiting for food to fall into its gullet. His heart raced as he glanced to either side, making sure his entire group remained behind him.

Krnar! Help!

Panic overwhelmed his mind and Krnar's blood turned to ice. Arkan called to him.

"Wait here! Don't move!" he yelled to those around him.

After cutting the line secured to his belt, he followed Arkan's signal along the edge of the fissure until he nearly tripped over the body of a Leroni huddled against the wind.

"Where is Arkan?" Krnar yelled.

The figure stretched one white-furred arm out toward the chasm and pointed.

"Krnar! I'm sorry!" Erknok, Arkan's closest friend, crawled toward him along the edge of the fissure. "I just reacted! I cut my line when I started to slide toward the hole! We might have been able to pull them out, all of us together!"

Krnar's mouth went dry and his hands felt numb, as if heart truly had stopped pumping blood to his extremities. He dropped to his knees and crawled toward Erknok.

The man pointed once Krnar had reached his side. Squinting against the blowing snow, Krnar could make out four glowing forms silhouetted against the darker ice on the opposite wall of the chasm. Arkan's hands gripped the shaft of his spear, which he'd driven into the snowpack on the opposite side. Ulletta, Mrkon, and Orvan dangled from the lines which connected their belts, twisting like bait on a hook.

"Krnar, I'm sorry."

Not able to tear his eyes away from the sight, he shook his head faintly from side to side.

"You did the right thing," he replied. "You'd all be at the bottom of that fissure if it weren't for your quick reaction. No apology is needed."

The muscles in Arkan's biceps bulged as he tried, and failed, to pull himself to the surface. Strong he might be, but his brother could not hold all that weight indefinitely.

Arkan, I'm here. Don't move. I'm coming.

No doubt saving his strength for the task at hand, Arkan did not respond, but Krnar felt a pinprick of relief pierce the bubble of panic which radiated from his brother's mind and threatened to undo him.

Unpacking and preparing his gear as quickly as possible, a plan took shape in Krnar's mind. A risky plan to be sure, but the best he could come up with given the circumstances.

With a grunt of effort, he drove the tip of his spear into the snowpack. As he lashed one long length of gut line to his spear he yelled to Erknok, "Do you have another length of line? This long?"

Erknok nodded and disappeared into the swirls of snow, reappearing just as Krnar finished the triple knot that connected the line to his belt. A few firm tugs assured him the knots were secure on both ends. Next he made three loops with the line from Erknok. He secured these loops with a sliding knot and then wound the trailing end around his chest, over one shoulder and under the opposite arm multiple times before securing this with another series of intricate knots. The three loops went over his head and finally he pushed one arm through the hole in the center. After one last check on his hand-hooks and boots, he gripped the line at the base of the spear and began to walk out over the edge of the narrow chasm.

I'm coming. Hold on a little longer. He projected this message to all four of the minds trying desperately to control their fear. He showed them his plan as he lowered himself into the abyss.

The wind did not follow him into the darkness. The sudden stillness surrounded him and helped to clear his mind but also made him acutely aware of the sounds of distress bouncing off the ice from the opposite side of the opening.

Descending as quickly as he dared, he finally reached the narrowest point of the chasm where two bulges in the ice reached toward each other like the hands of two loved ones unwilling to part. After digging the teeth of his right boot into the wall and wrapping the line once around his wrist, Krnar turned a hairsbreadth at a time. As he turned he reached with hand-hook and jagged boot sole toward the opposite ice shelf.

Every increment became a test of strength and will. He longed to rush forward, before it was too late, but he forced his body to move with deliberate caution. One wrong move and he would be no help to anyone. They would all end their lives together in the gaping black void below.

Once his right hand and foot were secure on the opposite wall, he released his left wrist and then pulled his body across the chasm.

Barely daring to breathe, he held his right side in an isometric contraction, straining with every ounce of strength until he finally dug both hooks into the ice.

With a long exhalation of relief, he allowed his body to relax and then reset for the next challenge.

The bitter chill of the cold air which rose up from the very core of the Great Ice enveloped him, sending shivers through his body. His breath condensed into puffs of semi-solid moisture the moment it passed his lips.

He climbed sideways now, toward Ulletta. Her eyes were closed. Her face tight with barely contained terror.

I'm here to help, Ulletta. We're going to make it out. Just hang on a little longer.

Ulletta did not acknowledge him.

Krnar began to climb up toward Arkan. He would secure his brother and together they would bear the weight of the rest. Together they could pull the others out.

Suddenly Ulletta screamed.

Krnar glanced down and saw that the line which connected Ulletta to Arkan had worked loose. Ulletta clung to the line now in desperation, already her arms trembled with the weight of those hanging below.

"Arkan!" Ulletta screamed her husband's name as she fought to hold on.

"Ulletta!" Arkan howled back.

Krnar's heart stopped for a beat. Without thinking he lowered himself until he was even with Ulletta.

Ulletta hissed as her fingers began to slip.

"Krnar!" Arkan bellowed his brother's name in a heart-rending explosion of breath.

Palms slick with fear and heart racing, he released his left hook and gripped the triple-looped line which rested on his opposite shoulder. After ducking carefully through the center hole, he reached out, stretching his body to the limits. He held the loop steady, centered it on Ulletta's dangling feet, and finally began to lift the loop upward.

The muscles in his back and legs screamed in protest as they simultaneously balanced and pulled his weight upward. His left arm trembled with effort of holding the line steady and raising it around Ulletta's swollen form.

Finally the loops were over her distended belly and secured beneath her arms. He tightened the slip knot.

Okay, I've got her, he projected to Arkan. Then aloud to Ulletta he called, "I've got you! Hang on to Arkan if you're able until I get the line taught. I'll tell you when I'm ready. You can do this!"

He released the loops and flicked a hook into his left hand. His body trembled with effort as he pushed upward with all his strength.

A hand span away from the surface he felt a pull against his chest and heard a scream below him. He instinctively hugged his body to the ice and felt one handhook begin to slide from the sudden addition of weight.

Are you okay? he projected.

I'm okay, Ulletta responded. *I couldn't hold on to the line.*

Okay. That's okay. Your hands are free now. Can you set your hooks?

Yes.

Every muscle in Krnar's body burned. He focused on breathing in through his nose, taking short shallow breaths as the line around his chest dug into his ribs and clavicle, preventing his lungs from expanding in a full breath.

He knew the moment she'd set her hooks. The pain of the gut-line digging into his shoulder eased enough to allow him to move.

Good, Ulletta. We're going to climb together. Ready?

Yes.

Krnar, I'm out. I'm lowering a line for you. Get your arms through and I'll help pull you to the surface.

Arkan hadn't wasted any time. The moment he'd felt the shift in the weight, and looked to see that Ulletta, Mrkon, and Orvan were secure, he'd scrambled to the top of the ice and retrieved more gut-line from his pack.

"Mrkon!"

Krnar heard Ulletta yell and glanced down. All he could see were his own glowing legs blocking the view of anything below him.

What happened? he projected.

Mrkon's belt is ripping, Ulletta replied. *He can't hold Orvan's weight by himself.*

Arkan, you're going to have to climb down to get Orvan.

Krnar's mind was a jumble of emotions. He tried to sort out the signals.

Orvan, can you reach the wall? Can you set your hooks?

I can't reach, the wall curves away from me here, Orvan replied.

Arkan is coming for you.

There's no time. You'll lose the boy as well. Orvan paused and then added. *Tell Ellall I said goodbye.*

The weight against his chest released suddenly and Krnar heard Ulletta's sob of grief.

What happened? Orvan?

He's gone Krnar. This came from Arkan, who'd witnessed the event from above. *He cut his line to save Mrkon. He's gone.*

Krnar felt frozen with shock.

Krnar, we need to move. Ulletta's message, wrapped with urgency, pushed him past his temporary immobility.

Yes, okay, here we go.

He and Ulletta climbed together. Mrkon wound the line between himself and Ulletta around his right forearm and held on for dear life.

Arkan lowered a line down. Krnar paused to work his arms through the loop and then continued to climb while Arkan pulled and supported his weight from the top.

Once Krnar's hooks reached the surface, Arkan was there. His brother gripped his wrists and pulled while Krnar walked up the wall with his lizard-tooth-lined boots.

Finally, enough of Krnar's body had cleared the edge that he could lean forward and crawl on his hands and knees across the surface. He continued to support Ulletta's weight while Arkan helped to pull her onto the snowpack, careful of their unborn child.

Krnar turned back toward the chasm and while Arkan supported Ulletta, Krnar hauled Mrkon bodily from the opening in the ice.

Mrkon trembled visibly. Silent and somber, he did not move toward Arkan and Ulletta, but stared at the clean slice in the line that dangled from his belt, the line which had held Orvan.

Finally, Ulletta knelt beside him and pulled Mrkon into her arms. She trilled and whispered soothing words as Arkan wrapped them both in a protective embrace.

Krnar lay on his back and stared at the swirls of white snowflakes which blew into his body and then rose in spirals of agitation until they once again continued on their journey.

Across the fissure he could hear shouts and trills. Eventually he became aware of the push of many minds against his own.

Reluctantly he opened his mind to the tendrils of thought, the questions, the worry, the curiosity.

Arkan, Ulletta, and Mrkon are safe. We must find a way for the rest of you to cross. He paused and took a deep breath before he added, *Orvan did not make it out.*

It took a moment for the message to register and then Krnar heard the rise and fall of voices, thick with sorrow. He, Arkan, Ulletta, and Mrkon added their voices.

The sounds of loss met and mingled over Orvan's final resting place.

Chapter 63

The wind ceased suddenly, like an over-tired child who fusses and fights until finally collapsing in exhaustion. The blowing snow settled and Krnar paused. After blinking several times to clear the ice from his lashes, he examined the horizon. Hoping for some sign that would reassure him, and his group, that they were on course, he squinted up at the sky. Mrkellan continued to hide behind a thick cloud cover.

Krnar felt as if he were trapped inside a giant endless snow cave; white below, white above, white as far as he could see.

"Krnar, what's that?" Arkan asked, coming up to stand at Krnar's left shoulder.

Krnar turned his head and peered in the direction that Arkan pointed.

At first he saw nothing, no change in landscape or sky. Then a sudden flash of light in the distance drew him forward like a fish to glow-weed.

"Did you see that?" Arkan asked.

Krnar nodded.

"What do you think it is?" Arkan asked, excitement creeping into his voice.

"It has to be the ship, the silver mountain. Nothing else out here would reflect the light like that."

Krnar met his brother's wide gaze. Arkan's white teeth showed in a huge grin.

"We did it, Krnar. We made it."

Krnar nodded but felt compelled to add, "Almost. Let's adjust course and keep it slow. Don't say anything yet. Not until we're sure."

Arkan nodded and side-stepped several paces in order to give his line room to move beside Krnar's. They simultaneously stabbed the ice ahead before signaling to their respective groups to resume their forward progress.

Krnar kept pace to Arkan's right, glancing up from time to time to squint at the horizon, hoping to catch another glimpse of that distant beacon. If the rest of the group noticed an increase in the pace, they said nothing. Perhaps they attributed it to no more than the break in the weather. Perhaps they were too weary to notice anything beyond the ache in legs and backs.

It pained Krnar to be this close and yet be forced to inch along like an oversized ice worm. He wanted to run, to shout at the top of his lungs. He wanted to see Jahira.

Had the other groups arrived already? Had the other leaders lost anyone?

The realization that once he reached the ship he would be forced to tell Ellall about losing Orvan dampened his eagerness somewhat. He used the time to rehearse his story.

The weary Leroni followed the curve of the world toward a hope beyond imagining. It didn't take long for those in line to begin to notice the intermittent glimmer on the horizon. At first a soft trill sounded behind him, followed by another. Seconds later a tug on the line caused a chain reaction in the connected belts when one of his group members stopped to stare.

"Krnar, is that the silver mountain?"

Having watched the shape grow in the distance, Krnar was now certain of what he saw.

"Yes," he replied.

Ululations of joy greeted his confirmation.

The line to his belt went slack and Krnar suddenly found it difficult to maintain a cautious pace without having his heels kicked.

Once they'd drawn close enough that Krnar had to tilt his head back to see the peak of the silver mountain, he could feel the hum of The People's minds close and plentiful. Krnar sought Allnall's signal and gently pushed against her mental wall.

Krnar! You made it! Allnall's thoughts opened to him. He could feel her wave of relief.

We're just outside. How long have you been here?

A full sun and sleep. Jahira told me this morning that you were approaching.

Has everyone else arrived?

Yes. Your group is the last.

Tension seeped from Krnar's shoulders with a long exhale.

The ramp is open. We will be inside soon.

I will tell Ellall...and Jahira...that you have arrived.

With a tingle like a finger trailing along his fur, Allnall retreated from his mind.

"I notified Allnall. She will spread the news of our arrival."

Arkan nodded then said, "What do we do now?"

"We enter the mountain," Krnar said, pointing the tip of his spear toward the ramp and the dark opening in the side of the ship.

Flashes of movement registered in Krnar's peripheral vision. The Leroni hastily cut their physical ties to each other and stepped hesitantly onto the slick silver surface which would take them into the mountain of the prophecy.

Arkan and Ulletta walked up the ramp hand-in-hand. They'd barely been an arm's length apart since the catastrophe on the ice. Mrkon followed close behind. His wide blue eyes and parted lips reminded Krnar of his own first impression of the foreign structure.

Gesturing his group forward, Krnar waited until all the others had boarded before following them into the cavernous room that Jahira called *the cargo hold.*

The Leroni looked about in awe.

The silver floor rose up into arching silver walls. Ladders, hooks, straps, and nets hung suspended from walls and ceiling. Krnar found it strange to think that he now knew the name and function of most of these objects that the rest of his people had never seen before in their lives.

Heads swiveled and trills escaped from many throats as The People pointed and whispered. Most fascinating were the tiny points of light pulsing within the walls, as if these humans had trapped the very stars.

All eyes snapped forward when a loud pop sounded from the ceiling followed by a long hiss. No one cowered but Krnar noticed many a hand resting on the hilt of a belt knife.

When a pair of wide, fur-covered feet appeared through the hole and rested on the first rung of the floor-to-ceiling ladder, hands were removed and shoulders relaxed.

Allnall descended first. She waited at the base of the ladder as Ellall made her way down.

Once safely on the floor of the room, these two came forward with smiles and greetings for the last of The People. Voices echoed in the hold as everyone began talking at once, exchanging greetings and firing questions.

A single gesture from the Akaruvel settled the crowd. She waited for silence and then addressed her people.

"The rest are here. You'll see them soon. We have been given rooms above where we will wait until the *ship* takes us to the alara grove."

More questions were initiated but stopped mid-sentence as a pair of thick-soled boots appeared through the hole in the ceiling. Before he even saw her face, Krnar knew it was Jahira.

He felt a desperate desire to go to her and, much to his amazement, to touch her. Having been among his own people for many suns, the only physical contact he'd had with another was his brother's initial embrace. It shocked him to discover how much he missed the occasional brush of her hand. This made him think of Arkan and Ulletta, their constant contact since their fall, and wondered if all couples felt that way.

Couples? he thought. *Is that what we are?*

His train of thought derailed when Jahira turned and smiled. Her face, so full of relief and joy, appeared exotic after his time away and at the same time achingly familiar.

When she moved toward him a jolt of realization struck. If he did touch her, or if she hugged him here, now, in front of his people, it was as good as a declaration of their union. He took an involuntary step backward and she stopped.

The mix of confusion and hurt almost made him reach out to her, but he could feel the eyes of his people boring into his back. He became acutely aware of her inability to block her mind and could only hope the erratic and intense signals were as confusing to his people as they had been to him at first.

Krnar nodded slightly, kept his expression neutral, and firmly blocked his own mind.

Jahira's smile faltered. Allnall saved him by engaging Jahira in conversation. Soon three more humans had joined the welcoming party. Krnar nodded to the General, Medic, and Ryan in turn.

Ellall instructed the members of Krnar's group to be seated, and then she and Allnall joined Krnar at the head of the assembly.

They engaged in the same brief but formal welcoming ceremony they'd performed now for each of the groups. Krnar took great satisfaction in his group's responses, most of all at the offering of fruit from the alara grove.

When his turn came, the sweet and tart combination awakened his taste buds. They cried for more with every juicy bite. Though he savored his offering, and even licked the juice from the fur of his fingers, an intense longing for more gripped him and would not let go.

It's amazing how quickly something you never needed before can work its way into your life and become a necessity, he thought.

When the formalities had been met, Krnar's group gathered at the base of the ladder per Ellall's instructions. They would now be shown to their rooms and prepare for the flight back to the grove.

Jahira and Allnall were first to ascend, accustomed now to their role in leading groups to their places and directing them in the use of seats and harnesses.

Krnar stepped to one side and waited.

Ellall joined him. Whether only to wait or because she sensed he had something to tell her, he did not know. She did not speak, only stood, calmly observing. Krnar could feel sweat forming on the back of his neck.

How do I tell her? he thought.

He shifted his weight from one foot to the other and finally cleared his throat.

"Orvan is not with you," Ellall finally said. Her voice remained low and calm, her eyes continued to watch the progress of those climbing the ladder.

"He is not," Krnar replied. His eyes cut to the side, watching for Ellall's reaction, but she remained unreadable. "We split into two groups during the storm. Arkan, Ulletta, Mrkon, and Orvan fell into a crevasse. They were connected by belt lines, and I tried to save them, but Orvan, he...Mrkon's belt began to tear and," Krnar swallowed against the lump which formed in his throat and then continued, "Orvan cut himself loose to save Mrkon."

The silence seemed to stretch for an eternity. Ellall pressed her lips together and then released them before she said, "That sounds like something he would do."

There was an edge to Ellall's voice that Krnar had never heard before.

"Akaruvel, there is more," he said. "Orvan told me, before he fell, he told me to tell you goodbye and...that he was sorry." Krnar had thought, at the time, that this was merely a courtesy, a show of respect to his Akaruvel, but now he saw Ellall's eyes close and her fingers tighten around the haft of her spear in a death grip.

"Ellall, I am sorry," he said softly.

Ellall opened her eyes and Krnar noticed the sheen of moisture which made the blue of her aged eyes much brighter than normal.

"Thank you for telling me," she said.

With that she stepped into place at the end of the line and seconds later began to climb.

Krnar was left full of questions and an even deeper sense of guilt than he'd carried for the last sun. He should have kept Orvan in his group. Maybe he should never have split the groups to begin with. What had happened in the past that would make Orvan, the eldest of The People, feel the need to apologize to the Akaruvel?

Chapter 64

Anxiety bloomed in the center of Jahira's chest and spread with every pounding footstep. A family of Leroni followed her through the ship, a male, a very pregnant female, and a young boy. Not just any family though, Krnar's family. His brother Arkan, his sister-in-law, and his nephew, or whatever the Leroni called such relatives, padded silently in their slippered feet. She felt acutely aware of the differences in her appearance, her clothes, even the way she walked. She wanted to talk to them but had no idea what to say.

Wary of embarrassing herself, she remained silent...outwardly silent anyway. Inside her thoughts bubbled like a pot of overcooked stew. Did they know about her? What had Krnar told them? Had he even mentioned her? Could they read her thoughts right now?

Maybe I'm overreacting, she thought.

Or maybe not, considering he had not said a word to her, mentally or aloud, the whole time they'd been in the cargo bay. He'd barely even looked at her.

The lack of acknowledgment in front of his people had stung more than she cared to admit.

Is this how things would be between them from now on? Now that he was back with his people would there be no place for her?

The fact that they might be aware of every emotion cascading through her brain only served to increase her uneasiness.

Stopping abruptly, she turned and nodded toward the door she'd almost passed, too lost in her thoughts to pay attention to her surroundings.

The door zipped open after she pressed the release button on the wall. Arkan and Ulletta started backward a step but followed willingly enough once Jahira walked into the room and waved them forward.

"Your hearth," Jahira said in the language of the Leroni.

Arkan's eyes widened and Ulletta smiled.

"Thank you," Ulletta replied. She bowed to Jahira.

Jahira returned the bow and then proceeded to show them how to strap in for takeoff.

"I have to go," Jahira said in her own tongue, jabbing a thumb over her shoulder to clarify her meaning.

"Thank you...Llahira," Ulletta said, pronouncing her name slowly, with the same initial sound error that Krnar made.

Jahira grinned in response.

Her smile widened when Ulletta elbowed Arkan in the ribs and looked pointedly between him and Jahira.

"Thank you," Arkan said, as if surprised to hear himself speak. He quickly regained his composure and added, "May Mrkellan shine on you."

He bowed and Jahira bowed in return before she left the room and closed the door.

She didn't hear Ulletta say, "You'd better be nice to her. That is the one Krnar could not stop thinking about."

Boarding proceeded quickly this time with only one group to usher in, not to mention everyone's familiarity with the routine.

A strong sense of urgency hovered in the corridors. Jahira felt it inside and out. Now that the waiting was over, and she knew Krnar was safe, she couldn't wait to get home.

The rest of the crew bustled around the control deck, preparing for takeoff.

Krnar, Allnall, Ellall, Frmar, and a few elders whose names Jahira could not recall at the moment had seats along the back wall of the observation deck.

After sliding into her seat, Jahira connected the visual feed from the control deck to the vid screens in each room. She'd explained as best she could how the system worked and that even though they couldn't all be on the observation deck, they would all have a chance to watch the flight. There really hadn't been a way to translate the concepts she'd needed. Jahira wished she could see the faces of the Leroni now, when the images appeared over the consoles in each individual room.

"Jahira, are you ready to take us home?" The General asked from his elevated seat in the center of the main floor.

"Very ready, sir," she replied.

The General nodded. Jahira synced the screens she's opened in front of her and completed her pre-flight checks.

"Flight status is green, General. Let's take these people home."

The ground began to drop away beneath them.

Jahira heard hisses and trills from the watching Leroni. Krnar and Allnall reassured them in hushed voices.

Once they'd reached elevation, Jahira prepared the rear thrusters.

"Here we go," she said.

The familiar sensation of gravity pressing her against her seat lasted no more than a handful of seconds. In minutes all traces of the third continent had disappeared behind the Colonizer.

The clear turquoise sky reflected off the water. Alternating patches of light and shadow created a trail of sparkling wave tips below the ship. From some angles it seemed as if they traveled on this path of light, pushing against the wave-forming winds.

Jahira couldn't help but glance back at their passengers who, for Leroni, were showing a considerable amount of animation. Some of the elders actually sat open-mouthed, staring at the scene before them.

Krnar caught her eye and smiled. Jahira smiled back, somewhat tentatively, and then returned to her screens.

"Weather looks stable all the way. Request permission to accelerate."

"Permission granted," replied the General. "But keep it at cruising speed and altitude. We want our guests to have a good view."

"Yes, sir."

A trill escaped from the observation deck when a laro became visible, no more than a dark blob on the surface of the water, but exciting in its being the first living thing they'd seen since leaving the third continent.

After about three hours of flying, land became visible on the horizon.

The extended silence of the Leroni shattered in a dozen excited exclamations.

The ship flew too far above the land to allow much detail. Nevertheless, Krnar and Allnall answered a steady stream of questions for the remainder of the flight.

Jahira felt a surge of relief mixed with a shiver of anxiety as they passed over the human settlement before landing in the field to the south of the grove.

Throngs of humans poured from tents, sod houses, and small gardens. They moved like streams, converging and expanding into a river of bobbing heads clearly visible through the transparent canopy of the control room.

The moment they'd all been waiting for had arrived.

Jahira hoped the two peoples could find some common ground quickly in order to make this co-habitation work.

Unfortunately, she mused, *humans are not famous for getting along well with others.*

Considering the fact that the Leroni had been exiled in some ancient war, their track record didn't appear to be much better.

A long exhalation rid her momentarily of the stress she could feel building in her chest. Right now she needed to focus.

"Powering down," she said. A slight shift and then movement and sound ceased. "Landing complete. Ready to commence deboarding, sir?"

The General's eyes were glued to the crowd of humans waiting at the edge of the field. A second later he nodded slowly.

"Let's hope we're all ready for this," he said.

EMPYREAN

Chapter 65

Tllomell shuffled across the warm silver surface which angled down from the ship and led to another world. She'd watched every second of the moving picture which had played on the wall of her room during the journey. She'd seen the ocean disappear, watched the landscape change shape and color, still she found the whole thing difficult to believe.

The sea of white heads before her blocked her view of anything aside from the brilliant blue sky and blazing yellow orb pulsing overhead. From her perspective, Allorkan seemed to take up more than its fair share of space.

Despite a faint breeze full of foreign smells, she could feel sweat begin to trickle through her fur, tickling her skin like a nest of ice worms.

The air felt thick, as if a wet hide which had spent all day warming by the fire now covered her face, stifling her breath.

When she stepped from the ramp, her feet sank slightly into the warm, spongy ground. The sensation made her nervous as she continued to follow the crowd. She couldn't help but imagine the ground giving way beneath their collective weight. Long strands of what appeared to be dried seaweed tickled the fur on her legs. The combination of sensations from every nerve ending threatened to overwhelm her.

The movement of the crowd finally ceased. Each individual carefully positioned an arm's length from his or her neighbor to avoid accidental touch. Tllomell scanned the group of humans who looked back with big eyes and bald faces that plainly showed every emotion which passed through their minds.

It was like staring at a sea of changing color. Everything from the various lengths and shades of hair sprouting from the tops of many-colored heads to the garish hides covering their bodies shouted for attention.

Behind them, and a fair distance away, Tllomell could just make out the tops of the silver trees of the alara grove. Red leaves rippled in the breeze. Sunlight glinted off their surface from time to time.

Her feet itched with the desire to walk straight to that refuge, to something familiar, if only from the Akaruvel's memories…somewhere away from the staring eyes.

A piercing cry sounded above her head, causing Tllomell to flinch. When she looked up, the dark underbody of a large flying creature sailed over. Trills of alarm rose around her as the long shadow passed over The People. Tllomell's mind immediately went to the tales of their ancestors, the Marked. They had had true wings, like those opened now above her, blocking out the light of Allorkan. Her heart raced. She felt numb with shock so that, initially, she did not notice the strong push against her mind.

When she finally eased open the block on her thoughts, Ellall's calming presence filled her, helped her breathe again.

It's called a bird, Ellall explained. *It is nothing to fear, only an animal that lives in the warm land. See how the humans pay no attention? It poses no threat. Be calm. We have forgotten much about this place but that does not mean it is not our home.*

Tllomell watched the bird circle back, moving higher and higher before it began to drift away from their gathering place.

Despite Ellall's reassurance, she did not completely relax until the creature had disappeared.

Finally, all the Leroni had exited the ship and now waited to see what would happen next.

The human faces shifted collectively to the ship and then burst into noise.

Shouts and whistles carried on the wind. They brought their hands together, creating such a clamor that Tllomell wanted to cover her ears.

Those around her shifted their feet and glanced at their neighbors, wondering what the ruckus was about.

At the top of the ramp, the humans who had first greeted them, and who were responsible for bringing The People here, smiled and waved their hands at the crowd.

Tllomell could feel the excitement in the air- a mix of relief, joy, anticipation, and only a hint of apprehension. She relaxed a little, realizing this must be some sort of welcome home ritual.

Krnar, Allnall, and Ellall stood with the humans. The representatives of The People joined their benefactors as they descended from the ship. The group stopped in the field between the two separated crowds.

The noise from the humans died down, which emphasized the fact that the world around them was anything but silent. Wind whistled through the plants. Clothes flapped in the breeze. Soft screeches rose at regular intervals from the depths of the swaying growth around them. Distant but urgent cries of foreign creatures vied for attention as one of the humans began to speak.

Tllomell let her attention drift until she felt another push against her mind. Krnar's voice inside her head, interpreting the words of the human, brought her focus back to the center of the clearing.

As you can see, our mission to rescue the Leroni from the third continent had been a success. More shouts and whistles rose and fell from the human side. *I have spoken to their leader,* the human gestured to the Akaruvel, *A woman named Ellall. I told her of our recent unfortunate loss of supplies. She has assured me that her people will help us in any way possible through this first long winter.*

More noises with the hands.

The Leroni are here as our friends and allies. We will treat them with respect and kindness. We will help them in any way that we can and we will accept their help in return. The human paused and spoke briefly to Krnar, who turned and spoke to Ellall, then replied to the human.

Tonight we will celebrate. We will welcome our new neighbors with feasting and dancing! For now, please allow them to explore and rest after a tumultuous journey. We will save introductions and questions for the celebration. Tllomell felt Krnar leave her mind.

Three of the humans nodded to Ellall before they broke away from the central group to join the human contingent. One lingered. The dark-skinned female who had flown the ship leaned in to speak to Krnar. As she did so, her hand brushed his. Krnar turned his palm to hers and squeezed before moving his hand back and shifting his body to a proper distance.

Tllomell's heart caught in her throat.

The human female smiled at Krnar and then turned to join her own people. Krnar, Allnall, and Ellall approached the waiting Leroni.

Ellall addressed the crowd but Tllomell did not hear her. A buzzing filled her ears, loud and insistent, drowning out all other sound. Heat, unrelated to the pulsing light of Allorkan, filled her body and pounded against her skin in rhythm with her heart.

How could that be possible? Had her eyes deceived her? How could Krnar accept the touch of one of these…humans?

The Leroni began to move.

Tllomell walked out of instinct, obligated to maintain her place in the group or risk contact with her neighbors.

At first she paid no attention to their destination, too numb to register anything beyond the wall of white before her.

When she did finally look up, she saw the silver trunks of the alara grove rising all around her. The majestic stalks were capped with vibrant red foliage and golden fruits hung heavy in the upper branches. The bottom branches had been picked clean.

The distant calls she'd been aware of while standing in the field, grew louder as her feet carried her into the shadows of the grove. Heads swiveled all around her as The People tried to take in every detail of this sacred place.

Even Tllomell, heartsick and confused, felt a sense of awe as the forest enveloped her. The power of this place vibrated up through the earth itself and hummed through her body.

Closing her eyes, she let it fill her up and expand, like hot tea whose warmth moves from the core to the extremities in waves.

Light pushed against the shadows, reflecting off sleek white heads as The People stepped into the vast ring of silver trees and stared at the hills rising before them.

The oranlodi.

Ellall dropped to her knees.

Others ran to the base of the hills.

Trills rose around her and the elders wept.

Tllomell could *feel* the presence of Aruvel. She prayed it would be enough to fix all that had been broken.

EMPYREAN

Chapter 66

Krnar waited, standing by Ellall's side. Those around him rushed forward to surround the first pool. When Ellall finally rose to her feet, Krnar followed at her elbow.

She passed the first pool, silently determined. The People fell in line behind her and followed their Akaruvel to the largest pool resting within the topmost hill.

Without a word they spread and surrounded the perfect circle of silver liquid. Here the Akaruvel of old had entered as two and emerged as one, filled with the memories of past, present, and future.

Krnar stared at his reflection in the mirrored surface, wondering if he would live to see the day a new Akaruvel emerged from the depths.

His musings were interrupted by the sound of Ellall's voice rising in song. More voices continued to blend and the music swelled until the valley filled with a song it had not heard in generations.

Before the echoes of the song had faded from the hills, Ellall's voice shifted to a familiar chant of sadness and loss. Now was the time to remember those who had not lived to see the warm land.

Krnar's voice caught in his throat as he joined the chorus. He knew he would have to share the memory of Orvan falling into the abyss, forever cut off from the light.

A gentle push against his mind forced him to open himself to his people. The effort to control his emotions proved futile. The intensity of both joy and sorrow which flooded him made it difficult to even maintain a sense of self. Like a school of fish moving as one, its individual parts indiscernible as they surround each other for comfort and protection.

Thankfully, he did not have to share his memories first.

A young woman by the name of Illdell shared an image of her son. Krnar swallowed back tears. Raw and intense, her grief tore at him. The boy in his mind had been two moons old, a sickly child who did not survive the crossing and would have never survived the Season of Ice.

But if he'd made it here, Krnar heard the thought and could not tell if it was hers or his own. Perhaps a collective realization that here, in the light of Allorkan, the boy may have had a chance.

The boy's father reached out and took his wife's hand. The memory shifted to the father's perspective, a vision of a tiny squalling face, the first sight of his newborn son.

The memory cut off abruptly.

Krnar glanced over to see the father's head bowed in grief, Illdell's hand on his back, her head bowed with his.

Soft trills rose from the circle before joining Ellall's again in a prayer to send the boy's spirit safely to Aruvel.

There were others, so many others.

Grandparents, parents, children, brothers, sisters, not only those who'd died in the final attempt to cross The Great Ice, but those who'd spent their years in the dark of the caves, hoping for this day.

Finally, Krnar felt the pull against his thoughts. Ellall drawing out memories, letting him know it was his turn to share.

Unbidden, an image of his father filled his mind.

His throat constricted. This was not what he'd intended to share. This was not a grief he'd ever planned to reveal.

Memories that he'd refused to acknowledge since the day his father had been lost to the ice overwhelmed him until tears spilled down his cheeks, releasing the bitterness he'd clung to for so long.

Eventually, when the memories of his father faded, he remembered Orvan. All of the raw, empty spaces filled with determination.

He had a duty now, to those around him, to those who had survived. Though he had not been chosen by his people, he believed he had been chosen by Aruvel. He and Allnall had succeeded where so many others had failed. Now there was work to do.

The Leroni were home.

Nicole L. Bates

EMPYREAN

Acknowledgements

This book has been in the works for a long time and there are so many people to thank for their support and for helping the story become what it is today.

First of all, thank you to my family: my parents, my husband, my sister, my mother-in-law and father-in-law, both of my brothers-in-law, and my four sisters-in-law, all of whom have shown unwavering support and confidence in me. Thank you also for reading and believing in my story. I appreciate you.

To my amazing friends and critique partners: Sara Fox, Vaughn Roycroft, D.D. Falvo, and Lara Schiffbauer, thank you for reading, in some cases multiple drafts, for your encouragement, keen eyes, and incredible feedback. Thank you also to my awesome beta-readers: James, Dana, Dan, Babak, Kate, Diane, Summer, Tammy, and Scott. Thank you to Cathy for helping work out the beginning of the book. You've all kept me going.

Thank you to Wanda June, for your expertise and for giving me hope, from the beginning, that this story should be shared. Thank you to Cherry for giving me a chance and some great advice when I was just starting this journey.

Thank you to Natasja Hellenthal of BeyondBookCovers for the gorgeous cover. You were great to work with and I'm so thrilled with the final result. You can check out more of her work at www.beyondbookcovers.com!

Just like raising a child, bringing the kernel of a story to fruition takes a village. I couldn't be happier with mine. Love to you all.

About the Author

Nicole L. Bates lives in Michigan with her family. You can find her website at www.nicoleLbates.com. You could also connect on Facebook with Nicole L. Bates (feel free to add her as a friend or follow her author page) or on twitter with @NicoleLBates.

Made in the USA
Monee, IL
21 November 2019